I0739858

THE TICKET

Loretta Miles Tollefson

The Ticket Copyright 2014, Loretta Miles Tollefson

All Rights Reserved
LLT Press, Eagle Nest, New Mexico

ISBN-10: 0692234810
ISBN-13: 978-0692234815 (LLT Press)

This is a work of fiction. Any resemblance to the living or dead is entirely coincidental.

“I wish I had a million dollars!”
It's a Wonderful Life

“Be careful what you wish for...”
Loretta Dawkins Miles

Chapter 1

I'm putting on my makeup on a bright Los Lunas, New Mexico Sunday morning, still in my robe and the mirror steamy from my shower. I have nothing on my mind beyond adding hand lotion to the grocery list. The trick will be remembering by the time I actually get into the kitchen. I wipe the mirror off again as my husband taps on the bathroom door.

"Come in," I call, pulling the mascara wand out of its tube.

Joe appears in the mirror behind me. "We won," he says.

"Hmmm?" I'm concentrating on my left eye, so I don't really look at him.

"I called the lottery phone line for last night's numbers. We won."

"That's a first. Was it enough to cover the cost of the ticket?" I dip the wand into the container again and start on the right eye.

"You could say that."

There's a suppressed excitement in his tone that stops my hand. I look at him in the mirror. He's trying not to grin. "How many numbers did we get?" I ask.

"All of them. Joe and Ruth Marsh, multimillionaires."

My hand is shaking. I concentrate on putting the mascara wand back in its tube and setting the container on the counter. "Are you sure?"

"I checked it three times. The amount for last night was $156 million."

My lungs are suddenly being cut in two by an iron band. My heart feels like it's going to come right out of my chest. I hold on to the counter and maneuver myself onto the closed toilet seat. "Oh, God," I gasp. "Oh, my goodness. Oh, Joe."

"You want to check the numbers?"

I force myself to breath. "Um, yeah, I would. Just to make sure I'm not dreaming."

A few minutes later we're sitting at our twenty year old kitchen table, looking at the slim piece of paper that has just changed their lives. "So I guess we need to sign it," I say.

"And then we need to call a lawyer."

"I guess so. That is what they always say to do, isn't it?"

"Except that we don't have one."

We grin at each other. "We certainly weren't prepared for this," Joe says.

"There's that guy who's been reviewing your book contracts," I say. It's more of a question than a suggestion.

"Yeah, someone from his firm should be able to help us."

"Except that it's Sunday morning, so we won't be able to talk to anyone until tomorrow." I feel a sense of relief as I say it. I need some time to adjust to this. I'm still having trouble breathing—or believing this is really happening. It's funny how, when something good happens to me, it doesn't feel real, but when something bad happens, it seems inevitable.

When Joe and I fantasized about winning the lottery, we never thought about the potential complications. We certainly didn't identify a lawyer who could help us through this. We didn't really expect to win, of course. At least, I didn't. So now I don't really know what to do. How to be. My head is still buzzing.

Joe seems to be adjusting a little more easily. "I suppose we should have some sense of what we want to do before we talk to anyone, anyway," he says.

This brings me back a little. This part I had thought about when we were fantasizing. And planning always helps me focus.

"Well, first I'd like to set up trust funds for the kids and a scholarship fund for my nephews," I say.

"No, I meant like an annuity or a lump sum."

And this is the part that we've always disagreed on, even when we were fantasizing. My heart starts thumping again. I take a deep breath. "And you think a lump sum is better, don't you? That just seems scary to me."

"What's scary to me is the idea of leaving control of our money in the hands of a government agency."

"The government agency that is giving us the money in the first place," I point out.

"Just because they can run a lottery doesn't mean they can keep our money safe in the long term."

I really don't want to argue with him, though the thought of us investing huge amounts of money makes me sick to my stomach. We'd lose it all. I just know it. "I think we need to talk to a financial adviser," I say.

"Yes, but who?"

"Someone from that legal firm?"

"I guess we need to do some research this afternoon. And make some phone calls tomorrow."

I laugh in relief. "I wonder if there's a website out there: Ten Steps to Take After You've Won the Big One."

He grins. "I wouldn't be surprised."

"How much do you think it will be, after taxes?"

"That's one of the things we need to find out. My guess is about $100 million."

"Wow. What would that be, if we just lived off the interest?"

He laughs. "Yes, oh practical one. You're going to budget this too, aren't you?"

I grin. "I have to get groceries today. I just want to know whether I should pick up caviar and champagne or a cheese ball and red wine to celebrate with. I wouldn't want us to get used to a style of living we won't be able to afford."

"I think you can probably get the caviar and champagne. At least this once. And those new shoes you've been trying to justify for the last month."

"Well, I'll need to check the credit card balance before I get too carried away." I look down at the ticket, the sense of wonder creeping up on me again. "All of that in that little piece of paper. And that's just a start. It doesn't seem possible. Aren't you going to put it in the safe or something?"

"Good point. We should actually take it to the bank and put it in the safety deposit box until we're ready to talk to the lottery people. I'll get an envelope for it."

As he gets up from the table, I say "I can't wait to tell Gloria!" then bite my tongue. We haven't even told our kids yet. "Though I suppose I should wait," I say reluctantly. "At least until we call the kids." This is going to be hard.

"I know she's your best friend, Ruthie, but— Can you at least wait until we call the kids?"

"When do you think we should tell them?"

"I'd like to talk to someone first to find out how much money we're actually going to get."

This makes sense. I nod. Though, depending on when we can meet with someone, it could be a couple days. "I think my phone battery needs to go dead," I say reluctantly. Although, if I run into Gloria at the store, I know I won't be able to not tell her. But I'll have to take the chance. She doesn't generally go shopping on Sundays.

"That's probably an excellent plan. Just leave it home. Are you sure you're going to be able to go shopping? You won't be distracted?"

"I'll be fine." I grin, suddenly buoyant. "I just need to check the credit card balance before I leave. And add shoes to my shopping list. And call the office to leave a message that I won't be in tomorrow."

He grins at me. "Are you assuming that we'll need to go into Albuquerque to talk to a lawyer tomorrow, or do you just feel the urge to take the day off?"

I laugh. "I just want to be prepared for all possibilities," I say. "Besides, I don't think I could walk into the office without it showing all over my face."

Joe does internet research while I buy groceries and shoes— the $80 ones I'd really wanted, not the $29.99 ones I'd settled on the week before. We spend the evening at the kitchen table, trying to figure out what the ticket will actually mean for us.

Given what he's learned, Joe calculates that, if we take the lump sum payment, we'll have about a million a year before taxes. But that doesn't account for anything we put into trust funds for our three adult children.

"With interest rates where they are right now, a million in a fund will only generate them $10,000 a year," I say, looking at his printouts. "That can't be right. It doesn't seem possible that it would be that little."

"Two days ago you would have been thrilled to be able to give them $10,000 each, much less each year," Joe says.

"Two days ago ten thousand was impossible." I grin at him. "That was then. This is now. So at one percent, ten million would give them each a hundred thousand a year."

"That's too much. Sam would never do anything constructive for the rest of his life."

"On the other hand, Jeanette would probably turn hers into a million a year."

"How did we get kids who are so different from each other?"

"It does make it complicated, doesn't it? I wonder what Paul will say?"

We look at each other. I roll my eyes and Joe laughs. "That's cool. Did you see the game last night?" we say in unison.

"So anyway," I say. "It seems to me that money enough to generate thirty or forty thousand a year would be about right. Enough to give them a cushion but not enough to make them lazy. Say three or four million in each trust fund and they can't touch the principal."

"What if Jeanette comes up with a business investment that needs more?"

I'm suddenly restless. "I need a snack." I get up and open a cupboard door. "You want some popcorn?"

"Sure, but you haven't answered my question."

"Your daughter drives me nuts." I pull out the new box of popcorn.

"How come she's my daughter all of a sudden? You're the one who taught her to budget and suggested she get a business degree."

"I didn't realize she was going to turn into a high-powered banker type."

"Actually we should ask her what she thinks we should do."

"Oh no we shouldn't. She'd talk you into some hare-brained scheme that would send all our money to Venezuela." This is one of the reasons I don't like the idea of a lump sum that we can invest ourselves.

"There is oil in Venezuela, you know. She was right about that."

"There is also money to be lost in Venezuela. Thirty five percent return, my eye."

"She was only sixteen."

"That was the scary part. How young she was and how thoroughly you accepted her judgment. You two are crazy. Fortunately, we didn't have any money to invest in that project, anyway." I put a bag of popcorn in the microwave.

"But now we do."

"And that's precisely why we need the advice of someone other than Jeanette about how to invest it. Even if she does have a degree now. You and she are a dangerous combination."

Joe gets up and pulls the popcorn bowl out of the cupboard. "I think I'm going to pop a second batch. The smell is making me hungry."

I sit back down at the table, suddenly deflated. There are just too many decisions. Right now, I'd love to get Joe's father's advice on the investing stuff. He was always so good with things like that. But he passed away ten years ago. This makes me think of my own parents.

"I wish our parents were here to help us enjoy this," I say. "I wonder if money to spend would have gotten my mother out of the house." It's only been three years since my mother died, and five since Dad passed away. It would have been so much fun to take Mom shopping. And finally replace Dad's old truck. Or at least get it overhauled.

I could take Aunt Marsha on a spending spree. Well, probably not. Aunt Marsha might be alive, but her dementia and frailty make shopping trips highly improbable. Even shopping for her is difficult. What do you buy for a heavily-medicated elderly woman enduring her final days in a nursing home?

Joe sits down across from me. "I know. We could have taken my Dad on that European art tour he was always talking about doing someday. Or bought a first edition Austen for my mother."

I laugh. "Yeah, she would have loved that!" I shake my head. "I wonder if winning would have helped my mother's depression. Maybe we could have found a doctor who could convince her to actually take her medication. Life could have been so different for her." I frown at Joe. I know I've told him before, but I can't help it: "You know she wanted to be an architect."

"Yeah, you've told me about that. Didn't she give it up after she had Carl?"

"Yeah. Even with two kids, she was still taking classes, and then the depression started hitting, and she stopped. That's when the agoraphobia set in. It's like she just felt so hopeless that she gave up. But she still kept fixing up the house."

I laugh, remembering. "We had the cleanest smelling house in the neighborhood, because she was always repainting. The only time she would go out would be to the hardware store to get more supplies. Dad bought groceries. She bought wallpaper, spackle, and paint. She'd fix up a room and then her energy levels would deflate and she wouldn't do anything for weeks. Then she'd decide to paint another wall or two." I shake my head. It still hurt to think about it.

Joe takes my hand. "I don't think any amount of money would have helped your Mom, Ruth," he says. "She was just the way she was. But knowing you didn't have to worry anymore would have made her happy, I think. You can bet she's watching right now, enjoying your pleasure in it and your plans for making life easier for your brother's children."

Carl's square blond face with its permanently creased brow flashes into my mind. I smile. "Knowing their education is taken care of will take such a burden off Carl. Maybe it'll even make his wife easier to get along with!"

Joe chuckles. "I wouldn't count on that. But you never know." He makes a face. "At least you know how you want to share with him. I don't have a clue what to do for Ruby."

I roll my eyes. His sister Ruby makes dealing with my sister-in-law Carla seem like a piece of cake. But then maybe that's just because Ruby is practically next door in Albuquerque while Carl and Carla are in Louisiana.

We're getting ready for bed when Joe asks the question I've been trying to ignore all day. "So what about your job?"

I pull on my nightgown and sit down on my side of the bed. I work as the office manager for an insurance agent named Andy de Vargas, who is also a New Mexico state representative. During the Legislative session each Spring and throughout much of the Fall, he's in Santa Fe for committee meetings, and I'm responsible for the agency and the other two employees.

Andy tells me often that I'm the heart and soul of the place, and that he can't do it without me, but that insurance just doesn't pay much. This drives Joe crazy. He's been telling me for years that I'm worth more than Andy is paying me, that I should look for something else. Gloria and Jeanette have been saying the same thing, though Jeannette, being our daughter, isn't quite as opinionated as Joe and Gloria are about it.

The trouble is, I like my staff. I can't bring myself to just up and leave them. Every time I think about it, I get depressed. I hired and trained both of them. Flora is a single mother with two teenage girls, and at least one day a week she has to leave early or arrive late because of what I think of as her "daughter duties."

Becky, on the other hand, is always there, making excuses to come in early and stay late, always looking for extra hours and the accompanying pay. I'm not sure that it's just the pay Becky needs. That live-in boyfriend of hers seems both possessive and abusive. I've never seen any evidence of this; it's just a feeling. But it makes me feel protective and helps me overlook the fact that Becky can take twice as long to do tasks that the undependable Flora does in record time. It's difficult.

"I don't know," I answer Joe. I rearrange the bed pillows.

"I know you feel responsible—" Joe begins.

"And you don't think I should."

"Come on, Ruth. I didn't say that."

"You've said it enough times before." I lean back against my pillows, knowing what he's going to say.

"I just think you're wasting your talents there. You know Andy's using you."

"But I don't know what I would do all day at home. Besides, the girls need me."

"The very fact that you call those women 'the girls' speaks volumes."

"Well, I'm taking tomorrow off, anyway," I point out. "Becky can cover for me. Though I'll have a stack of work to do on Tuesday."

"When will you tell them?"

"We haven't told our own kids yet. And I haven't called Gloria."

"Well, eventually you'll have to say something." He pulls off his shirt and reaches for his pajamas. "It's going to be pretty obvious that something has changed, when you show up in your new shoes."

They're very nice shoes, even if they are black and suitable for the office. I grin at him. "And go off on an extended vacation." I get up and pull back the blankets to get into bed. We could get new sheets now. I frown at Joe. "I don't know what I want to do. I suppose once we have the legal stuff settled and actually have money in the bank, I could give Andy a month or two notice, so he can start advertising for someone to take my place."

"And then what will you do?"

As I shake my head, a feeling of sadness creeps over me. "I don't know," I say slowly. "I really don't. To be honest, I'm not sure I even want to leave the agency. Yet it seems silly to stay." I slip between the sheets. "I'm going to have to think about it."

"It's easy for me," Joe says. He gets in beside me. "I'll just keep on writing my fiction. And now we'll have the money to do some real marketing. Maybe hire someone to put some advertising together and do it right. But you've been slogging away at that useless job, keeping us together all these years. Now you can finally break free of that, and I won't have to feel guilty any more."

I sit up. "My job isn't useless," I say defensively. "I provide a valuable service by making sure our clients get the insurance they need and the service they deserve. And I like my staff."

"I know you do. And what you do isn't useless. It's just that I wish my writing had broken through and made it possible for you to work only if you wanted to."

"I know," I say gently. "But I really haven't minded. And I do feel like I've helped people. I suppose I could just cut back on my hours rather than actually leaving. I'm really not sure what I'd do with myself if I were here all the time. I wouldn't want to get like my mother and become paranoid about leaving the house." I reach to set the alarm for seven. "On the other hand, it would be nice to not have to get up at five-thirty every morning."

Chapter 2

But I'm wide awake at five-thirty Monday morning anyway. Do I need to call the office about anything that wasn't finished on Friday? I don't think so, but I keep feeling like there's something I'm forgetting. I'm not used to taking the day off. I wonder when the lawyer's office will open, so Joe can call and set up an appointment.

There are two messages on my phone from Gloria. She's going to be getting worried. I'm going to have to get in touch with her. It's going to be difficult to not slip and tell her. We've been telling each other our secrets since we were ten years old. But we haven't even told the kids yet. And I promised Joe.

I'm regretting that promise, because it's easier to not tell the kids than it is to not tell Gloria. I talk to her more often than I do Jeanette, who's living in Oklahoma City and up to her eyebrows with work at the investment bank where she landed straight out of college. And I talk to Jeanette more often than I do Sam or Paul, even though they both live within a forty minute drive, Sam in Albuquerque and Paul in Rio Rancho.

I smile indulgently. I like my kids. I'm not complaining. They're great kids, and I think it's a good sign that they're busy with their lives. I've never thought adult children should be so dependent on their parents that they feel the need to check in every day. My mother thought I should and it drove me nuts.

On the other hand, I generally do talk to Gloria every day or so. Maybe I should send her an email saying I'm under the weather. No, she'd show up at lunch time with posole or green chili stew from Teofilo's. But I've promised Joe that we'll tell the kids before we tell anyone else. Ugh. I'll be glad when this day is over. Surely we'll be able to share our good news by then. And have some idea of how good the news really is. I never have liked waiting.

Joe rolls over, as if he can read my thoughts, and reaches for me. I snuggle into the crook of his arm. This is nice. I don't have to talk to anyone right this minute, anyway.

We wake two hours later, and Joe showers while I call the office to leave a message that I don't know if I'll be in, and then start fixing breakfast. By the time I'm done with my shower, Joe's made an appointment with the law firm for later this morning.

I stand at the counter drinking my coffee and look around the kitchen thoughtfully. I repainted it about six years ago. It needs it again. But new paint can only do so much. The appliances are twenty five years old and showing it. There's a dent in the side of the refrigerator. Something to do with one of the boys and a skateboard. I never was sure we'd heard the whole story. "We could renovate," I say.

"We could build a new one from scratch," Joe says, coming in from the hallway.

My hands are suddenly trembling again. I put my cup down. "It just isn't real to me yet."

He hugs me exuberantly from behind. "It is to me!"

I laugh and turn to face him. "I swear, I don't think you've stopped smiling since yesterday morning."

"I may never stop smiling again," he says, pulling his keys out of his pocket. "You ready to go?"

In downtown Albuquerque, the firm Joe called has assigned us to Randy Longmire, their person most knowledgeable about large lottery prizes.

He's pretty straightforward. "You know you're only going to get that total $156 million if you take the annual payments," he says. "It's basically an annuity paid out to you over the course of the next twenty-five years. The lottery has enough to cover the cost of purchasing the annuity and that's what they'll give you if you opt for the lump sum."

"So what would the lump sum be?" I ask. The annuity would be so much simpler.

Randy reaches for his calculator. "After taxes, about fifty million."

"That's quite a drop," I say, not looking at Joe.

"But if we invest it, we could be bringing in over a million a year," Joe says.

"How much would the annuity pay us each year?" I ask.

Randy runs some more numbers. "Roughly four million. Again, that's after taxes."

I look at Joe. "That seems like a better deal to me."

Joe looks at Randy. "How much would we need to set up trust funds for each of our three adult children that would guarantee them forty thousand a year?"

"It depends on where the money is invested and what happens with interest rates," Randy says. He pulls a chart from a file in his desk drawer and studies it. "If the income is covering both fees and payouts, right now you would need to fund two million per recipient."

Damn. Well, the kids are more important than my nervous system. We'll just have to find a way to do safe investments. "We can't do that if we take the annuity," I say. "There wouldn't be enough that first year."

"Of course, once you set up the trust, you can continue to add to it," Randy points out. "Say half a million a year for each child until it's fully funded."

"And we also want to set up scholarship funds for my nephews."

"Depending on how you wanted to structure that, you could do the same thing."

But there wouldn't be enough to do it all at once, which is what I really want to do. I don't want the kids to have to wait to get the full benefit of what we do for them.

"Pretty soon, there won't be anything left for us," Joe says. "We'll be back to budgeting every penny, just like we're doing now. Wouldn't you like to be free of that, Ruth?"

But I'm not giving in that easily. "I just wouldn't want to blow it all," I say.

Randy's watching our faces warily. Like he's afraid he's going to get in the middle of a marital spat. "It sounds like you two have a few things you need to talk over," he says. "You have some time, you know. You have 180 days to take the ticket to the lottery officials. Just make sure it's signed and locked away, and then you can take some time to sort through all of this. If you're going to set up trusts, you really ought to have the legal documents completed before you go to the Lottery folks. And of course the sooner you get all that done, the sooner you'll have the money. If you go with the lump sum, you'll also want to think about investment strategies. Any ideas on that front?"

"Well, we don't have to invest every penny of it," Joe says. "I'd like a little blow-out money."

Randy chuckles. "You'll want to decide how much blowing-out you want to do, of course. Have you celebrated at all?"

I grin. "I bought a pair of eighty dollar shoes, some caviar, and some cheap champagne."

Randy looks at Joe. "It sounds like you've got some slightly larger purchases in mind."

Joe nods, his smile widening. "Just slightly. And I think the kids are going to want to celebrate, as well."

"You haven't told them yet? I'm impressed with your self-discipline!"

"We wanted to get a feel for how much we were looking at before we told the kids," Joe explains. "Our daughter the banker is going to want to know details."

"Okay, so here are the details," Randy says. "If you go the payment route, you'll have an annuity of roughly four million a year for twenty-five years, after taxes. If you go with a lump sum, you'll have roughly fifty million dollars total after taxes. Of that, it sounds like you want to put aside about two million for each child in a trust fund. They'd have access to up to forty thousand a year from the fund's investment income. They won't be able to touch the principal at all—is that right?"

"Jeanette may argue with that one," I murmur to Joe.

He nods at me, then looks at Randy. "We may need to think a little more about the issue of when and how they can access the principal," he says.

"So the lump sum balance after the trusts are funded would be roughly forty four million, and it sounds like you had some other items in mind as well. So you're probably looking at investing roughly forty million if you go the lump sum route. A conservative investment strategy on that will give you a return of approximately two percent annually. You'll be paying capital gains on that investment income, not regular income tax, so at two percent--" He reaches for his calculator again. "You would have roughly $750,000 a year after taxes."

My chest tightens. For some reason that seems larger than the four million of the annual payout. Or maybe just more real. "I'm sorry. Did you say seven hundred fifty thousand? A year?"

Joe grins at me. "Having trouble taking it in?"

"You could say that." I take a deep breath. "Do you realize that's more than fifteen times the amount we've been making, before taxes?" I shake my head. "We really could buy a new house, couldn't we?"

"Do you still want to renovate?"

Randy grins at us. "Just don't start spending too fast," he cautions. "People do that, and then they end up with huge credit card bills that even the first checks don't cover. That can happen with the annuity route, too. You'd be surprised at how quickly that much money can go."

I feel my shoulders relax. This is more like it. We'll still need to budget. This is territory I'm comfortable with. "So how does that work?" I ask. "The lump sum approach, I mean. Wouldn't we have to use some of the principal to live on until the investment income starts coming in?"

"Investment dividends are typically paid quarterly," Randy explains. "You can set up a line of credit to cover your expenses until that first payment shows up. Of course, that will cost you. And you could get into a situation where you're never really ahead. You might be better off using some of the principal for initial living expenses. There are a number of different approaches, but I'm not the best resource for that. You'll need to get yourselves a financial advisor, if you don't already have one."

"Of course, that's assuming we go with the lump sum payout," I say. I can feel my chest constricting again. This is going to be more complicated than I thought.

"Either way, I would suggest a financial advisor," Randy says. "They can walk you through your options and help you figure out what will work best in your situation. We provide those services, as well. I can set you up to talk with someone this afternoon, if you'd like."

That's a little too quick, I think. I open my mouth to protest, but Joe has already said, "That would be great."

When we finally leave Randy's office, it's lunch time, and my anxiety is back in full force. It's all just happening so fast.

"Where do you want to eat?" Joe asks.

"Village Inn," I say. I roll down the car window. "Wow, it's stuffy in here."

"Nothing fancier?"

"No. You heard what he said. We're not going to see any of that money for a while. I don't want to end up with overdue credit card bills."

"Do you really think the French bistro would break our budget?"

"You need a reservation to eat there," I say irritably. "Besides, we need to talk and there's no privacy in that tiny place."

"There isn't much privacy in a booth at Village Inn either."

"Then let's go to Sonic and sit in the car."

"Yes, ma'am."

"Come on, Joe. Don't. I have a splitting headache and I'm really hungry."

"And this money thing is scaring you speechless, isn't it?"

"Well, I'm not speechless yet, but it is stressing me, I have to admit. I hadn't realized it was so complicated."

"I don't see what's complicated about it. We get the money, we set aside some for the kids and your nephews, we spend some, and we invest the rest of it and live off the interest. Seems pretty simple to me."

"It's all the details. And making sure we don't do something stupid that puts us in a hole. Or make bad investments."

"I have confidence that the woman who has kept us going on an insurance industry salary and sporadic book royalty payments can make $750,000 a year cover what we need. If we invest conservatively, we'll be fine."

And it's going to be my responsibility, I think irritably. "It scares the living daylights out of me," I say aloud. "And I'm not sure how safe conservative investments really are."

He pulls into a bay at Sonic. "Where does that phrase 'living daylights' come from, I wonder?"

"I'm not up to etymology at the moment, Joe. I just want a hamburger and a milkshake."

"Sweetheart, you're losing your sense of humor."

"Just get me something to eat, okay?" I close my eyes and breath in, trying to slow the pounding in my head. Actually, I'm not stressed. I'm even beyond scared. I'm completely freaked out about this. What is the matter with me? You'd think someone had died, the way I'm acting.

I take another deep breath and open my eyes. "Sorry," I say. "It's just happening so fast that it feels out of control. And I don't want us to make a decision that we regret later."

"What flavor milkshake?" he asks.

"Chocolate, I guess."

While we wait for our food, I say, "I'm not really comfortable with the way Randy was able to line up a meeting with a financial advisor this afternoon. It's just a little too quick. They're going to make a lot of money off of us if we're not careful."

"We're going to have to get advice from someone, and we don't know anyone else," Joe points out.

"I wish Jeanette was here."

"Yeah, she might know of someone. I hadn't thought of that. But we haven't told any of the kids yet. Besides, we've already set up the appointment. Though we do need to get through with it fairly quickly so we can go by the bank and get that envelope in the safety deposit box."

I rub the back of my neck. It feels as tight as a board. I have to admit I'll feel better when the ticket is locked up. Randy has taken a photocopy of it and it's in his files, but we'll need the real thing to actually claim the money. And as spooked as I am, I wouldn't want to lose it now. "Let's just make sure we don't make any decisions this afternoon, okay?" I say. "I'm feeling really pushed by all this, and it's making me nervous. Let's just make this a fact-finding mission."

"That sounds reasonable. But we are going to need to call the kids tonight. And I expect that you're going to want to tell Gloria pretty soon."

I grin and feel myself relaxing. I'd sent her an email this morning saying I was swamped and would get in touch tomorrow. Telling Gloria is going to be fun. "I'm sorry I got so stressed out," I say to Joe. "I am happy about this. It's just not something I'm used to dealing with. And the question of work is still hanging over my head."

A server appears at Joe's window. Joe hands him the credit card and lifts the bag of food into the car. He grins at me as he hands me my milkshake. "Better get used to it, Ruthie. I do like Sonic burgers, but I would also like to eat at that French bistro a little more often!"

Chapter 3

We start our calls to the kids with Paul. He's the oldest and most laid back of our three children, so I'm not expecting a big reaction. He'll probably say "that's cool" and start talking about last night's football game.

Instead, he says "So how much is it after taxes?"

My work cell phone is face down on the kitchen table, acting as a speaker phone. Joe raises an eyebrow at me. "You sure you dialed Paul?" he murmurs.

I chuckle at him. "We're not sure exactly," I say to the phone. "It depends on whether we go with the annual payments or a lump sum. At the very least, it will be about $750,000 a year, after taxes."

"This is so cool," Paul says. I haven't heard this much excitement in his voice since he got his first vehicle.

"If I didn't know that was you on the other end, I'd say we dialed the wrong number," I tell him.

"Well, this is pretty exciting," he says. "The thing is— Well, I'm assuming you'll be wanting to share some of it with us kids—"

"Of course," I answer.

"Did you have something particular in mind, son?" Joe asks.

"Well, I know you spent more than you could afford helping me get through auto body school, but now that I've been actually doing it for a while, I'm wondering if it's really what I want to do for the rest of my life."

I open my mouth and shut it again. I roll my eyes at Joe, who's grinning at me. During Paul's last year of high school almost every evening ended with me telling him that working on vehicle bodies was going to get monotonous, that he had the brains to do something more with his life.

Joe's still grinning as he says, "It's getting old, huh?" to the phone. "I always suspected you chose auto body school because it cost less than college. So now we can afford to ask the question your Mom and I have always wanted to ask you: What would you do if you could do anything you wanted?"

"Actually, I've been thinking about that a lot lately," Paul answers. "In fact, I've already turned in a non-degree application so I can get set up to register for an evening class at UNM this fall. It would be kind of a test of whether I could work days and go to school at night."

I shake my head. Of our three children, Paul is the most superficially predictable and yet the most fundamentally surprising. "What program were you thinking about enrolling in?" I ask.

"Well, you know how I've always been interested in sports. I was thinking I'd like to get a degree in journalism and a minor in physical education or athletic coaching, with the goal of becoming a sports writer or maybe a sports broadcaster."

"You mean like a sports reporter on the news? Do you need a degree for that?"

"I've been doing some research and talking to people at the University. It sounds like the best approach is a degree in journalism with a minor in a sports field, and then an internship. I didn't see how I could do the internship, since those are typically unpaid, and I'd have to work. But if you're willing to share some of the money—" He pauses. "I'm sorry. This is really selfish of me. You tell me you've won the lottery, and I ask how much I can have."

"It's not selfish. You're our child," I say. "And we've been trying to figure out how to share it with you guys. We want you to be able to do what you want, not just what you have to do in order to survive."

"We've been talking to a lawyer and a financial adviser, to figure out how much we'll need to set aside in a trust fund for each of you," Joe explains. "We want to work it so you'll each have about forty thousand a year."

"Wow. You mean for like the next ten years or so?"

"No, this would be permanent. The rest of your lives."

There was silence on the other end. "You still there?" I ask.

"Umm yeah. I'm just trying to process. You mean I could go to school full time and have money to live on while I interned, and then choose wherever I wanted to work, without worrying about pay?"

Joe grins at me. "If that's what you want to do, Paul, then yes, that's what it means."

"Holy shit. Sorry, Mom. Now I'm really having trouble processing it."

"Just don't go quitting your job just yet," I warn. "It looks like it's going to take a couple months to set all this up and maybe longer than that to actually get the money flowing."

"I won't. It's not that I don't like what I'm doing. It's just that it doesn't seem like a productive use of my time."

My mouth twitches. And sports casting is. Well, it's his life, not mine. At least he knows what he wants to do with himself. I'm twenty five years older than Paul, and I'm still not sure how to answer the question Joe has just asked Paul. Yet the thought of actually quitting work twists my stomach into knots. I push the anxiety firmly away. This isn't the time to be thinking about that.

We've decided to call the kids in order of age, so Jeanette is next, but she doesn't pick up. I leave a message asking her to call. "Probably out with friends," I say as I put the phone down.

"You hope. It could be a business dinner." Joe takes a sip of the champagne we still have left. "You really do think she works too much, don't you?"

"I do. It's not healthy at her age."

"She'll settle down and have babies eventually, you know."

"I didn't say she should settle down and have babies. I just meant that her life should be a little more balanced, that's all. Besides, I don't want any grandbabies until our children are ready to have babies."

"I guess we should just go ahead and call Sam."

Unlike Paul, Sam has decided to go to college. Also unlike Paul, Sam at twenty still hasn't made a decision about the kind of work he wants to do when he finishes school. This means that, in the second half of his sophomore year, he's still in the American Studies program, a program that seems unlikely to enable him to get what Joe calls a "real job."

On the face of it, this seems unfair. As a novelist, Joe himself doesn't have what most people would call a real job. But on the other hand, he knew when he was fourteen that he wanted to write fiction and he's never wavered from that calling. He earned his English literature degree in three years.

I'm a lot more patient about Sam's lack of direction, which is a good thing, since I'm the one managing the family budget. Even with his restaurant job, federal grants, and state lottery scholarship, Sam still needs parental financial support from time to time.

"I hope he's not at work," Joe says as I dial the number.

"Then we can just leave a message," I say. But when Sam picks up, I can hear restaurant noises in the background. "If you're busy, I can call you later," I say.

"What? No, that's okay. Hold on. Hey Jack, I'm going on break, okay? Just a minute, Mom. Okay, I'm outside now. It's God-awful hot in there. I needed a break. How you doin'?"

"I'm putting you on speaker phone," I tell him. "Your Dad and I have something to tell you."

"Hey Dad. What's up?"

"We hit the jackpot."

"Huh?"

"Really, we won the lottery."

"You're shitting me. Seriously?"

"Seriously."

"Oh, wow, I can quit my fucking job!"

Joe grimaces and I laugh. "I knew you were going to say that!" I say. "Though not necessarily in those words."

"Wowee, we're rich! How rich are we?"

"Pretty rich," I tell him. "But we don't have any of it yet, so don't start getting too carried away. We're hoping to get all three of you kids home next weekend, so we can talk about it. Can you do that?"

"If the truck can make it that far. I think the timing belt is going out. If Paul's going to be there, maybe he can take a look— Hey, I could get a new truck!"

"We'll see," Joe says. "So if you have to work Friday, then I guess we can expect you Saturday morning?"

"Um, yeah. I think so. I'll have to check the schedule."

"Sam, it's Monday. Surely you know whether you have to work on Friday."

"They keep changing the schedule. I don't think I do, though."

"In that case, we'll see you late Friday, okay?"

"I think so. I'll be there Saturday for sure. I gotta get back inside, so I better go."

"Okay," I say. Joe looks like he's going to blow a gasket. "Love you, son. And Sam, don't tell anyone just yet, okay?"

"Okay. Love you too, Mom. Bye."

"That kid is the most selfish, irresponsible—" Joe paces irritably back and forth the length of the kitchen.

"Okay, Joe. Let me make sure this is off before you start ranting." I turn the phone over and push the "End" button.

"The only thing he can think about is himself. I can quit my job. I can buy a truck. I, I, I, I. That's the only word he knows, I swear. Besides curse words."

"He's only a kid."

"He's twenty years old!"

The phone rings and Jeanette's name pops up on the screen. I grin in relief. "And now for the third possible response."

Jeanette's voice is as cool and professional as ever. "Hello, Mom and Dad. I'm sorry I couldn't pick up earlier. I was on a conference call with Japan. It's actually tomorrow morning there, so scheduling calls gets a little interesting."

"Wow, Japan," Joe says. "What's going on there?"

"Just a property purchase we're helping to facilitate," Jeanette says. "Sometimes I think I'm in the wrong business. The real estate commissions on these transactions are substantial."

"Well, we have a substantial transaction to tell you about, ourselves," Joe says, grinning at me.

"Really, what's that? Is Mom finally going to quit the insurance agency?"

Her too. I had expected this, but it's still irritating.

"Well, if she wants to," Joe says. "There's certainly nothing stopping her now."

Jeanette chuckles. "So what happened, did you win the lottery or something?"

"The woman is psychic," Joe says.

"Really? Truly? Oh my goodness! That's terrific! Have you seen a lawyer yet?"

I laugh in spite of myself. "You are so predictable! We spent all day talking to a lawyer and a financial adviser. Aren't you proud of us?"

"I am! And so happy for you! So are you going to leave the insurance agency?"

My lips tighten. "I haven't had time to even think about that yet."

"So I'm assuming you're taking a lump sum, right? Have you thought about how you're going to invest it?"

"That's one of the things we were talking to them about, only we're not sure how much we're going to have to invest," Joe tells her. "We need to decide first how much money to put aside in trust funds."

"You mean for scholarships for Roger and Ralphie? By the way, have you told Uncle Carl yet? Or Aunt Ruby?" She laughs. "She'll be wanting Mom to come in to the shop to buy clothes."

"No, we haven't talked to either of them," I say. "I don't know whether Carl is on the oil rig or not right now. I can never keep track."

Jeanette's right about Ruby, but I don't even want to think about that. "The first thing we want to do is set aside money for you kids," I tell her. "A trust fund for each of you to give you an income, a fall-back position if you should need it."

"Oh my goodness. I'd say you don't need to do that, but there are some things I've wanted to do that I just haven't had the resources for. This would open a whole set of possibilities for me. Oh my goodness. I need to sit down!"

I laugh. "We thought you'd have a different response than your brothers did."

"Let's see," she says. "Paul said, 'That's cool, but I don't really need it,' and Sam said, 'Now I can quit my job and buy a new truck.' Am I right?"

"Right on the second one, wrong on the first," Joe says. "Paul wants to go to college."

"Good for him! And Sam wants to spend it all right this minute, right?"

"Something like that," I say. "We'd like to sit down with all three of you on Saturday to talk this over. Do you think you could fly in on Friday night?"

"That should work. I'll get on line right now and see if I can find a flight. I'll send you an email when I have something, okay?"

"Sounds good. If you come in early enough, Sam can pick you up at the airport. He didn't seem to think he had to work Friday evening."

There's a pause on the other end. "It might be simpler if I rented a car," Jeanette says. "That'll make it easier to get back to the airport on Sunday without disturbing everyone else's plans. And I'll probably want to drop by and see Virginia while I'm home." Virginia, a former county treasurer, was a kind of mentor to Jeanette while she was in high school, and they still keep in touch. "So what kind of investments did you talk about with the financial adviser?"

It's ten o'clock by the time we get off the phone with Jeanette. Too late to call Gloria. Instead I send her another email, this one asking if she's available for lunch tomorrow. "My treat," I add just before pressing the Send button. I grin. The financial decision stuff is complicated and scary. I can't seem to shake my fear that we're going to get into a huge hole of debt. But telling Gloria is going to be fun.

Chapter 4

There isn't much time to think about the ticket at work on Tuesday morning. I dig into the pile of stuff on my desk with a sense of relief. This I know how to deal with. Flora is late due to an appointment with the high school guidance counselor, and Becky's eyes are puffy and red, a sign that her boyfriend is behaving badly again.

I start working through the stack of mail. This is supposed to be Flora's first task of the morning, but we'll be behind all day if the processing doesn't get started now. Becky's at her desk in the far corner, blond head bent anxiously toward her computer screen, carefully processing payments.

Flora comes rushing in at a quarter to ten. "So now my next problem is how to pay for college!" she announces proudly.

I smile at Flora as I slit open the next envelope. "I gather the girls' grades turned out to be better than you thought?" I ask.

"They did!" Flora pops her purse into a bottom desk drawer and grabs her coffee cup. "They both have almost straight A's!" She bounces over to the credenza in the waiting area and pours herself some coffee. "Anyone need a fill up? No?"

She runs her free hand through her short red-highlighted black hair. "I knew their grades were good, but I didn't know what their averages were. And I wasn't sure what the SAT scores they had gotten really meant. I am so proud of them! But don't tell them that, of course!" She laughs and heads back to her desk.

Becky looks up from her computer. "Why not tell them you're proud?"

"They'll get big heads and think they don't have to work no more," Flora says as she drops into her chair. "The counselor says they've got good chances to get into college, but they're gonna have to work their butts off if they want scholarships, and that's the only way I'm gonna be able to afford to get them through school."

She stops suddenly and stares at me, her eyes soft. "My twins. My girls. College graduates. And me barely making it through high school. I just can't believe it."

"They're only sixteen," I remind her. "You'll have a while to get used to it."

"And a lot of things can happen between then and now," Becky says. She closes her eyes. "The allergens must be really bad today. My eyes are killing me."

"Maybe you should go lie down for a bit," I tell her. "Andy won't be in today, so you're safe on his couch."

"Maybe I will," she says. "I just feel wiped out." She disappears into Andy's office and closes the door.

Flora collects the stack of payments off Becky's desk and begins processing them at twice Becky's speed. "Becky doesn't realize what an accomplishment this is for me," she says as she works. "A single Mom, with an ex-husband who hasn't paid child support in ten years, and twins on top of that. I've given my life to those girls, and now I'm seeing the rewards. It just makes it all worth while."

I smile at her and make a mental note to check the payments for accuracy after she's left for the day. "I know you've worked hard to give the twins a decent upbringing," I say. "I'm really pleased for you. You know, there's a Federal savings program you can start now that allows you to set aside pre-tax money for future school expenses. You might want to check into it. Even a little bit now will make a difference in a couple years."

Flora shakes her head. "I don't know where it would come from. I've gotten further in debt this year, what with the girls' school clothes and all. If that stupid ex of mine would just get himself a decent job and pay some of the child support he owes, I wouldn't have such problems."

I smile but don't say anything. I've seen the twins' school clothes. Personally, I think Wal-Mart jeans are just as good as ones from the mall, but Flora is convinced they need what she calls "good clothes" to boost their confidence.

And maybe there is something to that theory. After all, it's my own oldest who experienced the worst of my and Joe's poverty, and he's the one who decided against college. I know he thought we couldn't afford even to help him with the incidentals not covered by his scholarships and grants. Life is complicated, and no one is ever certain that they've made the best of the choices available to them.

I rub the back of my neck. Well, except for possibly Gloria. She's always seemed so confident and comfortable with the choices she's made. It's one of the things I love about her.

"We're going to the Luna Mansion for lunch," I announce as we leave the agency at 11:30. "I'm paying, so I get to decide." She's looking at me in amused confusion. I laugh. "You should see your face."

"I'm just not used to you being that decisive, or so ready to eat at the priciest restaurant in the county," Gloria says. "You look very pleased with yourself." She slides into the passenger seat of my battered Ford Aspire. "What's up?"

But I just smile at her. I keep it up until we're in the cozy back parlor of the Mansion and have placed our orders.

"Okay, so now are you going to tell me?" Gloria demands. "I don't have all day, you know. I have a showing at two." She grins at me and takes a sip of her diet coke. "I know it has to be good news. *Te pescaron en las moras*, to quote my grandmother."

I wrinkle my forehead at her. "Huh?"

"You've been caught in the mulberries," she explained. "Your mouth is giving you away."

I grin. "The cat that ate the canary, huh?"

"One that's avoiding the subject," she says, pushing her hair away from her face. "Come on, Ruth. I can't stand it!"

This is fun. "It's a secret," I say. "We haven't told anyone so far, except the kids."

"You're pregnant."

"That is not funny."

"You're finally going to quit your job."

"That's what Jeanette said. What's wrong with my job, anyway?"

"Nothing, nothing. Sorry. And you're avoiding telling me what you actually want to tell me. Which means you're either freaking out yourself or you think I'm going to."

Gloria pushes her long curly black hair away from her face and sits up straight. "Okay, I'm ready. Tell me."

"We won the lottery."

"What?" she shrieks. Everyone in the room turns to look at us. Gloria claps her hands over her mouth, eyes wide. "Sorry."

She leans toward me and lowers her voice. "Are you serious? Really? How much? When do you want to start looking at houses? We need to buy you a whole new wardrobe!"

I start laughing. "Oh Gloria, I do love you. You are so predictable. First you scream and then you start planning a shopping trip!"

Gloria claps her hands together and taps her feet, almost dancing in her chair. "I'm just so excited! It's so great! You've always done without, and now you get to have whatever you want!"

"I have what I want."

"I know, I know. You have great kids and a great husband and a tiny house and a lousy job. I know you want the first two things on that list, but are you sure you want the third and fourth?"

"I like my house and there is nothing wrong with my job."

Gloria grimaces. "Well, you do have a nice house. You've done a great job fixing it up. But you have to admit it's on the small side." Our food comes just then. Once the waiter leaves, she asks, "So have you told Andy yet? Or the girls in the office?"

"No, I wanted to tell you first. And I'm not sure how to break it to Andy."

"You really don't want to quit?"

"Maybe eventually. But right now too many things are changing. I need some stability in my life. I'm not sure what I'd do without some sort of routine."

"I can understand that. But you're going to be pretty busy, aren't you? Will you have time to work?"

"I took the day off yesterday so we could meet with a lawyer and a financial advisor. But I don't expect we'll be doing that every day. In the meantime, what would I do with myself?"

"I could think of a few things." Gloria grins. "What did the kids say?"

"You're never going to believe what that oldest son of ours said." I launch into a report on my children's reaction to the news and, because this is Gloria I'm talking to, my own anxiety. "I guess I just feel like someone's just given me a really gorgeous pair of shoes that are way too big for me," I say, winding up.

Gloria bursts out laughing. I shake my head at her.

"I'm sorry, but you are just too funny," she says. "I don't think these shoes are too big for you at all. We're just going to have to get you used to them."

She pushes her hair away from her face. "In fact, I just listed a gorgeous house on the golf course in Rio Communities that you really ought to look at. It has a mother-in-law unit that would be a perfect office space for Joe. And a big room with lots of light that would be a great room for your own personal space."

I have a sudden vision of my mother's darkened "personal space." I push it away and signal for the check. "I like the house we have," I say. "And converting Jeanette's old room into an office for Joe has worked perfectly well. I don't see why everything has to change just because of one little piece of paper."

"Well, just let me know when you're ready," Gloria says. "If you become ready, that is." She grins. "And I want to know exactly what happens at the office when you tell them the news about your little piece of paper."

This is another thing I'm feeling anxious about. I'm not sure how to bring it up, but I really ought to let the girls know what's going on. Especially since I'm going to need to take more time off for meetings with lawyers and financial advisors before things get themselves completely organized.

It's all pretty unsettling. Just getting both my employees in the same space in a quiet frame of mind is going to be a big enough challenge. And then there's the problem of how to tell Andy.

But when I get back to the office I discover that both Flora and Becky are at their desks and moving steadily forward with the afternoon's tasks.

"Good lunch?" Becky asks as I come in the door.

"It was nice," I say, heading toward my desk.

"Where'd you go?" Flora asks.

"Luna Mansion."

"Wow, you must be feeling rich!" Flora says. "That place is way outside my price range."

"Or just celebrating something?" Becky asks. She smiles at me. Her eyes are clear now.

"Both at the same time." I put my purse on the top of my desk and smile at them. This is going to be easier than I thought. "We won the lottery last weekend. All of it."

"You and Gloria?"

"Joe and I."

"Oh wow!" Becky jumps up, runs across the room, and gives me a hug. "That is so exciting!"

"You mean like the whole jackpot? But it was huge! I am so jealous!" Flora laughs and comes to hug me also. "Is Gloria looking for a house for you already? What did you and Joe do to celebrate?"

"Gloria is looking for a house, not that I want one!" I laugh and shake my head. "She's incorrigible. And to celebrate I bought a new pair of shoes and some caviar and champagne."

"And I'll bet they're the practical pair of black pumps you have on right now!" Becky laughs and looks at my feet. "You are so funny."

"So why are you still here?" Flora asks.

"Flora!" Becky says.

"I just meant that she doesn't have to be, so why would she be here? I wouldn't be, if I didn't have to feed those daughters of mine."

"Maybe she likes us."

"Maybe she can't picture herself anywhere else," I say ruefully.

"There's nothing wrong with that," Becky says. "There hasn't been an announcement about this on the news. Are you going to keep it quiet?"

"It hasn't been announced because we haven't gone to the Lottery people yet," I explain. "We're still trying to figure out how much to put in trust funds for the kids, and what kind of investments to make. All sorts of stuff has to be done before we claim the prize. There are so many things to decide, that I don't even want to think about it. Working is much more restful."

"I know how that is," Becky says with a sigh. She goes back to her desk. "Working can keep you sane."

"I don't find balancing work and kids very restful at all," Flora says. "I would love to be able to just talk to lawyers and financial advisors and stuff."

"So that's what you were doing yesterday?" Becky asks. "Your message was a little mysterious, you know. I was worried that you might be sick, but you seemed okay this morning, so I didn't want to ask."

"I'm sorry about the mysterious phone call," I say. "I wasn't sure whether it would take all day or what all was involved. I'll probably have to take some more time off, so I'll try to be a little more explicit next time. I should know in advance, anyway, which will help."

"I would think the lawyers would be willing to meet whenever you wanted them to," Flora says. "Seeing that you're the ones with the money and all."

"Hmmm," I say. Time to change the subject. I sit down at my desk and move my computer mouse. "The Davises are coming in at two-thirty to discuss their life insurance policy. Flora, could you pull those files for me? My phone light is blinking and I have a couple email queries I need to take care of before they show up."

Fortunately, Andy won't be back in the office until the middle of next week. That'll give me time to think about how to tell him. Hopefully, Flora will be late that morning, as usual. I want to tell him about this change in fortune myself.

"Oh, and both of you, please don't tell anyone else about this. We're trying to keep it quiet. Until we actually claim the prize, anyway. I don't know how much we'll be able to control after that."

"You can count on me!" Flora says. "So are you going to fund any scholarships or things like that?" I pretend not to hear this as I pick up my phone receiver.

Chapter 5

The first child to arrive on Friday is Sam, who calls me from the house at one p.m. and announces that he wasn't on the restaurant's work schedule for this evening after all.

"And Dad says Paul won't be here until after seven and Jeanette is flying in tomorrow morning," Sam says. "So I have nothing to do until then. I thought we were starting this party early, but Dad says he has a chapter to finish."

"He's behind on his deadline because he took Monday off to meet with lawyers and go to the bank and stuff," I tell him. "The trumpet vine in the back yard needs to be pruned, if you really have nothing to do. Don't you have homework you can work on?"

He chuckles. "I could probably find something to do besides pruning. It's not exactly warm out there. I'll see you when you get home, okay? Five thirtyish?"

But of course he isn't there when I get home. And he didn't tell his father where he was going, or when he'd be back. "Naturally," Joe growls when I ask.

"He isn't a child anymore, and you had said you were busy with your chapter," I point out as I open the refrigerator door. I chuckle. "I can see he's been here, though. The milk level is down a couple of inches."

"But I doubt he'll stop and get some on the way home," Joe says.

"We still have plenty," I say. "So I guess we'll wait to eat until Paul gets here. You okay with that?"

"Yeah, I had a snack."

"How'd the writing go?"

"Not very well. I keep thinking about things I want to check into and possible investment opportunities. Anything but my characters and what they're up to."

"Well, that happens sometimes, even when you haven't won the lottery," I remind him. I pour myself some water. "What things are you thinking we need to check into?"

"Oh, just wondering if we could have found a better financial advisor, and what kind of houses are on the market right now." He moves to the sink and begins washing out his coffee cup. "And how much flights to the Bahamas would cost."

"Flights to the Bahamas?" I put my glass down on the counter. "I didn't know you were interested in the Bahamas."

"We never had the money to be interested with. And it might be fun to do something major as a way of marking the beginning of our new life." He refills his cup with the last of the coffee in the pot.

I study him. "Did you say that the other thing you were wondering was what kind of houses are on the market?" I ask. "You're beginning to sound like Gloria."

"I imagine that was the first thing out of her mouth on Tuesday."

I grin. "Well, first she thought we should go shopping, remember? But she does know of a nice big one on the golf course with a separate building you could use as a writing space."

"Always looking out for number one, isn't she?"

"Come on, Joe. That's not fair. Of course she thought about a larger house for us. She's a realtor. That doesn't mean she was thinking about her commission."

"First you defend Sam and now Gloria. Why do you protect people when they're selfish?"

"I'm not protecting either of them," I say evenly. "I'm just suggesting that their actions may reflect other motives besides selfishness."

"But they may not."

"Are you sure you had a snack? You sure are grumpy."

"Sorry. I guess I'm feeling anxious about tomorrow. I know they're our kids, but we've never really had to discuss money with them before."

"We've never had any to discuss." I sit down at the kitchen table and put my chin in my hand. "It is weird, isn't it? It does feel like it changes the dynamics. I mean, just little things like paying for lunch on Tuesday. I liked it, but it was still scary. Like there was a new me signing that credit card slip, one I didn't really know very well."

I grin at him. "I started to add up the credit card balance in my head, the way I always do, wanting to make sure we'd be able to cover it at the end of the month. And then I realized I didn't have too. There would be enough, and it didn't really matter if it rolled over to the following month. There would be enough then, too. But it's still kind of a scary feeling. Like I'm not being responsible if I'm not worrying."

"You think maybe I'm worrying about tomorrow because I feel like I should, not because I really need to?"

He sits down across from me. "I suppose there's some truth to that. It just seems like it's all too good to be true. You see stories on TV about wealthy kids who hate their parents, and children who try to put their Mom and Dad in mental homes so they can get their money, and the message is clearly that wealth is a curse more than a blessing. On the other hand—"

He looks down at the scuffed Formica of the kitchen table. "It would be fun to go shopping for new furniture." He grins at me. "And a new house, even with Gloria."

"If we decide that we want a new house."

"Do you really want to stay here? I know you put a lot of work into it, but it is pretty small."

"I don't know. I just feel like everything is happening so fast. I think I'm in too much of a daze to feel worried about the kids or to want to spend money." I grin. "Except for small things like lunches with Gloria."

"Or new shoes."

"Which wasn't such a small thing a week ago," I admit. "I guess I'm just adjusting. But really, Joe, I don't think you need to worry about the kids. You've already seen how they're reacting. Paul wanting to go back to school. Jeanette getting excited about the investments she can make. They're not going to be greedy."

"It's Sam that I worry about."

"If I remember right, you were worried about Sam before last Sunday."

"That's for sure. He just doesn't seem to know what he wants. Where does he get it? Is it because he's the baby of the family, or is he some kind of genetic aberration?"

"Actually, I think it might be genetic code." I get up and move my empty glass from the counter to the sink.

"Not mine," Joe says.

I open the cupboard door and contemplate the bag of craisins and almonds I bought on Sunday. "Mine, I'm afraid," I say into the cupboard. "I'm his mother, and I still don't know what I want to do with myself."

"Have you been thinking about that?"

"Hmmm." I pull out a small bowl and pour nut mix into it. "You want some?"

"No thanks. I'm hoping the fact that you're thinking about that means you're also thinking about not staying on at the insurance agency."

"Andy will be in next week," I say evasively.

"And you told the girls."

"Yeah. Becky was happy for us, and Flora wanted to know if we were going to fund any scholarships."

"Sounds about right."

The back door opens, and Sam comes in. "Hey Dad. Hi Mom. What's up?"

Joe says, "Hello, Sam," and I give him a hug. "Hi, kiddo. Are you hungry?"

"Nah, I'm good. I was down at the chicken place hanging out, and I had some chicken and grease there. Sara says hi."

"For Pete's sake," Joe says.

Sara is Sam's ex-girlfriend. "Oh really? What's she doing in town?" I ask. "I thought she was in Las Cruces going to State."

"She is. She's in town for the weekend. She says congratulations about the money."

Joe stands up, his chair scraping the floor. "I thought we told you not to tell anyone. Who else have you informed about our good fortune?"

"Just Sara. She's cool. She won't tell anyone."

"I'll bet she won't." Joe picks up his coffee cup and nods at me. "I need to go put my stuff away, and clean up my office so it's fit for Jeanette to use tomorrow."

I watch him go and then turn to Sam. "You know your Dad thinks Sara's not very reliable," I say mildly.

"Well, he's wrong about her, like he is about so many things," Sam says. "I told her we're trying to keep it quiet."

The same words I'd used at the office. I've told Flora and Becky. And Gloria. Who am I to judge? "Just try to not tell anyone else until we get things arranged, okay?"

"Okay. How long will it take to set things up, do you think?"

"We're not quite sure yet. But we'll talk about that tomorrow when all three of you are here. How is school going? And how is Junie?" Junie is the latest girlfriend.

"Oh, I dumped her," he says. "She's been spending way too much time with Alfred, her gay best friend. I think the whole gay thing is an act. Gives him access, you know."

"Seriously? Why would anyone pretend to be gay when they're not? It just seems like it would make life more complicated."

"Not if it lets you hang out with girls and get all close to them and learn all their secrets without any commitment on your part. Sounds like a pretty sweet deal to me, if you're not interested in actually sleeping with them. Until you decide you're not gay, anyway. Or maybe you're bi or something." He moves restlessly between the table and sink, leaning against each one in turn.

"He sounds confused."

"So is Junie. I'm not dealing with it." He opens the back door. "I'm gonna get my shit out of the truck. Hey, do you think Paul would have time tomorrow morning to look at it for me? The timing belt is screwing around on me and it's making this shitty whining sound whenever I turn it on."

"I don't know," I say, ignoring the language. "Jeanette's going to be here about ten, so if you guys get up at a reasonable hour, I suppose you'll have time."

Sam, who likes to sleep until noon on weekends, ignores this comment, and heads out the door. A few minutes later, I hear the television go on in the living room and know we're safe from conversation between my husband and youngest son for a couple hours, until Paul gets here. Paul's presence always seems to act as a kind of invisible referee between the other two.

And Paul, or perhaps Sam's concern about the truck, even manages to get the three men together in the driveway and grouped around the open hood the next morning before Jeanette's rental car pulls in. I'm watching for her, so I'm at the open kitchen door when she gets out, wiping my hands on my apron.

"Hey, a convertible!" Sam says, by way of a greeting.

Jeanette grins. "Hi, Sam," she says. "Yes, who could pass up a free upgrade to a convertible, even if it is too cold to put the top down? Hi, Dad. Hey, Paul, how's it going? What's wrong with the truck now?"

They'll never leave the driveway if I don't interrupt. "Jeanette!" I say. "Hi sweetie. Have they got you attached to that truck, too?"

Jeanette laughs. "Not really. I expect Sam already has his eye on a new one, anyway. Right, Sam?"

Sam grins at her over the top of Paul's bent head. "We're not supposed to talk about it until everyone's here."

"Well, it looks like everyone is here now," I say. "The waffles are ready when you are."

"You didn't hold breakfast for me, did you?" Jeanette asks. "You didn't need to do that."

"Well, call it brunch," I say. "There are definite signs in the kitchen of men eating eggs. So I don't think anyone starved."

After we eat, we all adjourn to the living room, cups of tea or hot chocolate in hand. "Okay, do we get to talk now?" Sam demands.

Jeanette puts her cup down and reaches for the tablet and pen she placed on the coffee table before we ate. "So you said the ticket was worth $156 million, right? Have you made a decision yet about a lump sum versus an annual payment?"

Paul laughs. "You're not at work, Jeanette," he says.

"This is serious stuff," she replies. "I just want to make sure I understand what's going on and how I can help."

"Well, what's going on," Joe says, "is that we bought a ticket for last Saturday's $156 million lottery jackpot. The lawyer and financial advisor we met with on Monday told us that will mean about fifty two million if we take the lump sum, or about four million a year if we take the annual payments."

"Wow, you lose that much if you take the lump sum?" Paul asks.

"But you've got it all at once," Sam says. "Holy shit."

"Sam," his father says. "Watch your language."

"Sorry, Mom."

"So what have you decided?" Jeanette asks.

"We're leaning toward the lump sum," I admit. "I wasn't sure about that at first. It's so much money that it's just plain scary. But the more we think about it, the more it makes sense. That way we can set up trust funds right away for each of you and give you a financial cushion."

"That was one of the things we wanted to talk to you about," Joe explains. "We're thinking about funding enough to give you each about forty thousand a year."

"Wow," Sam says. He's currently making about six thousand a year at his restaurant job.

"Hmmm," says Jeanette, who's making twelve times Sam's salary at her banking job. I brace myself for further comment, but she has her head down as she draws designs on the edge of her notepad.

"I don't know what to say," Paul says. His income will almost double with this windfall. "I really could go back to school. 'Thanks' seems kind of inadequate."

"If you're expecting that to cover tuition and living expenses, it may be tight," his sister warns.

"That's fine."

"I really could buy a new truck," Sam says. "And quit the restaurant. Holy shit. Sorry, Mom."

"Before we go any further, I do want to say thank you," Jeanette says. She looks from me to Joe. "I know we're your kids, but you don't have to do this. Setting up trust funds and giving us that kind of security, I mean."

"But we want to," Joe says.

I look at Paul and I can feel the tears starting. "It makes it so much better, if we know that we're making your future brighter. And your present," I say.

"So the idea is that you'd invest the rest of it and live off the interest?" Paul asks. "How much will that give you, do you think? Will it be enough?"

"The lawyer estimated about $750,000 a year." I smile at him through my tears. "I think it will be enough."

"Holy shit!" Sam says again. "Sorry."

"This really has left you speechless, hasn't it?" Jeanette shakes her head at him, grinning. She turns to her father. "So have you started putting a financial team together yet?"

"A who?" Sam asks.

"A group of people they can go to for financial advice. Or people who will actually manage their portfolio for them." She nods at me. "That will take a lot of pressure off you when perfect strangers start suggesting that you invest in their get-rich-quick schemes."

"The financial advisor we talked to didn't mention that," I say. It makes a lot of sense. She does have some financial experience, after all.

"It gives you more than one set of eyes on any given proposal," Jeanette explains. "It's worth thinking about doing. I know a few people in Albuquerque who might be good contacts for putting a team together."

"Would that include you?" Sam asks.

"I wouldn't think so," she says. She looks from Joe to me. "My plan is to add my trust income to what I'm already investing." She twirls her pen. "I'm pretty excited. This is going to turn my ten year plan into a five year plan, if I'm careful."

"And I bet you will," Joe says. "We may want to get some suggestions from you, if you don't mind."

I bite my tongue and make a mental note to pursue the financial team idea.

"Of course not," Jeanette tells him. She glances at me. "Of course, I could get there even faster if I started with more."

I decide to ignore this. "I think your father has visions of playing the market himself," I say. "A financial team to give us advice sounds like a good approach."

"So when does all this start?" Sam asks. "'Cuz I want to call the restaurant right now and tell them I'm not coming back."

I laugh. Trust Sam to get back to business. "Slow down a little, Sam," I say. "We haven't even gone to the Lottery office yet to claim the prize."

"We wanted to talk to you guys about all of this first," Joe says. "And we need to get the trust fund papers drawn up and ready to go, so that gets taken care of right off the top. Apparently it changes the tax picture on the remainder."

"Yes, there are tax advantages to making the trust amounts larger," Jeanette says. "What amounts did you have in mind?"

I feel my jaw tighten.

"The financial advisor says two million each should do it," Joe says.

"So that's about four percent for each of us kids," Jeanette says.

"That's right," I say, more sharply than I mean to. "And it could have been zero."

"Sorry, I guess I'm more in work mode than I thought," Jeanette says apologetically. "It's just automatic reflex to do the calculations." She looks down at her pad of paper. "Didn't you say something on the phone about scholarships for Uncle Carl's boys?"

"Yeah, we figure twenty five thousand invested now for each of them should be about right," Joe says. "And we're setting aside about a million in what the lawyer calls 'mad money.' I was thinking we could use some of it for a vacation to the Bahamas, or something."

"The idea is that you spend the money like you're crazy?" Paul asks.

"For all of us?" Sam asks. "Can I bring a friend?"

"That forty thousand from the trust funds was a rough estimate," I say to the room at large. "It could be more, depending on the rate of return."

"It's plenty, Mom." Jeanette looks up. "I need five years, anyway. I won't be ready before then."

"Ready for what?" Sam asks.

Jeanette doodles on her pad of paper. "I know you all think that all I'm interested in is making money," she says. "But money for its own sake gets old pretty fast. I've been thinking for a while that I'd like to use what I know to help nonprofit companies invest their funds. A lot of them have capital but it's usually not a lot and they don't have the expertise to invest it well."

She shakes her head. "The rates that really good investment firms charge are too steep for a small nonprofit to justify, so the staff members try to do it themselves and they end up making poor decisions. My idea is to get a solid enough financial base with my own investments that I can afford to open a small investment firm that will be specifically targeted toward assisting nonprofits."

She shrugs. "We have a nonprofit section at the bank, but it's really small. The guy who's running it thinks my idea of a nonprofit to assist nonprofits is a viable business model. But I need more experience and contacts before I can do it. He's willing to partner with me, but he won't be financially ready for another five or six years, himself."

"Wow," Paul says. "I'm impressed."

"That's why I got so excited on the phone." Jeanette looks at Joe, then at me. "I had estimated that it would take about ten years before I had enough capital. This will cut that time frame in half and put it in sync with his."

I feel a pang of jealousy. Everyone knows what they want to do. Everyone has a plan, except me. And Sam, of course. You can't call quitting your job and buying a truck much of a plan. Yet that's essentially what Joe, Jeanette, and Gloria all think I should do. Well, buy a house instead of a truck. But it's the same concept.

"This is moving us all along a little faster than we could have reasonably expected," Paul says. "I downloaded an application for the university yesterday. There's a late application deadline, so I may be able to actually start my program this fall. If all else fails, I figure I can take a couple courses as a non-degree student, just to get my feet wet."

"So what is it you're going to study?" Jeanette asks.

Paul explains about the journalism/sports program.

"You mean I'm gonna be an upper-classman while you're a freshman?" Sam asks. "How cool is that?"

"You better watch out, or you'll still be in school when he graduates," Joe says dryly.

Sam's phone buzzes. He pulls it out and starts punching buttons. He looks up at me. "Some of my buddies are going skateboarding at the park," he says. "Is there more stuff we need to talk about?"

"No, I think we're done for now," I tell him. I'm exhausted, and I don't think it's from standing in the kitchen for an hour cooking waffles. "You go ahead. We can talk more this evening."

"Have you had a proper celebratory dinner, or did Mom make you go to Village Inn?" Jeanette asks her father.

He chuckles. "Not even that. We went to Sonic."

"Maybe we should make reservations for tonight at Luna Mansion," Paul says. "I don't think Mom should cook."

They all look at me.

It's just too much right now. It's not the money. And I like eating at Luna Mansion, although dinner for all of us is going to cost a lot more than lunch with Gloria. But I just feel exhausted. On the other hand, I wouldn't have to cook. It's sweet of Paul to think of it.

"Whatever you want to do," I say, avoiding their eyes. "I'm going to go lie down for a little bit."

"And I want to go see Virginia," Jeanette says. "I know you're trying to keep this quiet and all, but do you mind if I tell her our news?"

"Well, seeing how your brother has told Sara, and your Mom has told her staff and Gloria, I don't suppose one more person would hurt," Joe says. "So yeah, go ahead. But do ask her to keep it to herself."

"Oh, she will," I say from the door to the hallway. "Just as the girls and Gloria will." I don't look back to see Joe's response to this. I really do have a headache.

Chapter 6

But I'm feeling much better on Monday, when we have more meetings scheduled with the lawyer and financial advisor. I've taken another day off and after our morning appointments stipulating trust fund terms and gathering names for potential financial team members, Joe talks me into a movie and then some shopping. He needs clothes, he says.

Using the credit card still makes me nervous, but I take a deep breath and do it anyway. There actually is enough credit line to splurge a little, as long as I know we'll have the money for the minimum due when the bill comes. And he really does need some new summer shirts. The weather will be getting hot pretty soon.

Once Joe's chosen what he wants, he steers me across the store into the women's section and talks me into a couple blouses, a cardigan, and a new pair of shoes for myself. "And they don't have to be on sale," he reminds me.

It feels weird, but I go along with it. He's getting so much pleasure out of my choosing clothes that I begin to suspect him of ulterior motives for his own shopping. "I think you decided you needed shirts just so you could get me into the store," I say as we leave by the mall entrance.

"I would never do a thing like that." He grins at me. "Want some ice cream?"

We sit on a bench in the mall, eating our sundaes and watching other shoppers go by. I sigh contentedly. "This is nice," I tell him.

Joe smiles at me. "It is, isn't it? I think I'm finally starting to relax."

"I wouldn't want to do it every day, though." I lean against him and suck the chocolate off my spoon. "We might get a little too relaxed."

"Though I can definitely see us doing this more often."

"Before or after I go to work and you're finished writing for the day?" I tease.

"Well, we would have to work around my writing. But do we really need to work around your work schedule?"

"I don't know, Joe. At the moment, I'm enjoying the moment. But I can't imagine not having some work to go to."

"Is Andy in tomorrow?"

"Wednesday. But I don't want to think about that right now."

But apparently Flora has been thinking about Andy's schedule and my announcement, because she's at her desk when I walk into the office early Wednesday morning. She looks up from her computer. "Andy's here already," she says.

I nod. "I saw his car." I put my purse into the desk drawer, sit down, and switch on my computer. The message light on the phone is bright red. I'm picking up the receiver when Flora says, "He wants to see you."

There's something in her tone that stops my finger from hitting the voice mail button. I lower the receiver and look at Flora. "You told him, didn't you?" I ask. My voice is surprisingly nonaccusing.

Flora scrunches her eyes apologetically. "It kind of slipped out," she says. "Sorry."

"Well, I would have liked to have chosen the time myself, but I guess now is as good as ever." I grab a notepad and pen and stand up.

"I really am sorry," Flora says as I knock on Andy's door.

My stomach is churning. Damn. I had pictured this happening quite differently. I square my shoulders and open the door as Andy says, "Come in." I can tell from his voice that he isn't happy.

"Hi Andy. How was the Capitol?" I'm trying hard to sound normal, but I don't think it's working.

"Just as usual," he says. He pushes away from the computer section of his desk and swivels to face me. He leans back in his chair. He runs his fingers through his thinning though still black hair, laces his hands over his protruding belly, and nods at the chair facing him on the other side of the desk. "Have a seat. I hear from Flora that you have something to tell me."

I sit down and lean towards his desk. "I'm sorry she did that. I asked the girls not to say anything, because I wanted to tell you myself."

"You could have called me."

"I felt it was better if we talked in person. This doesn't change my commitment to the agency."

"Is that why you've taken two days off in the last week?"

"I took one day off last week and one yesterday," I say evenly. "There were a lot of things we had to discuss with the lawyer and financial adviser."

"And I could have helped you to identify those, you know. I have connections."

I hadn't thought of Andy as a resource. "I guess you could have," I say. "To tell you the truth, I left identifying the legal resources to Joe. We're still working on putting a financial team together though, so if you have any suggestions, that would be great."

He swings himself out of his chair and paces to the window, where he pushes aside two of the slightly-dusty vertical blinds and looks out the window. This is a habit he has, when he needs to buy time to think. He squints up at the sun and says, "So, what are your thoughts about investment strategies?"

"We want to be fairly conservative with the bulk of it. Our daughter has some ideas, but of course she won't be part of the financial team."

"Have you thought about investing in insurance?"

"I imagine we'll want to increase our life insurance. I don't think either one of us has really thought about that yet."

He turns and smiles at me. "No, I was thinking of more long term investment strategies like investing in an insurance agency. Like this one."

"I suppose that would make sense," I say slowly. "Since I know something about the business."

He sits down again and leans toward me. "You do know a little something, don't you?"

He laughs. "Hell, you've been running the place for years, while I'm at the legislature. And even when I'm not. You're the glue that holds the place together. What do you say we go fifty-fifty and you work for a percentage instead of a paycheck?"

"You mean as your partner?" I hadn't anticipated this. I'm surprised at my own confusion.

"Sure. Why not? You'd get a percentage of the profits, and that'll make work a lot more enjoyable for you."

"I'm not sure, Andy. I'll need to talk it over with Joe. And the financial team."

"Which you don't have in place yet."

"No. In fact, we haven't even gone to the Lottery office yet." I'm glad to be back on logistical grounds. "I was going to ask if it was okay if I take Tuesday morning off next week to do that.

It sounds like the legal stuff will be completed then, so we can make this official."

"You mean it's not official yet? From the way Flora was talking, it sounded like you were quitting tomorrow."

"I don't know where she got that idea. Of course not. I wouldn't do that to you, partnership or not."

"Well, that's good to hear. I hope you have that ticket safely locked up somewhere."

I smile. "Yes, it's safe and secure in the safety deposit box, right next to Grandma's pearls and electronic copies of Joe's manuscripts. Will Tuesday be okay?"

"Sure, it'll be fine. Just let me know when I can catch the announcement on the ten o'clock news."

I shake my head. "Sorry to disappoint you, but it turns out that we don't have to have our names announced. So we don't plan on being on the news."

"Well, I'm sorry to hear that. It would be good for business. Publicity is always good, you know."

"In this case, it could backfire," I point out. "People might think we don't need the business. Or that I'll get sloppy because I have other things on my mind."

"You sloppy. That's a laugh." He looks at his watch and stands up. "I need to head to the Chamber Board meeting. And I have a Rotary lunch meeting, so I won't be back until about two. The News Bulletin editor is supposed to be here then, to discuss the Civitan golf tournament publicity. Can you keep him entertained until I get back?"

I nod, glad our discussion is over. "No problem. And I'll have the monthly summaries ready for your signature then, too. We need to fax them to the home office this afternoon."

He has his hand on the door knob.

"I do have one favor to ask of you," I say.

"No telling?" he grins at me jovially.

"Yes, please."

"I'll try to be more discrete than Flora was," he promises as he heads out the door.

Becky and Flora look up at this, and Flora grabs a tissue as I leave Andy's office.

"Flora, did you really tell him?" Becky asks reproachfully as I go back to my desk.

"It just kind of slipped out," Flora says. She dabs at her eye make-up with the tissue.

"Boy, you wouldn't survive very long at my house," Becky says. "Things slipping out can cause a lot of trouble." She moves her computer mouse. "When I was growing up, I mean," she adds.

I sit looking blindly at my computer screen. My head is throbbing. I rub my temples. "Well, that wasn't much fun," I say. "But it's done, so I guess it's for the best, Flora."

I smile at her wryly. "I probably would have spent all day trying to get in there to tell him, only to have him leave before I had a chance. Given his schedule today, it's just as well that it's over with. So you probably did me a favor."

"Really? So you're not mad at me?" Flora squeezes her tissue into her hand and jumps up to give me a hug, which I return half-heartedly. "Oh, thank you Ruth. I just felt awful. He came in and he asked how everything was, and it just sort of came out. And then when you went in there— I just couldn't concentrate the whole time you were talking!"

Still sitting, I hug her more firmly now. "It's okay, Flora. It all worked out, I think. But now I'm running late. And it looks like I have a lot of emails. Would you mind if I forwarded them to you to take care of, so I can get the monthly summaries done? If he doesn't sign them this afternoon, I can't get them to the home office today, and none of us are going to get paid this month."

I have a feeling that it's going to take longer than usual to complete the summaries, because my head is still spinning. I'm not sure what I think about becoming a partner in the agency. Even though it seems like an answer to the question of whether and how I'll continue to work, for some reason the proposal unsettles me. I need to talk it over with Joe. I rub the back of my neck as I reach for the phone to begin checking my voice mail.

Chapter 7

I tell Joe about Andy's offer of a partnership in the agency while we're eating dinner, a frozen lasagna baked in the microwave and a pre-packaged salad, with some cherry tomatoes thrown in.

He looks up at me across the table and then spears a runaway tomato. "So what did you say?" he asks.

"That I'd have to talk with you and our financial team. Jeanette was right. That's a great way to get out of stuff. Though of course, we don't actually have a team together yet."

"It wouldn't really matter if we did, because this isn't really a financial team issue, anyway," Joe says. "This is about what makes you happy. How do you feel about it?"

"I absolutely do not know." I push back my plate and put my elbows on the table. "This question of what I want to be when I grow up is something I've never had to answer before now, and I don't know what to do with it. I mean, when I was in high school, I knew what I wanted— I wanted to get out of the house and go to work and be as little like my mother as possible. I wanted to be independent. That meant working, preferably in a nice clean office. But now that I can be independent of the work world itself, I really don't know what I want to do."

"My poor Ruthie," he says with exaggerated sympathy.

I grin at him. "Well, not exactly poor. But I really don't know what to think about this. I like helping people with insurance issues, and I like my staff. And I thought I wanted to continue working at the agency in spite of how you and Jeanette and Gloria all feel about it. But for some reason the idea of actually being co-owner makes me uncomfortable. Even though being a partner would probably eliminate the need to get up at the crack of dawn every morning. I don't know why, but becoming a partner doesn't feel right. And yet if I'm not there, I don't know what will happen to the girls."

My thoughts veer off. "I can't believe Flora told Andy about the ticket." I shake my head. "Actually, I can believe it. I just don't think it was quite the innocent slip she says it was. Poor girl, she doesn't realize that she really doesn't want my job. She just wants the money."

"Do you have to make a decision right away?"

"He didn't ask for one, but I think I probably need to. It's not fair to string him along."

"That sounds like you've made up your mind." He leans back. "If you were going to stay, you'd say you were anxious to get things settled in the new direction, or something like that. 'String him along' sounds like you've decided that the answer is no."

He knows me well. "I guess I have, haven't I?" I grin at him, then sober. "On the surface, being a partner sounds like the perfect plan, but something tells me it's a bad idea."

"Are you sure? This is a big step for you."

"I think so, yes. I mean, I'd be happy to just work there part time, but I don't think Andy could handle it. I either have to invest or I have to leave. And I just don't feel good about being his partner."

I sigh, then add, "But the thought of leaving is spooky. What am I going to do with myself?"

Joe ignores this. "So what will you tell him? That you're quitting?"

"Well, I can't just up and leave. I mean, there are things like the bookkeeping and the monthly reports that only I know how to do. I can train Becky to do them, but that will mean promoting her, and then Flora is going to have a fit because she'll think she deserves it more than Becky. Which she would, if she would ever slow down enough to do things right the first time. Or show up on time."

I smile wryly. "Although she did show up this morning, didn't she? She would probably be more prompt if she was in charge. At least at first."

He reaches for the lasagna pan. "I think I'm going to finish this off. It's pretty good, even if it isn't yours. So you'll give him a month's notice?"

"That's what I'm thinking. Effective tomorrow, I guess. It seems so strange to be actually talking about quitting the agency. I've been there for so long."

He puts the pan down. "You don't have to if you don't want to, Ruthie," he says. "I know I've been bugging you for a long time about finding something better, but if you're happy there, you should stay. Maybe there's another alternative."

"Maybe I should sleep on it." I get up and start clearing the table. "Maybe the idea of being Andy's partner won't seem so bad in the morning."

But the whole partnership concept seems just the same in the morning. It just doesn't feel right to me. I try to tell myself I'm being unreasonable, that I'm just afraid of the responsibility, but I can't shake the sense that becoming a partner at the de Vargas Insurance Agency would be stressful at best and a financial disaster at worst. Even though we have money to throw around, that's not a place I want to throw it.

I decide that I'll give Andy four weeks notice, effective immediately, and suggest that he go through an official interview and hiring process with the girls, to decide who should replace me. It never occurs to me that he might not take my advice about this. After all, he told me only yesterday that I'm the one who really runs the place.

Once again, he's in the office when I get there at eight. This is unusually early for him. Generally, he has a breakfast meeting and doesn't show up at the office until about ten. His door is open and he waves at me when I come in. "Hey, Ruth! How are you this morning?"

Okay, if he's in a good mood, this should be easier. Although I still need to actually write the letter of resignation. I wasn't expecting him to be here yet. "I'm good, Andy," I say. "Have you seen the girls yet?"

"Flora's gone to check the post office box, and Becky went to get us some donuts. My treat," he says. "Are you ready to come talk to me?"

"Um yeah, I guess so. Give me a minute to check messages, okay?""No problem. Gotta keep the customers happy!"

This uncharacteristic joviality and lack of impatience is a little unnerving. My stomach tightens. I check voice mail while I wait for the computer screen to come up.

But there's nothing urgent on the phone or email, so I'm going to have to face it. Funny that I should be so anxious about doing something that I feel so positive about when I think about having already done it. I straighten my shoulders and go to knock on Andy's open door.

"Come in, come in!" he laughs. "You don't have to knock!"

I smile at him and shut the door. "You're certainly in a good mood," I observe.

"Well, the thought of you as my business partner fills me with cheer," he says, smiling at me and fiddling with his pen.

I know that sign. He's anxious. I sit down on the edge of the chair opposite him.

"I've been thinking about how we could do this," he says. "The profit and loss statement for last year pretty much tells the story, and then there's the good will. We'd have to look at the income stream and calculate a viable split—"

I lean forward and put my hand on his desk. I take a deep breath to steady my voice. This is going to be harder than I thought. "I'm sorry Andy, but I'm not sure I want to come into the agency after all," I say. "What with everything that's happened, and all the financial arrangements that Joe and I are making, I don't know that I want to be tied down to an office job, if I don't need to be."

He smiles at me benevolently. "Well, in that case, we can hire someone to take over as office manager and promote you to silent partner. That would give you plenty of time to take care of your personal financial arrangements."

I shake my head, and his smile fades. "I'm really thinking it would be better if I left the agency altogether," I tell him. "I can give you plenty of notice, so there'd be time to train my replacement, whether that's one of the girls or someone else."

"So you're going to just up and quit on me?"

"I was thinking a month's notice would be enough." There's a hard ball of pain in the pit of my stomach.

"You can leave right now." He tosses his pen onto the desk and stands up.

Surely he doesn't mean that. "Andy—"

"I thought we had a good working relationship, and yesterday you were all excited about becoming a working partner, but apparently I was completely misled by you." He stands up. "I should've known you would do this, given the amount of time you've been taking off."

I look at him blankly. Surely he's joking.

"You obviously weren't as committed to this agency as I thought," he continues. "I know what you've been up to. Taking time off, long lunches. You've just been sitting here waiting to leave, haven't you?" He brushes past me and opens the office door. "I'll send you your final paycheck in the mail. Not that there's any rush, now that you have other income coming in."

I get up automatically and then sit down again. Then I'm back on my feet, facing him, hands clenched at my sides. How dare he. "I have worked for you for twenty years."

I have to fight to keep my voice steady. "In that time, I've taken maybe one week of vacation a year and three or four days of sick leave, all together. And you haven't paid me for any of them. I've been loyal and honest and kept the office running smoothly when you were gone. You said yourself just yesterday that I was the glue that held this place together. If you fire me, who's going to keep the agency functioning while you're in Santa Fe or going to Rotary Club meetings?"

"Those meetings bring in business," he says. "It's called networking. You may be doing the paperwork but I'm the one bringing in customers. And I can see now that you had no intention of joining with me in making this place bigger and better. You were just looking for something to tide you over until you cashed your first check!"

I shake my head. "I was trying to ease my way out, so I wouldn't just drop everything in your lap," I say, more calmly now. "If I walk out of here today, who's going to do the payroll? Or the monthly summaries? No one else knows how to do them."

"We'll figure it out."

"I can stay for a couple weeks and get Becky trained to do it."

"Becky? Who said she was going to take over for you?"

"Well, or Flora. Someone is going to have to do it."

"Well, that will be my lookout, won't it?" He runs a hand through his hair, yet another sign that he's worried, but the tightness in his jaw says he isn't backing down.

A wave of pity sweeps over me. He is so stubborn. He's said that I'm fired, and now he can't take it back. "Fine," I say. "I'd like to stay and say goodbye to the girls. Is that okay?"

"No," he says. "I'd rather you leave now. I'll explain to them." His tone softens slightly. "You can leave them a note if you want to."

That he can read. Or tear up. But I can always call them later. "All right," I say. "It will take me a few minutes to clear out my desk."

But as I'm doing this, Flora comes back from the post office. Becky is right behind her with the box of donuts.

"Man, there was a line at that post office like you've never seen," Flora says, dramatically dropping the mail on her desk. She pulls off her coat. "And it's unbelievably windy out there!"

"I bought a whole dozen," Becky says to Andy, stopping in his office doorway. "I hope that's not too many."

He's standing at the window, peering through the blinds at the parking lot and the street beyond. "That's fine," he says absently. "Could you shut the door?"

She pulls it closed with one hand and places the donut box beside the coffee pot on the credenza. "Well, here they are, if any one wants one," she says, looking puzzled.

Flora looks up from her desk. "I thought we were celebrating, or something. That's what he said."

"I guess he's changed his mind," Becky says. "I got a chocolate filled one for you, Ruth. How come you're cleaning out your drawers? Did you lose something?"

I finally look up. "Um, no, I—" I get up and go to the copier. The box we use for recycled paper is half full. I dump the paper into the copier trash can and carry the box to my desk.

"What're you doing?" Flora asks.

"Are you okay?" This is Becky, moving toward me.

I put the box on my desk, next to the pile of things I've pulled from the desk drawers, and sit down again. I look at them. "I don't know how to tell you this," I say.

"You're leaving," Flora says. "You lucky thing."

"You're quitting just like that?" Becky asks. I shake my head wordlessly and Becky kneels beside me. "I don't believe this. He fired you, didn't he?"

I nod, my lips quivering. Becky hands me a tissue from the box on my desk. "I've never been fired before," I whisper.

"What?" Flora asks.

"She said she's never been fired before," Becky tells her. She turns back to me. "I can't believe he did that."

"I was fired plenty of times, before I came here," Flora says. "It was never a good fit, that's all. You get used to it."

Becky puts an arm around my shoulders. "What are you going to do?"

"Well, I don't have to do anything," I say. "About working, I mean. So at least I don't have to worry about that."

I pause and shake my head. "But it still hurts. I mean, I was going to quit and give him plenty of notice so I could get you guys trained to take over, but he just—" I gulp back my tears. "He just fired me."

"Wow," Flora says. "Well, I suppose that's his privilege."

"But it must really hurt," Becky says.

I nod and use the tissue Becky has handed me.

Flora jumps up and grabs a donut from the box. "Wow," she says again.

"I hated to think of leaving before you came back," I say. "But I didn't want to make a scene."

"Here, have a donut," Flora says. She puts the chocolate filled one on a napkin and brings it to my desk.

"Thanks, Flora," I say. I smile at her. "Chocolate always helps."

Flora and Becky both laugh.

"You must want to just get out of here," Flora says.

"I don't know what I want," I say.

"I bet you don't want to talk to Andy again," Becky says. She looks at his closed door and then at her watch. "He's going to be leaving in a few minutes for his Lion's Club meeting. We need to get you out of here before he comes out of his office."

She grins mischievously at me. "Unless you want to stay long enough to tell him what you really think of him."

I shake my head. I'm not up to that at the moment. I start packing the pile of stuff on my desk into the empty box. "I think I have everything," I say. "Except the plant."

I look at it ruefully. Andy gave it to me when my mother died. A small thing then, it's grown luxuriantly and now takes up a quarter of the desk. It reminds me more of Andy than of my mother. I don't want to take it home.

"I'm going to leave the plant," I say. "If either of you want it, just take it home. Otherwise, leave it here. Hopefully, one of you will be using this desk soon, and you can decide then what you want to do with it."

I can hear movement in Andy's office. I need to get out of here before he comes through the door. "Well, that's it," I say.

I put the tissue container into the box with my other things. I haven't eaten the doughnut. My throat is too tight. "Shoes, photos, extra nylons, coffee cup, sewing kit, fingernail file, and tissues."

I smile at Flora and Becky. "It looks like I'm all set."

"I'm going to miss you so much," Becky says.

"Stay in touch," Flora tells me.

I give them each a hug, sling my purse over my shoulder, and pick up the box. "Good luck with everything," I say. "And call me if you need anything."

That reminds me. I dig into my purse for my cell phone and hand it to Becky. "Here's my phone, since it belongs to the agency. Which means you don't have a number for me. I'll have to replace it. I'll let you know as soon as I do, so you can get in touch with me if you need to."

"Good luck to you," Becky says. "And— Oh Ruth, it's been such a pleasure working for you. Thank you for everything you've done."

I shake my head at her, my eyes watering. "You're going to make me start crying again." I turn abruptly toward the door. "I'd better go."

Flora holds the door open for me.

Becky follows me through the waiting area. "I can't believe this is happening," she says. "Goodbye for now."

I turn at the door. "Goodbye. Do call me if you need anything, okay?"

"We will. Bye."

I put the box in the car trunk and glance through the glass door into the agency. Andy is standing by Flora's desk talking to the girls. He turns and looks outside, then turns quickly away. He's waiting for me to leave.

For a split second I consider lingering, just to make him late for his meeting, but then I get into the car and drive away.

So it's nine o'clock on a Thursday morning and I've just been fired from the job I've held since Sam was a baby. Almost twenty years. Even though there's no financial ruin staring me in the face, it's still hard to take in.

I don't want to go home. I don't know what I want to do. Go some place and cry my eyes out. But where? I shouldn't be driving, I know that much. I'm far too upset to be driving. And I don't want to talk to Gloria, either. Right now, I don't want to talk to anyone. I just need some time to adjust.

I step on the brake and turn sharply right, into the Los Lunas Library parking lot. A horn blares from the delivery van behind me. I pull into a parking spot and turn off the car. I fumble in my purse for more tissues.

"Why am I so upset?" I ask out loud. "I was going to quit anyway."

It's the lack of gratitude on his part. The ferocity of his turning on me. The anger. What have I done to deserve this, besides work for him for almost twenty years?

Joe, Jeanette, and Gloria—they were all right. He really is a jerk. What a waste of my time that job has been. But I'm really more hurt than angry. Even if he'd wanted me to leave, he could have been nicer about it.

I smile ruefully. I've worked for him long enough to know that he's essentially a selfish person. It's probably the main reason I felt so uncomfortable about being his business partner. I should have realized he'd do just what he did. I just hope he doesn't take it out on Becky and Flora. I wipe my eyes, blow my nose, and rub the back of my neck.

I sit there for a long time, willing myself to relax. Finally, I stir. As chilly as it is outside, the sun on the windows is making the inside of the Aspire uncomfortably warm. So now, what am I going to do with the rest of my day?

I don't want to go home. Joe is so far behind his deadline it just isn't funny. My going home with this news would be a major distraction. Besides, I'm just not ready to tell him yet, to dig up all the emotions that are starting to settle down a bit.

I could go shopping. I smile, considering this option. I really could, couldn't I? The financial adviser contacted the credit card company yesterday and arranged for a ten thousand dollar expansion of our credit limit. I could actually go to the mall and spend whatever I want to. I smile and shake my head. It's pretty incredible.

I could use some clothes. Though not for the office, apparently. I push the thought away. But I don't really want to go by myself. I wonder whether Gloria is busy. That could be fun. Just the two of us playing hooky at the mall in the middle of the day. We haven't done that since high school.

I reach into my purse for my phone and then remember that I don't have one any more. I chuckle. It had been the cheapest phone and lowest cost plan I could find, and even then Andy complained about it. But it was useful when he or one of our clients needed to get in touch with me on weekends or after office hours.

"Well, first things first," I say aloud. "I guess I'd better go buy myself a new phone."

Chapter 8

The first call I make on the new cell phone is to Gloria, who actually is free this afternoon. "But instead of going shopping, I think we should treat ourselves to a visit to the spa," Gloria says. "I closed on a house yesterday and you know I always give myself a special treat when I make a big commission. Let me see if they have an opening."

I go to LotaBurger to get an ice cream sundae and watch the traffic go by while I wait for Gloria to call me back. I'm just finishing when the phone rings.

"Two slots for a full salon treatment at Ageless Living at two o'clock," Gloria announces. "Are you game?"

"Aren't you going to ask me why I'm available for this on a Thursday afternoon?"

"I kind of figured Andy fired you. Am I right?"

"Yes, but I don't want to talk about it."

"No, we have better things to talk about," Gloria says briskly. "Like spa treatments. Meet me there at two?"

"Sounds good." Not that I know what I'm going to do until then. It feels so strange to not have to get back to the office to the piles of work on my desk.

But I do need to put gas in the car. I fill up at the nearby Giant station and go into the store to buy a bottle of water. The sundae has made me thirsty.

Ahead of me in line, a young woman is balancing a baby on her hip while she rummages through her purse. When she gets to the counter, the girl places a handful of quarters in front of the clerk and then digs into her jeans pocket for another handful. "I need as much gas as that will buy," she says.

The young man behind the counter counts the money and looks up at her. "It's five dollars and sixty four cents," he says. "That'll get you about a gallon and a half."

"Okay."

"That's not going to get you very far," he observes.

"It's what I have."

He shrugs and reaches for the pump switch. The girl straggles out, her baby sucking on his bottle and looking blankly back at me over his mother's shoulder.

By the time I get back outside, the young woman has placed the baby in his car seat and is inserting the gas nozzle into her car. Impulsively, I go toward her.

"Could you do me a favor?" I ask.

The young woman turns toward me. Her faded pink t-shirt says "Baby on Board," but she has no pregnancy bump. Her face is completely bare of makeup and looks tired. "Sure," she says. "If I can."

"Would you let me fill your gas tank for you?"

She frowns. "Is this some kind of scam? Because I have no money in the bank, so it won't do you any good."

I shake my head. "It's not a scam." I'm surprised at how confident I sound. "I've just been lucky and I want to share my luck."

The girl sucks in her upper lip. "With me? I don't know what to say."

The pump clicks off at five dollars and sixty four cents. We stand looking at it. She replaces the nozzle into its slot on the pump.

"You'll need to put the nozzle back in the car," I say.

The baby in the car starts to cry and the young woman opens the back door. "It's okay, Henry," she says. "Mommy's almost done. What did you do with your pacifier, silly boy?"

I move to the pump, swipe my credit card, punch in the zip code, and reinsert the nozzle into the car. I punch the mid-grade button and start the gasoline flowing as the girl emerges from the car.

"So he loses pacifiers too?" I ask. I'm grateful to the baby for giving me something to say. I smile. "My youngest one was horrible that way."

"He gets mad at it and spits it out and then howls because he can't find it," she tells me. She grins. "It's pretty funny if I can find it right away. If I can't, it's not funny at all." She looks at the traffic flowing by, then at me. "I really appreciate your doing this."

"I appreciate your letting me do it," I say. "How old is your son?"

"He's nine months old."

"Oh, they're so fun at that age. They change so quickly."

We chat about babies while the tank fills, me trying to cover the awkward spaces with reminiscences about my own children. When the pump clicks off, I put the nozzle back and collect my receipt.

The young woman stands awkwardly, her pregnancy t-shirt limp on her thin frame. "I really don't know what to say," she says. "I can't tell you what this means to me."

I smile at her, feeling buoyant. "I can't tell you how much it means to *me*. Thank you for letting me help you." I suddenly realize that there's a pickup truck sitting behind my own car. The driver is glaring impatiently. "I need to go," I say, moving away.

"Thank you again!"

"You're welcome. And good luck!"

When I glance back, the young woman is sitting in her car with her head turned, talking to the baby in the back seat. I tuck my card and receipt in my purse and pull out. When I look back again, the girl is gone. A propane company truck is moving into the now-empty space.

I smile. Even though the final goodbye had been awkward, I feel good.

More than good. Wonderful. I can do this now, if I want to: Impulsively help others without worrying about the consequences to my own or my family's survival. A rush of energy surges through me.

I tell Gloria about the girl at the gas station that afternoon while our nail polish is drying. She laughs. "You're more excited about giving that young woman a tank of gas than you are about spoiling yourself with an afternoon at the spa or the thought of buying a new house."

She shakes her head at me. "What a woman you are. You're so happy because you finally have the money to indulge yourself by helping others."

"I wanted to come to the spa, too," I say defensively. "It just felt good to help her, that's all."

"You just seemed more stressed than happy when we had lunch," Gloria says. "But this thing at the gas station made you really happy. I think it's great."

She bounces a little in her chair. "But now tell me what happened with Andy."

I give her the long version, with Gloria muttering "Idiot!" and "I'm not surprised" at the appropriate moments.

"What a jerk," she says when I've finished. "Have you told Joe yet?"

"No, I didn't want to interrupt his writing," I say. "He's seriously behind deadline now, what with everything else that's been going on. Besides, I just didn't feel like going home. I was too restless."

"Well, I hope you're feeling calmer now. And I want you to notice that I didn't say I told you so."

I chuckle. "Although I bet you were thinking it! But thank you for not saying it. We'll see if Joe can restrain himself."

"I always knew Andy was a selfish bastard," Gloria says. "But I'm still having trouble believing he did that to you. I mean, just from a business point of view, it was stupid. Besides the fact that he's going to lose your business, which could be substantial when you replace your car or buy a new house, who is he going to get to replace you at a moment's notice?"

Joe says exactly the same thing that evening. "And I'll bet Flora and Becky don't last more than a couple of weeks," he adds.

"Oh, Joe, don't say that! I'll feel so badly if they lose their jobs!"

"Well, maybe he'll settle down and think twice before he does something that stupid," Joe says. "He can't replace all three of you at once, or he's not going to have anyone to keep things going. Wow, this fish is delicious. Where'd you get it?"

"I got it at the spa. They have that little bistro attached to it, remember? It's always been outside our price range, but today I decided to splurge."

"It's sure not the usual takeout." He reaches for another helping of salad. "So, what was it like to be a leisured lady and spend your afternoon at the spa?"

"Pretty weird. I'm not sure I like massages. They make me feel overly relaxed. I could hardly move, I was so sleepy. But the pedicure and manicure were nice." I wiggle my fingers at him. "I wonder how long it will take before I chip the polish?"

He grins. "How long has it been since you wore nail polish? Twenty years?"

"More than that. I gave up after Jeanette was born. I had no time. I had pretty much stopped while I was pregnant with her anyway, because that's when Paul started being so sensitive to everything, and I was worried about the smell of the remover bothering him."

"Everything bothered that child's breathing. But he ended up working with auto body paint and epoxies, and they don't seem to bother him at all."

"I worry about it, though. I'm glad he wants to do the sports journalism stuff."

"Me too. By the way, I had a call from Randy today. We can go to the Lottery office with the ticket at any point now. I was waiting to check with you about whether you can take next Tuesday off, but I guess that doesn't have to factor in now, does it?"

"No, I guess not." My stomach tightens. Yes, Andy had been a jerk, but I've been planning my life around my office duties for so long that it's hard not to automatically factor in my work schedule when planning anything else. That has to be why I feel sick every time I'm reminded of what happened this morning.

"I'm going to miss the office routine," I say to my salad.

"I suspect you'll get used to not having it," Joe says. "You'll just develop new routines, is all."

Easy for him to say. "You have a purpose, no matter what happens to the rest of your life." I get up and begin clearing the table. "I don't. I'm not sure what I'm going to do with myself. I was already trying to figure that out, but now there's no buffer while I think about it."

I pull the shrink wrap out of the drawer. "I wonder how well the rest of this fish will hold up until tomorrow."

He gets up, takes the shrink wrap out of my hands, and wraps his arms around me. I lean into his warmth. He means well, he just doesn't understand, that's all.

"My darling wife," he says into my hair. "My thoughtful, sincere, loving wife. You've never had the chance to think about what you wanted to do because you were always doing for others. Now you have that chance. Just give it some time, sweetheart."

He nuzzles my neck and slides his hand down my back. "We could maybe sleep on it?"

What a man. He does know how to distract me. I chuckle and turn in his arms to kiss him, moving closer. "Sleeping on it sounds like an excellent plan."

The next morning, I'm cooking pancakes when Joe comes into the kitchen. He shakes his head at me. "Just because you're home doesn't mean you need to spend all your time cooking," he says. "Not that I don't appreciate it. It smells wonderful. But I'm not sure it's a good habit to start spoiling me."

"I know. And pancakes and eggs every morning aren't exactly on your food plan." I wave the spatula at him. "But I couldn't resist. I was thinking though, that I could help you get back on track with your work schedule if I took over some of the Lottery process stuff. Like calling Randy to set up a time to meet with the Lottery people. Oh, and we're going to have to give him my new cell number. I guess I'd better call the office—"

I stop short. He's grinning at me. I make a face at him and grin back. "I mean, I should call Becky and Flora and give them the new number in case they need me, or someone calls me about non-work stuff."

"So it sounds like you have a few things to do this morning," he says, sitting down at the table. "This does look good. I'm not complaining, you know. I just don't want you thinking you should be spending all your time on house work, if you don't want to."

But there's not much else to do besides house work. By one o'clock I've arranged for us to meet Randy on Monday to formally submit the ticket at the Lottery office. I've also called the kids to give them my new cell number, and left a message at the office for Becky and Flora with the new number.

The kitchen is spotless, the living room and bedroom are dusted and vacuumed, and the laundry is in process. Joe is in his office, back at the third and, he says, hopefully final revision of his fourth novel.

"I have an idea for the fifth one," he'd told me as he put the lunch dishes in the dishwasher. "It's about a family who wins the lottery and the kids go berserk and drive their parents to bankruptcy."

"That's not funny, Joe."

"No, seriously. I got to thinking about how great our kids have been about this, and that got me thinking about what life would be like if they had been stupid and greedy. I think there's room there for a serious look at greed and selfishness."

"Since when did you start writing horror novels?" I put the milk back in the refrigerator.

"Well, maybe it would sell. The first three haven't done much."

"They've done all right. Five thousand a year isn't bad."

"And that's a generous approximation. I didn't set out to be a minor novelist, Ruth."

"I know, but the market is what the market is, and you are the kind of writer you are. You aren't seriously going to try to write for the market, are you? You never have, and now that we don't have to worry about finances, it seems like an illogical time to start."

"No, I'm just going through my usual dilemma about what to work on next," he'd said evasively.

I shake my head now, as I sit in the quiet and overly-clean living room. Joe's always been convinced that advertising is what he needs to really break through as a writer, but his publishing firm doesn't have much of a budget for that kind of thing.

I wonder how much it would take to hire a competent firm. And how I can find out. I wander into the spare bedroom and look at the old desk I use for paying bills. The family financial center, Joe calls it. I'm going to need a computer if I'm going to be any real help in finding out about things like marketing firms or managing finances and the email. Our only computer is on Joe's desk.

I go back into the kitchen, pull out a pen and the scratch pad that serves as our family communication center, and begin jotting down a list. I need a laptop. Maybe one of those notebook things? They're awfully small. Maybe not. And a printer.

And, now that I think about it, we could get a faster internet connection—wireless instead of the dial up that's so painfully slow that Joe has to send his novels to his publisher in sections. I've been using my computer at work to download the proofs for him during my lunch break. Now that I can't do that, a faster connection is actually a necessity.

I grin. It's funny how having money results in the need to spend money. Though it's really not having a job that's resulting in this particular need. But I'm not going to think about that.

I look at my nails. There's already a small chip on my right thumb, where I whacked my hand against the side of the dryer door this morning.

I make a face at it. The spa with Gloria was fun, but I don't intend to spend my days being pampered and manicured. That would get old pretty quickly. And be pretty pointless, the way I bump my hands on things.

Chapter 9

Since we don't want to publicly announce that we're jackpot winners, Joe and I don't ask the kids to join us for the trip to the Lottery office on Monday. Joe still hasn't called Ruby, and I'm not sure whether Carl is on the oil rig or not, so I haven't tried to get in touch with him yet, either. We've tacitly agreed to wait until after the win is official.

Neither of us wants to admit that we aren't looking forward to telling our siblings. Though in my case, it's really my sibling's spouse that I don't want to talk to. I'm hoping Carl will be home when I call.

I'm still feeling a little nervous about the official process for collecting the ticket money. Even though the numbers have been vetted and Randy's been in touch with the Lottery office to confirm that everything is good with the ticket and that we're the sole winners, I'm still anxious. What if it all falls through? What a mess we'd be in then, when we've promised the kids financial security, and I've lost my job. And added to the credit card debt.

As I sit in the car waiting for Joe to close the garage door behind us, I will my stomach to stop churning. "Everything is fine," I tell myself yet again. "It's going to be okay."

"You okay?" Joe asks as he slides into the car. "You seem a little quiet."

"Just feeling a little anxious," I answer.

"Scared it somehow won't be true?" He asks, and I nod wordlessly. "Me too," he says. "But there's no logical reason for that fear."

"It's pretty ironic, really," I say. "I've spent a lot of time the last couple weeks trying to get used to the fact that we have money now. And now I'm feeling anxious that we might not have it, after all."

"It would be pretty weird to go back to not having it," he says.

"And Randy would have been the first person to tell us if there was a problem."

"Yep." He starts the car. "And the sooner we get there the sooner this will be over."

We go by the bank to retrieve the envelope containing the ticket from the safety deposit box, then on to the Lottery offices. Randy is waiting for us in the parking lot. "Got the ticket?" he asks.

I hold up the envelope.

"Signed, sealed, and ready to be delivered," Joe says.

In the lobby, Randy asks for Katherine, the person he's been communicating with.

A middle-aged woman with pale skin, jet black hair, bright red lips, and three large silver necklaces draped over her sizable chest comes out to greet us.

"Katherine, these are the clients I've been speaking with you about," Randy says.

"Hello!" she says cheerily. "Come on back."

We follow her down the hall and into her office, where I hand her the envelope. Katharine solemnly pulls out the ticket, turns it over and looks at the signatures, then pulls a magnifying glass from a desk drawer. She studies both sides again through the magnifying glass, while Joe and I exchange glances. My stomach is still churning.

Katharine picks up her phone and dials a number. "Gary, can you come in for a minute?"

A thin young man in glasses appears in the doorway, and Katharine hands him the ticket. He looks at it carefully, shakes his head, and then hands it back to her and leaves the room.

Katharine turns to us. "So you think this is a winning ticket?"

I can hardly breathe. A picture of Andy's angry face rises in front of me.

Joe's hand covers mine. "Based on what we know, yes, we believe it is a winning ticket," he says. His voice is unexpectedly aggressive in the silent room. I glance at him and he looks at the floor.

"Well, you're right!" Katharine beams at us and I feel a sudden surge of anger. How dare she. Joe laughs and his hand moves away from mine as he settles back in his chair.

Randy chuckles. "Do you do that to everyone who comes in here?" he asks.

"Just trying to keep the suspense up a little." Katharine smiles at us again and reaches across her desk for a stack of papers. "Based on what Randy had told me and the copies you provided, I was pretty sure we were good to go, but we have to be certain, you know. Gary certified that it was legitimate. Now, are you certain you don't want to go public with your good news?"

"Yes," Joe says before I can open my mouth.

"Well, I'm disappointed because the press conference is always a lot of fun for everyone. And you get all sorts of attention. It's a great opportunity to publicize the lottery program and all the scholarships that it provides to our young people."

She studies our faces and then nods. "But if that's the way you want it to be, that's the way it is." She hands the paperwork to Joe. "And of course, if you should change your mind at any point, we can go ahead and make arrangements for a press conference, so it's no work for you at all. It's a great way to thank the lottery program for what they've done for you."

"We'll think about it," Joe says, taking the forms.

"We'll need you to sign those forms and then we can go down to accounting and get your deposit processed," Katharine says.

We sign forms for fifteen minutes but I don't really calm down until we get to the accounting office, where Katharine turns us over to a young woman who reminds me of Becky, even though this girl is Native American. There's that same attentive, gentle look in her eyes and expressive mouth. The deposit forms are already prepared; it's just a matter of getting our signatures, and then she'll deposit the money into the accounts we've specified.

We'll be able to make a withdrawal any time after 3 p.m. today.

The girl smiles at me as she hands Randy copies of the forms. "I'm so happy for you!" she says. "I hope this is a great experience for you."

Impulsively, I reach to give her a hug. "Thank you," I say. "That means a lot."

We agree to meet Randy at the Ranchers Club for a celebratory lunch and head for the car. As he turns the ignition, Joe looks at me quizzically. "What was the hug all about?" he asks. "You aren't a hugger person with people you don't know."

"It was just so nice to have someone genuinely happy for us," I say. "That Katharine person was horrible."

"She was just trying to be funny."

"She wasn't. That was just mean." It's stuffy in here. I roll down the window.

"It's all she has, Ruthie," Joe says, maneuvering the car into the University Boulevard traffic. "Can you imagine being in a job like that, watching other people win millions while you and your family are barred from even buying a ticket? It must be pretty tough."

"I can imagine being more gracious about it," I say stubbornly. "She should look for another job, if she hates that one so much."

"Maybe it's all she can do."

I grin ruefully. "It's evident who the fiction writer is in this family, isn't it?" I take a deep breath. "And I'm sounding like a smug rich person who doesn't have to worry about putting food on the table. Sorry. I just thought the suspense was unnecessary. And the young woman in accounting was so sweet."

We have a long relaxed lunch, then Randy pleads work and heads back to the office.

"So what do you want to do now?" Joe asks me.

"Since we're in town, I'd like to go to the mall," I tell him. "I'm realizing that I have plenty of office clothes, even though they did mostly come from the thrift shop or my sewing machine. But I have almost no at-home clothes that are fit to be seen in."

He laughs. "If you've suddenly gotten picky about what you're wearing at home, then we have definitely come into money!"

"I feel a little weird about it," I admit. "Like I'm suddenly this clothes-conscious snob, or something. But everything I own does seem a little tired or out of style."

"Do you want to go to the shop and give Ruby the commission?"

"I'm not sure that's the best way to tell her," I say dryly. "You still haven't called her, remember?"

"Oh yeah," he says, looking guilty.

I laugh. "You look like a kid who got caught raiding the cookie jar."

"I don't know why I'm so reluctant," he says.

I raise an eyebrow. "Do you want me to tell you?"

"Not especially."

I chuckle. "So, I was thinking more Penney's."

"You can spend more than that, Ruth."

"But why should I? That's silly. I just need some jeans and some tops. And maybe some new walking shoes."

"Shoes, huh?" He grins at me. "How long is this going to take?"

"We'll be at the bank by three."

It's more like three-thirty when we get to the bank, but I've managed to find a couple knit tops and a pair of bright green tennis shoes that put a spring in my step. At the teller window, Joe hands the young man behind the counter his driver's license and a withdrawal slip for one thousand dollars. "How do you want that?" the teller asks.

Joe looks at me and grins. "Hundreds, I think."

"We'll need some twenties, too," I point out.

"Give me nine hundreds and one hundred in twenties," he says to the teller, who checks his drawer and says, "I'll be right back."

My heart is pounding and I think Joe knows this, because he grins at me conspiratorially. "I feel like I'm doing something illegal," he says.

I glance around the room and grin back at him in spite of myself. "I feel like someone's going to come out and arrest us."

The young man is back now and counting out our money. "There you go," he says cheerfully.

Joe tucks the money into his wallet and I flash the teller a big smile. "Thanks," I say happily.

"Any time," he replies with a little grin.

Joe grabs my hand, and we head toward the door. "Careful, he's going to think you're flirting with him," he mutters.

"I was just being friendly."

Joe laughs as we go through the door. "You were just relieved he didn't call the cops."

I giggle. "I do feel like I've just gotten away with something."

He puts an arm around me. "Well, what do you think? Want to split some of my cash with me?"

"What do I have to do to get my share?" I tease.

We get into the car. Joe pulls out his wallet and a hundred dollar bill. He holds it up to the light. "Just look at that," he says. "You know how long it's been since I held a hundred dollar bill?"

"I don't think I ever have," I say. "When did you?"

"My first job, when I was a junior in high school," he tells me. "I was doing that haying, remember? And he paid us cash. A hundred a week in hundred dollar bills. I took it to the bank and deposited eighty into my college account and kept the rest for gas and extras. I thought I was rich."

"And now you are." I smile at him and reach to touch his face. "And so am I, because I have you."

He reaches for my hand, and kisses it. "We are very lucky, you know."

"I know."

"So do you want to go spend more money?"

"Not really. I'm kind of burned out. And hungry, actually. That wasn't much salad at lunch, for the price we paid for it."

"Do you want to grab an early dinner? And then we both need to make a phone call. And write some checks for the kids."

"Yeah. Let's go to some place simple, though. I've had enough fancy food and restaurants with atmosphere for one day."

He grins at me. "You're just a Village Inn girl, aren't you?"

I laugh. "Yep, and proud of it!"

Chapter 10

We go back to Los Lunas to eat at the Village Inn on Main Street. As we're looking at the menu, Joe points out that no matter where we eat, we can splurge on the more expensive meals, so we both order steak and, of course, pie for dessert: Joe, coconut cream and mine triple berry, my favorite.

As we're waiting for our pie, an elderly couple is seated at a table nearby. As they consult their menus, I hear the woman ask "Are you sure that will be enough, dear?" and the man answer, "It'll get me through, Elva."

When they order, the man asks for a baked potato and coffee, and the woman asks for toast and tea. Then the old man says, "Are you sure that prescription was really seventy-five dollars?"

"Seventy five dollars and ninety-eight cents," she answers. "It went up from last time. I think I'm going to try taking a half dose every other day. It should still work. And then we wouldn't have to get it again so soon."

The waitress comes with our pie.

"You better check with the doctor before you do that," the old man says.

"I am not going to the doctor and paying that co-pay just so he can tell me whether or not I can do something I would do anyway," the old woman says sharply.

Joe looks up from his pie. I lean toward him. "Did you hear that?" I whisper.

"You can't save the whole world, Ruth," he says.

"Can we at least pay for their meal?"

"It's not much of a meal," Joe says. I smile at him. So, he's been eavesdropping, too.

I glance around the restaurant. Our waitress is at the front counter, flirting with the cashier. I reach into my purse for my wallet. "I'm going to go talk to our waitress," I say, sliding out of the booth.

Joe's scraping the last of the crumbs off his plate when I come back. "You look very pleased with yourself," he says.

"I am," I say with a grin. I pick up my purse. "Are you ready?"

"You haven't finished your pie," he points out.

"That's okay. I really didn't have room for all of it," I say impatiently.

He raises an eyebrow at me. "Okay, then," he says, and slides out of the booth.

As Joe is paying our bill at the counter, I see the waitress approach the old couple with menus. They look up in surprise. "I'll wait for you outside," I tell Joe, and head toward the door.

He follows me out a minute later. "What did you do?" he asks.

I hurry him toward the car. "I gave her two twenties and told her to make sure they had a good meal and some food to take home."

He smiles at me, shaking his head over the top of the car. "You really can't feed the whole world, Ruth. And one meal isn't going to solve that woman's prescription problem."

"I know, but it's something. And it will make them feel like somebody cares." And it makes me feel good. The bad feeling from the Lottery office has completely dissipated.

"An anonymous someone who gave up her pie to make sure they had a good meal."

"I ate part of it. And she was so frail looking, Joe. Besides, it was fun. And I didn't need the pie."

He chuckles as he starts the car. "I know you're feeling rich when you start not eating all your food."

I laugh. "I suppose so. You'll have to tell that one to Ruby, the family dieter."

"Oh yeah, I get to call Ruby when I get home. And you need to call Carl. Do you know if he's off his rig yet?"

"I don't think so. Which means I get to talk to Carla." I make a face.

"So we both have our work cut out for us."

"Well, I'd rather talk to Carla than Ruby, I can tell you that much!"

"Besides, you just did your good deed for the day, so you're feeling very pleased with yourself." He grins at me. "So are you telling me you don't really care what Carla says?"

"Well, just a little bit," I say. "Though I don't know why I should feel defensive when we've just made sure her kids are going to have the money they need for college."

But Carl is home when I call, so I don't have to talk to his wife, whose passive aggression had become somewhat legendary in the family. Carl isn't effusive in his thanks, but then, he isn't exactly the effusive type.

"You're sure you want to do this?" he asks, after I've explained that we're setting up college trust funds for his two boys. "You're not obligated or anything."

"Of course we want to," I tell him. "We're so happy we can, Carl. If Ralph or Roger decide they want to go to trade school or something, they can use it for that too, of course. The language isn't specific. But I am going to need their social security numbers."

He gives them to me, thanks me again, tells me he's going back to the rig in another week, makes sure he has my new phone number, and then hangs up. I look at my watch. Fifteen minutes. Carl really does hate to talk on the phone. It's downright funny sometimes.

I lay my checkbook on the kitchen table and collect envelopes and stamps from my desk. We've decided to send each of the kids twenty thousand dollars to tide them over until the trust income starts coming in. Well, it's really "just because" money. Because we can.

I smile as I seal the envelope containing Jeanette's check. Then I begin writing the one for Paul. I pause and look at it. I've never written checks for this amount before, even when we bought the house. It still doesn't feel real. I've just finished and am paying the mortgage and electricity bills when Joe comes in.

His conversation with Ruby has taken three times as long as mine with Carl, and he doesn't look very satisfied. He stands in the doorway looking down at his phone, turning it over in his hand.

"Ruby has pointed out that now I can get a decent cell phone," he says.

"I suppose you can." I put a stamp on the envelope containing the mortgage payment. "Do you want a smart phone like mine?"

"Which you can still barely use." He grins at me. "And you have a lot more technological patience than I do." He slips the phone into his pocket. "No thanks. Though I probably should think about a gizmo to hold it on my belt instead of carrying it in my pocket."

"We'll have to look for one next time we go to the mall."

"Your new favorite shopping place."

I grin at him. "From Wal-Mart to Coronado Mall. What can I say? I haven't gotten to ABQ Uptown yet."

Joe chuckles. "And Ruby wants to know why."

I make a face at him. "I knew this was coming."

"She was just kidding, Ruth."

I shake my head and go to the fridge. "If you say so. I'm thirsty. You want some water?"

"No thanks. So Ruby says congratulations, and she hopes she'll see you in the shop soon, so she can help with your makeover. Apparently there are some new mules that she thinks you'll like. Whatever a mule is. They have other stuff too, but I've forgotten what all she said."

I chuckle. We certainly have different siblings. Carl, who says as little as possible and Ruby who can smother you with a blanket of seemingly gracious words. "Mules are a kind of shoe," I tell him. "Little backless totally impractical things. But very cute."

"So the next time we're in Albuquerque we should go in there."

I raise an eyebrow at him and put my now-empty glass of water on the counter. "Wow, you're getting brave. Are you sure you want to spend a couple hours in an upscale woman's clothing shop watching me get irritated with Ruby for trying to sell me everything in the store?"

He grins at me. "Well, you can't blame her for trying."

"That's a matter of opinion. But I notice that the refrigerator is getting empty. I'm going to make a grocery list for tomorrow. Is there anything you're particularly hungry for?"

"Not off the top of my head." He heads out the kitchen door. "Oh, and Ruby wants to know if we're available for dinner at her place on Sunday."

I open my mouth, and he turns in the doorway. He holds up a hand. "I didn't commit," he says. "But it has been a couple of months since we saw her."

"Six weeks, actually."

"So maybe we could do it a couple weeks from now?"

"I suppose." I make a face at his departing back and find a piece of paper to use for the grocery list. Ruby. So seemingly gracious and so full of little barbs, all of which feel like they're pointed directly at me. And Joe just can't see what the problem is.

I've always suspected that I actually make more money than Ruby, which isn't saying much. Well, made anyway. When I was earning a paycheck. But Ruby has always made it seem like I was the unsuccessful one, making snide comments about my thrift shop clothes and loading Jeanette down with impractical things Ruby's picked up from the shop's closeout rack with her employee discount. Ruby has no children or husband but she's made that seem like a positive, rather than a negative, aspect of her life.

I sigh and rub the back of my neck. It's ridiculous. Even though I now have millions of dollars in the bank, Ruby can still get to me. And I haven't actually talked to her. And Joe wonders why I want to put off going to Ruby's apartment for dinner.

Joe still hasn't decided what to do for his sister out of our sudden windfall. He says he doesn't know what she needs. I suspect a check would be the best option, but how much and how to present it are still open questions. Having dinner with her might help with that dilemma, although giving her something beforehand might make dinner less uncomfortable. Of course, that will depend on what Joe decides to do.

It's ironic that I can get so much pleasure out of anonymously giving a little old couple a meal, but dread helping my own sister-in-law. I have to admit that it's a lot simpler if you can just walk away.

Since we only need a few things, I go to Albertsons the next day for the fruit, milk, and vegetables run. I know it's silly—I can shop here all the time now, if I want to. But I find myself clinging to my old shopping habits: Wal-Mart for paper and cleaning products, canned goods, and meat; Albertsons for veggies and fruit.

As I'm standing in the freezer aisle considering whether to buy ice cream, I hear Gloria's voice. When I turn around, there she is, on her cell phone with a client while she piles her cart with low-calorie frozen entrees. She shuts her phone and sees me at the same time.

"Ruthie!" she says, hugging me. "How are you?"

I laugh. "Still trying to get used to shopping for groceries in the middle of the day in the middle of the week. How are you?"

"Oh good, good. Just trying to make sure there's something in the freezer when I get home at night!" She lowers her voice. "I was going to call you, actually. I was at a Chamber of Commerce lunch yesterday, and I heard something that you ought to know about."

"What's that?"

Gloria puts her phone in her purse and pushes back her hair. She frowns. "Someone asked me how you were, like you were sick or something, and then said they were concerned because Andy told them you had up and quit on him without warning."

Damn. This sounds so much like something Andy would do. "Did he say why I supposedly quit?"

"Well, this guy asked if you were okay, so I don't think so. But I think Andy might have said more to other people, because the marketing woman at Wells Fargo was admiring my new ring and asked if it was a gift from my best friend."

I swing around, pace across the aisle, and swing my arms out. "Great. So the whole town knows. And thinks that I was a total jerk and left Andy in the lurch."

Gloria shakes her head. "Well, not the whole town. But a lot of it. Oh Ruth, I'm so sorry."

"And Joe was worried about you telling people." I bite my lip and scrunch my face at her. "Sorry. Joe didn't want to tell anybody, is all."

"Well, you can tell him I didn't," she says dryly. "It was your wonderful boss that he and I both like so much."

"You were both right about him, too." I frown. "I'm just not sure what I should do about it."

"I'm not sure I'd do anything," Gloria says. "At least not right this minute." She grins. "I felt like marching across the room and yelling at him, but it didn't seem like the best time and place. And maybe he hasn't told that many people. It might just sort of die down, you know."

"Maybe." I shake my head. "I hope so." I grin at her. "By the way, I may need your help. Joe told Ruby about the ticket last night, and she's invited me to come get a clothing makeover in her shop. I'm going to need some style protection, and I don't think Joe will be much use in that department."

Gloria laughs. "Oh, that should be fun!"

"I'm not sure I want to get decked out in her shop's particular style."

Gloria grins at me. "Of course, the only way to combat that is to decide what your particular style is."

I groan. "I know, I know. But that means I have to figure out who I am and what I want to do with my life."

"You're our sweet loving Ruth and you can do whatever you want with your life," Gloria says, hugging me.

I roll my eyes at her. "Well, that's definitive!"

Gloria's phone rings. She pulls it out of her purse and looks at it. "I have to take this," she says hurriedly. "Call me, okay?"

I nod and turn back to the ice cream. I envy Gloria at this moment. She has things to do and people to talk to. I push the feelings away, decide we don't really need ice cream, and head to the deli counter.

As I'm waiting in line, a local businessman gets in line behind me. I assisted him with a water damage claim last month when the bank of the flood control ditch next to his property collapsed. "How are you?" I ask now. "Did you get your repairs completed?"

He looks at me blankly. "Repairs? Oh yes, they're completed." Then his smile widens. "But I guess you don't need to be worrying about that type of thing anymore, do you?"

"I suppose not," I answer, suddenly wary.

"I hear you've had some good fortune," he says.

I move forward in line, toward the counter. Good, they have roast beef today. "You could say that," I say over my shoulder.

"I wouldn't worry about anything Andy says right now," he says. "He'll get over it and realize he needs your business."

I nod, my eyes on the counter.

"If you're looking for business opportunities, I hope you'll come talk to me," he adds.

"I don't know that we are," I reply. "We would need to vet it through our financial advice—our team of financial advisers. But I'll let you know if we're interested."

In spite of my smile, my stomach clenches. Now that the word is out, is this going to happen every time I go to the store? But the deli attendant is waiting for my order. I move forward.

The attendant looks at me with no curiosity in her eyes. "What can I help you with?" she asks. While she's cutting and wrapping the roast beef I keep my eyes firmly on the various salads behind the counter glass.

When I turn to leave, I find that the businessman has drifted away to examine the cheese and fruit display. "Have a good day," he says to me as I pass. I nod without speaking.

Maybe we really should buy a new house. Somewhere else, that is. Damn. I happen to like living here. I push the cart through the produce section, toward the dairy cases at the back of the store.

One of the things I like best about grocery shopping is that Virginia and I seem to have similar shopping patterns. I often run into her when I'm at the store. When this happens, we stand in the aisle and chat until someone comes by and we have to move to keep from blocking the way.

I don't really expect to see her today, since I don't normally shop during the week, but as I pass the seafood counter, I see her ahead, her gray head with its tidy bun bent over the container of Greek yogurt in her hands.

"Boo!" I say, coming up behind her. Virginia jumps.

"Oh, I didn't see you!" Virginia says as we hug. "How are you? And my sweet Jeanette? I haven't talked to her since she was here to discuss your news."

"She's well. Working harder than ever, now that she has resources of her own to invest."

Virginia shakes her head. "I love her to pieces, but that girl needs to learn how to have fun. I keep praying she'll get a boyfriend who can teach her how to relax."

"Me too," I say. "And how are you?"

"I'm good! I'm just trying to decide if I should pay for yogurt that sort of tastes like my mother used to make or just make it myself."

"I've never tried making yogurt. Is it difficult?" This is what I love about Virginia. She goes right to practical stuff.

"Not really. It just takes time, is all. But I have that. It's keeping it at the right temperature that's the tricky part."

"Don't they have some kind of machine you can buy? Like a crock pot thing?"

"Or I can just buy the yogurt," she says. She looks at the back of the container again. "It probably tastes just like my mother's. It just doesn't have the same memories attached to it."

I chuckle. "Memory does color the flavors of our childhood, doesn't it? I still don't like pink lemonade and my dislike has more to do with the boy cousin who teased me about its girly color than the taste of the lemonade!"

We chat about yogurt and memories for a few more minutes. "And is Jeanette investing all of her money?" Virginia asks abruptly. "Not enjoying any of it?"

"So I hear."

"And what about you? Are you and Joe doing anything special?"

"We bought some new clothes. That's about it. And we want to put some money into marketing Joe's books, when he has time from his writing to think about it. And we've had our share of people making suggestions for so-called investments."

"And charity?"

"I've had a lot of fun playing Secret Santa," I confess.

"Well, if you decide that you want to do something a little more formal with it, you might keep the orphanage in mind," she says, looking up at me.

"Oh Virginia, not you, too!" I try to laugh, but I can feel the tears rising.

"Oh, you poor darling. I am so stupid." She reaches for my hand. "I am so sorry, Ruthie. You have enough burdens right now, and here I am making it worse." Her eyes peer into mine anxiously.

"It seems like it shouldn't be a burden," I say, gulping. "I mean, I should be happy and just spend it, shouldn't I?"

"It's always more complicated than that." Virginia looks at me sympathetically.

A teenage boy comes up behind us and tries to reach around me for some flavored yogurt. I move out of his way, and Virginia hugs me. "I'm sorry, darlin'," she says. She looks at her cart. "This yogurt isn't going to be fit to eat if I don't get it home. And we're in the way." She pats my hand. "I'll be praying for you." She grins mischievously. "That you'll learn to be happy and just spend it."

I watch her go, a little gray haired woman whose grocery cart handles come up to her shoulders. So small and so strong. As she turns into the paper goods aisle, she looks back at me and points her finger at me. "Have fun!" she calls. "That's an order!"

I laugh. "Yes, ma'am," I call after her. I shake my head ruefully. Even Virginia has ideas about how we should spend our money. And Jeanette had been given permission to tell her.

Andy hadn't. The more I think about it, the madder I get. And the next morning I'm even more irritated. I'm at the post office with a package for Carl containing the education trust fund information. I've mailed the package and am walking out when I'm accosted in the lobby by a woman who owns a title company that the de Vargas agency works with. "I hear you're buying a new house!" she says.

"Not that I know of," I answer. I'm having trouble placing her, though I recognize her face.

"Well, it sounds like you can afford it." She laughs and pulls a business card from her pocket. "I just wanted to give you this and let you know that we have plenty of experience with completing large transactions quickly. So I hope that when you do decide to purchase, you'll come to us."

I take the card and nod. There doesn't seem to be any other way out of it. So this is what it's going to be like. Damn Andy. He needs to stop. When I get home, I dial the agency. A strange voice answers the phone. "Is Becky there?" I ask.

"Becky is no longer employed here," the voice says briskly. I frown as I finally recognize the voice. It's Christine, Andy's wife. How odd. Of course, if Becky is no longer there, she might be pinch hitting.

"Christine?" I say. "This is Ruth Marsh. I need to come in to talk to Andy about our insurance coverage. Can you tell me when he'll be in?" Very good, I tell myself. That was quick thinking. Insurance coverage indeed.

There's a pause on the other end. "He's not available this afternoon," Christine says. "Do you want me to have him call you?"

I smile. "Not available" is code for "he's here but he doesn't want to talk to you." Andy's a stickler for not actually lying to callers. "No, that's fine," I tell her. "Just leave him a message that I called and will try to catch him tomorrow."

I tuck my phone back into my purse and pick up my keys. Well, this is as good a time as any. Joe is still in his office working, so I won't have to explain what I'm doing. He'd probably try to talk me out of it, say it was pointless. Which it probably is. But I'm not going to let Andy make my life miserable without at least letting him know I don't appreciate it.

Not that I really know what I'm going to say to him, I realize as I pull into the agency parking lot. The blinds in his office window move. So he's feeling a little anxious, is he? Knows I'm here? Good.

I walk firmly in the door and do a double take. One of the three desks has been removed. There's a new poster on the wall facing the door. It contains a picture of the ocean at sunset and the words "All things are possible to them that believe in God."

Christine is sitting at my old desk, which has been repositioned so she has to turn her head to see the door. She seems to be studiously avoiding looking in my direction. The other desk is occupied by a young blond woman with spiked hair, red eyeliner, and a nose ring. "Hello," I say to her. "Where's Flora?"

The blond smiles at me companionably. "Oh, Flora doesn't work here anymore," she says. "How can we help you?"

Christine has finally turned. She gets up and comes forward, her hand out. "How are you, Ruth?" she says sympathetically. "I hope things are going well for you."

What an odd thing to say. Sympathy seems misplaced, somehow. I feel a sudden urge to laugh, along with a surge of power that I've never experienced in this office before. "I need to see Andy," I tell her.

"Andy's not available right now—"

I shake my head. "There are no other cars in the parking lot," I point out. "I know he's in there. I saw the blinds move when I drove up."

Christine's lips tighten. She gestures toward the two chairs in the waiting area. "If you'll have a seat, I'll see if he's available," she says. I remain standing as she goes to Andy's door. She knocks and opens it simultaneously, then slips inside, shutting the door behind her.

My lips twitch. This would be kind of fun, if I only knew what was going on with Becky and Flora. I turn to the blond. "What happened to Flora and Becky?"

She shrugs. "I guess there was some kind of disagreement when the former office manager quit, and Christine fired them."

"I hope they got severance pay."

She shrugs again and goes back to her computer. "I wouldn't know."

Christine comes out and holds the door open for me. "He can make time to see you now, since you're already here," she says.

Chapter 11

Andy moves away from the window when I come in and comes forward with his hand out. "Ruth!" he says, trying to sound pleased. "How are you?"

I ignore the hand. "Hello Andy," I say. "I understand that half the Chamber of Commerce is under the impression that I suddenly came into a lot of money and got arrogant as a result. So arrogant that I up and quit without warning."

He backs away. "Have a seat," he says, as if I haven't spoken. He sits down and stretches his arms behind his head, trying to look casual. I remain standing. "How are things, Ruth? I understood from Christine that you wanted to talk about your insurance coverage."

"No, I don't want to talk about our coverage," I say. "I'll deal with that some other time. I want to talk about what you're telling all your business cronies."

"Now, Ruth, I had to tell them something when you left so abruptly—"

"I left because you fired me!"

"Regardless of why you left, I still had to tell them something. After all, you'd been here a long time. People notice that kind of thing in a small town like this."

"It's not that small and I'm not that important," I say impatiently. "And even if people did ask, you could have just said we'd had a disagreement, or I'd found a better opportunity, or something,"

Now I'm really feeling angry. My voice rises in spite of myself. "I told you that Joe and I didn't want everyone knowing about the lottery win, and you flat out lied when you said I quit."

He opens his mouth, shuts it, then opens it again. "I don't recall telling anyone you quit. He leans forward. "I don't know where your information is coming from, but I think maybe it's a little lop-sided. I did answer some questions when people asked me if my wife becoming my office manager meant I was having income problems."

"You could have told them I finally had the good sense to leave for more money," I say dryly. I drop into the chair, suddenly tired. There's really no point in being angry with him. He isn't going to apologize. Or change.

"You never asked for more money," he says.

"But I did ask you several times for more money for Flora and Becky. And you seem to have fired them, as well."

"No, I didn't. Christine did. They weren't cooperative."

"Flora wasn't cooperative? I find that hard to believe."

"Becky wasn't cooperative. And you know that Flora was always late and leaving early with some made-up crisis with her daughters. Also, Christine thinks she had a second job she never told us about."

I push back the urge to raise my voice again. "Flora did have a second job. I told you, about that, remember? She's been working at a convenience store in the South Valley on weekends to earn extra money. It never interfered with her work here. And she's a single mom. Of course she had kid stuff to deal with. But she's very quick and knew what she was doing. She was also good for business because she knew just about everyone who walked in the door. I swear she's related to two-thirds of the county. I can't believe you fired her."

"Christine did."

I resist the urge to roll my eyes. I could remind him that Christine is his wife and therefore acting on his behalf, but there's really no point.

"And what about Becky?" I ask instead.

"Becky quit."

"Like I did?"

"No, she actually quit. Christine established some new rules, and Becky didn't agree with them. She said she had been going to quit anyway, so if she could have her final paycheck, she would leave without creating a scene."

I frown. "What new rules?"

"Appropriate business attire, daily devotions, things like that."

And now they have red eyeliner and a nose ring at the receptionist's desk. That's appropriate business attire? My lips twitch but I manage not to smile. "Daily devotions?" I ask instead. "You can't make employees do that."

"We're a private business based on biblical principles," he says. "We can require that our employees follow those principles. And if you're wondering about Rosalind, she's a homeschooled born-again Christian girl who Christine is mentoring."

And who's going to be trouble, if I'm any judge of character. "And when did all this happen?" I ask.

"Friday morning."

"So they probably never got my message with my new cell number."

"I have no idea." He opens his top desk drawer and pokes at the pens and pencils in the upper tray.

I look at him thoughtfully. Under his defensiveness, he seems depressed. "So is Christine going to remain your office manager, or are you looking for someone permanent?" I ask. "Just in case I know of someone who might be interested."

"For right now, she's permanent," he says. He closes the desk drawer. "Juggling the house and kids and the office may get to be too much, but for now, this is the way we're working it. The boys are coming in after school so she can supervise homework."

He stretches out his arms, still trying to look relaxed, then runs his hands through his hair. He picks up a pencil and starts flipping it between his fingers. "It creates a nice homey atmosphere. It's making me more productive, that's for sure."

Poor man. There go the long lunches and afternoons on the golf course. His wife is going to make sure he stays at his desk making phone calls and doing paperwork.

There's really no point in prolonging this. He isn't going to apologize, and it sounds like fate is making sure he pays for his actions. I stand up. "So where did Becky go?" I ask. "Or do you know?"

"I haven't heard from her." He jumps up and opens the door for me, suddenly animated. "I hope you'll consider leaving your insurance policies with us," he says, more loudly than strictly necessary. "We have some great life insurance products, as you know."

"We'll see," I reply.

Christine looks up from her desk. I nod to her and start toward the door, then turn back. The work cell phone I left behind had contained Flora and Becky's home phone numbers.

Christine, could you give me the home numbers for Flora and Becky?" I ask. "I need to get in touch with them. The numbers are in their personnel files."

Christine makes a show of unlocking a desk drawer and looking through the files in it. "I don't seem to have those files here," she tells me. "They must be at home in the archives. If you'll give me your new number, I can get those for you."

I give her my number and leave. As I settle back into the car, I wonder if giving her my number was a smart thing to do. Well, if I start getting odd phone calls from people wanting to sell me something, I'll know where they got the number. But I also know that Flora's cell phone is unlisted—protection against the ex-husband calling her. So Christine really is my only source.

And Becky. She and her boyfriend only have a land line, which is also unlisted. Why would she just quit like that? It's so unlike her. Has the boyfriend insisted? And why? Since I'm heading home anyway, I could just drive by Becky's place and see if her car is there. It's only a couple miles out of my way.

But when I drive down the dirt road in Becky's subdivision, there are no vehicles in front of the single-wide trailer on its half-acre lot.

I pull into the driveway and study the trailer. It's always seemed so unBeckylike to me, with its sand-blasted exterior and tumbleweed-strewn yard. A pickup truck pulls in behind and around me. A heavy-set man in his late twenties gets out. He's wearing jeans, a dirty white t-shirt, and at least a three-day old beard. He comes toward me, a slight frown on his face. I roll down my window.

"Can I help you?" he asks in a surprisingly pleasant voice.

"I'm looking for Becky."

The frown deepens. "So am I," he says grimly. Then he smiles at me, the charm of the smile belying the grimness in the voice. "We had a bit of a misunderstanding, and she hasn't been around the last few days," he says lightly. "I've been trying to get in touch with her, but since she doesn't have a cell, that makes it difficult."

He shakes his head. "I kept trying to get her to buy one, even if it was just a prepaid thing. But she always said we couldn't afford it."

So this is Al. He's quite the charmer. The cell phone story isn't what Becky told me. "If you do see her, could you tell her that Ruth Marsh wants to talk to her?" I ask. I give him my number and head home.

Joe is still working when I get there. I pour myself a cup of coffee, then drop into a chair in the living room. I'm still chewing over my conversation with Andy. I suppose there's no point in being angry with him. Christine, with her poster and her daily devotions and her knowledge of his every move is going to be punishment enough. It won't be long before he's wishing Flora is rushing through the door, late again, and Becky is spending the afternoon inserting invoices into envelopes that should have already been mailed.

Though my conversation with him has reminded me that Joe and I need to reconsider our insurance policies. I'm inclined to think we probably should move them, but I'm not sure where.

I go back into the kitchen and grab the pad of paper we leave on the counter for notes to each other. Now that the initial money is in the bank, we really do need to start figuring out what to do with it.

Insurance is one thing. And we need to get cable internet installed. Which will mean cable TV, too, instead of the antenna on the roof. We're the only ones in the neighborhood who still have an antenna. And I really do need a computer. I'm still sitting at the table making lists when Joe comes in.

He kisses the back of my neck. "Getting us organized?" he asks. He opens the refrigerator. "What are you planning for dinner?"

I raise an eyebrow at him and grin. "Once upon a time you were the weekday cook," I point out.

He closes the refrigerator door. "Sorry," he says, looking boyishly guilty. "I guess you being home so much has made me forget the routine. Do you want me to continue cooking during the week?"

"Actually, I like cooking during the week," I admit. "I'm just teasing you. I bought some rotisserie chicken at the store, which is a good thing, because I turned around and forgot all about dinner until just now."

He sits down across from me. "What's on your list?"

"Well, I started thinking about all the little things that we've wanted through the years. Cable TV, internet service, stuff like that."

"There's actually a big thing that I've wanted that we still haven't talked about."

"Book marketing?"

He nods. "I've been doing a little research on our painfully slow dial-up connection and there's someone in Santa Fe that I think might be able to help us. She's a former marketing professional from New York and apparently still has connections there. I called her but she said she couldn't give me a cost estimate until she had a better sense of my product and what I had in mind."

"Does she market books?"

"She said she'd done books as well as other products and that there were examples on her website. But when I tried to look at the website, the dialup was so slow the computer froze up."

"I'm planning to call the cable people tomorrow," I tell him.

"Or we can do the dish thing."

"We'll need to look at the cost."

He grins. "Was that an automatic reaction, or do you really think we need to be careful about the cost?"

I laugh. That is going to be a hard habit to break. "I guess it was an automatic reaction. The other thing I want to think about doing is changing insurance agents."

"Really? How come?"

I tell him about my experience at the store and my visit to the agency. By the time I'm done, he's pacing the kitchen floor, his jaw tight. "What an asshole," he says. "So now half the county knows we won the lottery. Oh, that's just great."

"I doubt that it's half the county," I say mildly. "But apparently he's told quite a few people, and they all think I'm an ungrateful jerk who up and quit the minute she got some money." In spite of my pity for Andy's situation, I find that I'm still irritated.

"Well, the ones with any sense are going to think you did the right thing, given what a bastard he is," Joe says.

"What really bugs me is that he fired Flora and Becky."

"I thought you said Becky quit."

"Under duress, it sounds like. She wasn't planning on quitting on Thursday, as far as I know. I wish I could get in touch with her. Both of them, actually. I wonder how they're doing."

"I would be careful about getting in touch with Flora," Joe says. "She's likely to want a handout."

"Well, I was hoping to do something for the twins," I tell him. "So I'd just be following up on that. But even if we weren't going to do that, I'd like to see how she's doing. She's going to need a job reference, and she doesn't have my new phone number. I guess I could go by the house or that convenience store she's been working at on the weekends."

"The one in the South Valley? Isn't that in a rough area? Could you wait until we can go together?"

"Joe, I'm over fifty years old and drive a beat up Ford Aspire. No one's going to bother me."

"You know, that's something else we should upgrade."

"My age?"

He grins at me. "No, I like your age. The car. It's twelve years old, losing paint and needs a new radio. I think we should start car shopping for you."

"That reminds me, have you heard anything from our youngest son about whether his truck is still holding up?"

"No. No news is good news, I suppose."

"I hope so. At least he has a way of getting in touch with us." I put my elbows on the table and my chin in my hands. "I wish I knew Flora and Becky did. I thought they had your cell number. But you haven't heard from either of them, have you?"

"No. I would've told you if I had. And given them your new number. But don't you think you're feeling a little too responsible for them, Ruth? They're grown women, after all."

"Grown women who were working for me and who are no longer working because of me. Yes, I do feel responsible. And I think I should."

He raises both hands at me. "Okay, okay. Just keep in mind that this might be the best thing for them both, in the long run."

Chapter 12

But when I go by Flora's house, I find that she doesn't share Joe's certainty about the benefits of the situation. When she sees me at the door, the tears spring into her dark eyes. I brace myself.

"Oh Ruth, what am I going to do?" she wails, running her hands through her hair. "You leave, and Christine fires me and my ex still hasn't paid his child support, and the unemployment office says I'm not eligible, and welfare says I have too many assets."

"Oh Flora," I say helplessly, moving past her into the house. "I'm so sorry for all this. I still can't believe it. I called and left my new phone number but you must have already been gone by then."

Flora follows me into the living room and drops onto the couch. There's a pile of clean clothes on one chair and a school backpack with a torn strap on the other. The television is on. I sit down on the other end of the couch.

"You're looking good," Flora says, brightening. "How are you?" She reaches for the remote and turns off the television.

"I'm fine." I fidget with my purse. "I can't believe Christine fired you."

"I can," Flora says flatly. "She's always had it in for me 'cuz I'm not a church person."

"Did she give you severance pay?"

"Of course not. She didn't even give us our final paychecks. Said we'd have to wait until the regular payday, with no advance at the middle of the month. So I don't have hardly any money and both the girls need new backpacks." She nods to the one on the chair. "Stephi had so many books in hers Friday that it just ripped the strap right off."

I get up and bring the backpack to the couch. "It looks like this would be fairly easy to mend." I turn it over. "The strap could just be shortened a bit, or replaced. The fabric on the backpack itself is still good."

"But I don't know how to sew," Flora says. "And I don't have a machine."

"The cleaners have a repair service," I tell her. "I don't think it would cost much to get it done."

"And then Stephi would be going to school with a mended backpack. She's better than that." Flora lifts her chin. "I'd rather have her carrying her books until we can get her a new one, than having her look all cheap and poor."

I drop the back pack onto the couch between us. I've worked with Flora long enough to know when there's no point in arguing.

"Well, it's your money," I say. "I just wanted to see how you were doing and give you my new phone number." I dig into my purse and bring out an envelope. "I put it in here with a note, because I didn't know if you'd be home or not."

Flora takes the envelope. "Cute purse," she says. "Is it new?"

I look down at it. "No, I bought it a couple years ago at Thrift Town. I just don't use it much because it's a little larger than what I like to carry." I stand up. "I need to go. Keep in touch, okay? And if you need a job reference, make sure to use me, and not Christine."

Flora laughs bitterly. "No problem. The guy at my weekend job says maybe I can go full time there, but I know that's not gonna pay enough, so I'm gonna have to find something else. Do you have any ideas?"

"Not off the top of my head." I move into the hallway. I really don't want to be here when Flora sees that there's a check in the envelope. She's either going to get gushy or hint that it should be more. Or do both at the same time.

I start out the front door, then turn back. "Do you know what happened with Becky? I went by the trailer, and Al said he hadn't seen her since last week."

"I haven't heard from her," Flora says. She starts to open the envelope. "I'll give her your number if I do."

"Yes, let her know I want to see her." Impulsively, I give her a hug. "You're going to be fine, Flora. You'll find something so much better than working for Andy."

Flora looks like she's going to cry again. "I wasn't working for Andy," she says reproachfully. "I was working for you."

I bite my lip. "I know," I say. "And I wish you still were. But I don't need an insurance assistant."

Flora giggles. "Not that rich, huh? Well, I do a great manicure and pedicure, if you need one. Just let me know!"

I chuckle. "That's not really my style, I'm afraid. But do keep in touch, okay? And let the girls know that I want to help supplement that scholarship money when they've received it."

"Oh Ruth, really? That is so sweet! You don't have to do that!" Flora beams at me. Then her face falls. "I'm just worried about getting them graduated, if I can't even afford things like new backpacks."

"It'll be okay. You'll see." Flora is fiddling with the envelope again. I head out the door and down the porch steps. "I'll talk to you later."

She follows me onto the porch. As I put my key in the car ignition, I see that she's finally opening the envelope. Her mouth opens as she pulls out the check. She looks toward the car with a huge smile as I back out of the driveway. I wave at her and pull into the street as she runs down the steps toward me. I shake my head, smile, and wave again. I press on the accelerator.

Well, that was kind of fun. And the twenty five hundred will do more than get Flora over the hump until her paycheck comes in from Andy.

But I suddenly feel more tired than anything else. Flora's energy levels have drained me. And why a new backpack is better than one with a repaired strap is beyond my comprehension. I shake my head. I should have just mailed that note and check, instead of going to the house. Flora doesn't know where Becky is, anyway.

But I have other things to do. I drive to Staples and spend an hour choosing a laptop computer and printer for myself and, on a whim, a new filing cabinet and box of printer paper for Joe. The filing cabinet in his office is a battered black cast-off from a garage sale we attended ten years ago. Two of the three drawers don't close properly because the front panels are creased.

I ponder the desks, then decide that Joe really needs to make that decision. The file cabinet box barely fits in the back seat, so I head home.

I spend the rest of the afternoon getting familiar with my new computer and setting up the appointment for getting cable service installed. They'll be here next Monday, some time between nine and five.

I make a rueful face as I end the call. It doesn't matter how much money you might have, you're still at the mercy of the cable guy's schedule. Monday is going to be something of a black hole. But it'll be great to have internet service.

In the meantime, my new printer also acts as a scanner, which means I can finally organize all the pictures I've been collecting in boxes all these years.

However, whether I'm ready to stir up the memories the photos of my parents will raise is a whole other question. I'm still sitting in the kitchen, laptop in front of me, chin in my hands, thinking about what could have been, when Joe walks in.

"Hi, honey, I'm home," he says with a grin. He reaches for the refrigerator door. "I got a lot done today. It felt good." He pulls out the water pitcher and holds it toward me. "Want some? What are you up to?"

I shake myself. "Just wondering if I want to start tackling a family photo organization and scanning project."

He cranes his neck at the machine in front of me. "So you finally broke down and bought yourself a laptop?"

"And a printer with scanning capability. And we're getting cable service installed on Monday." I frown at him. "They're going to be in your office, putting in the connection. Is that going to mess up your schedule?"

"What time?"

"Anywhere between nine and five."

He rolls his eyes. "Well, I guess I'll just work around them. I have a bunch of organizational stuff I have to do, so I can just plan on doing it then."

"And I bought a new filing cabinet for you, to assist you in your organizational efforts." I grin at him. "But it's still in the car. I couldn't figure out how get it into the house by myself, without pulling some muscles or something."

He laughs. "Well, once I get it out, I'd like to head down to the car dealership after dinner. I made a phone call today, and it sounds like they may have something that would make hauling new file cabinets home a little easier."

I raise an eyebrow and grin. "How many more do I need to haul?"

But when we get to the dealership, I start feeling anxious. The SUV's the salesman has on the lot are beautiful, but do I really need this? It's not the same as the filing cabinet or even the laptop. Those are things we've needed for a while, anyway.

But my Aspire is still functioning. Replacing it isn't critical. While Joe talks about gas mileage with the salesman, I walk around the dark red SUV with the leather seats, five disk cd player, and voice-activated radio. This is all just a little too luxurious for me. I shake my head.

Joe breaks off his discussion with the salesman and comes over to put his arm around my shoulders. "You okay?"

"I'm just not sure I'm ready for this, Joe." I frown at the car's gleaming finish. "It's just too much."

"Too much money?"

"Too much spending too quickly. Too fancy." I look up at him. "Do we need to make a decision right now?"

"If I told you I wanted a new truck, would you be willing to buy it?"

"You know, we probably should replace the truck," I say thoughtfully. "It's been breaking down on you every time you turn around. At the very least, we should get new tires on it. And do something about the upholstery."

He smiles at me. "It seems to me that the Aspire has been breaking down almost as often as the truck. And the tires on it also need to be replaced. The upholstery has seen better days, for that matter. And the radio doesn't work."

"The radio is fine. The cd player died, is all."

"But you don't want to replace it."

"These vehicles are all so fancy they just seem like overkill."

"You've been poor for so long you don't even know what it's like to be middle class, much less rich."

I look around the showroom. The salesman is coming toward us with brochures in his hand.

"Hush, he'll hear you. We don't want to spend more money than we have to."

He grins at me. "Shall we just take one for a test drive?"

"The simplest one they have."

"Or do you mean the cheapest?"

"I just don't want the equivalent of a Lexus."

"I know. But since we have the money, I thought we might want to look at a hybrid."

"As long as it's not complicated."

"You just plug it in," says the salesman, coming up behind us. "We have a baby blue hybrid Escape that you might want to look at. It gets great mileage and has a lot of space for hauling groceries or sports equipment."

Two hours later, we leave with the Escape. As we drive off the lot, I glance out the window at the Aspire, which is sitting off to one side. The dealership has given us a $1000 trade-in value for it. I'm not sure it's worth that much, but then, the salesman was happy to accept a check for the full amount of the new vehicle.

I look at Joe, who's experimenting with the air conditioning controls. "Paying cash certainly makes the car-buying process simpler, doesn't it?"

He grins at me like a little kid. "That was fun."

I laugh. "I have to admit that it was. As was buying that laptop and printer this afternoon. I guess I'll have plenty to do for the next few days, what with reading all the new manuals and figuring out how things work."

"That'll be a good project for Monday, while we're waiting for the cable guy. You are going to be there when he comes, aren't you? Because I don't know what you've told them about what we want done."

I grin at him. "Yes, I'll be there." My stomach tightens. "Though I really want to sit down and figure out how much we've spent. The money isn't infinite, you know."

He reaches across and pats my hand. "I know. And now you can set it all up on the accounting software that came with your laptop. That should simplify the bill-paying process."

"All I have to do is figure out how it works," I tell him. "Though I did take a look at it this afternoon and it didn't look too complicated, as long as I don't try automating everything or running elaborate reports. Did you know you can set it up to automatically pay your bills online from your bank account? That seems a little too automatic for me."

"Welcome to the middle class, my love."

I shake my head at him. "Why do you keep calling us middle class? I hate to tell you this, Joe, but I think we might actually be rich."

He looks out the passenger window and fiddles with the lock button. "I don't know. I guess I'm just not ready to think of myself as rich yet. Seems too much of a jump from the poverty we've been living in."

"I have two things to say about that," I say as we turn into the subdivision entrance. "First, anyone who can walk into an auto dealership, write a check, and drive off with a new vehicle is pretty rich. And second, we were lower middle class, not poor."

"I'm beginning to realize just how on the edge of poor we were," he says ruefully. "Now that we have the ability to buy all the stuff we've been doing without all these years, I'm realizing just how much stuff we've been doing without. If that makes sense."

"I never felt poor, Joe." I touch his knee. "I had you and the kids. What more could a woman want?"

"Besides a smart phone, new laptop, a printer that also scans, and a new car, a hybrid no less?" He grins. "Oh, and new shoes and some new clothes and cable internet service. I'm not going to suggest a new house yet, because I think that might be pushing your limits a little. But I do think you ought to take Ruby up on her clothes-hunting offer."

I stick my tongue out at him as I steer the car into the driveway. "Or maybe I'll just find a seamstress to make all my clothes."

He leans over and kisses my cheek. "If that's what you want, my love, then that's what you should do."

I shake my head at him. "I'm not quite to the point yet where I want to set up as a clothes horse. Though I have asked Gloria to go with me to Ruby's shop."

"So you don't need me to go with you?" he asks hopefully.

I laugh. "No, I don't think so. And don't look so disappointed."

Chapter 13

In preparation for the shopping trip with Gloria, I buy half a dozen fashion magazines and a book on determining your fashion style and spend the weekend and Monday studying them, alternating with the computer and printer manuals while I wait for the cable guy.

But when Wednesday morning comes, I'm still not sure what look I'm after. Casual, but not sloppy, I suppose. Minimal jewelry. Not too trendy. And what I buy needs to be able to be washed and dried at home. I'm not going to add to the earth's chemical load by taking my stuff to the dry cleaners.

That reminds me that the washing machine is once again making a whining sound. I'm going to have to have someone take a look at it. Though it is twenty years old, after all. Maybe we should think about replacing it.

I chuckle at how easily that thought slipped in. Replacing instead of repairing or just putting up with the problem. What a novel idea. Maybe I really am getting used to having some money. I wonder how much I'm going to end up spending before the day is over. I have no idea what to expect, or what a reasonable level would be.

And Gloria doesn't help. "I'm going to hide the price tags from you," she says as she settles into the new car. "You need to think about what you like and what fits, not about price. Promise me?"

"Sort of like what I did with the car?"

"Sort of. Though you didn't exactly get a Rolls Royce, did you?" She pats the fabric seat.

"Not my style. But it has a cd player that actually works. And it gets really good gas mileage. So I'm happy."

"It's really nice," Gloria says. "And it's a lot higher up than the Aspire was. It feels kind of weird."

"Yeah, driving it is taking some getting used to," I tell her. As we pull onto the freeway ten minutes later, I say, "I can actually get in the fast lane now as we're going uphill, without worrying that I'm blocking traffic!"

"Wow, you are in the big time!" Gloria laughs. "Ready for a new house yet?"

I scowl at her.

"Just kidding," she says with a laugh, holding up a hand to ward me off. "Though I have to tell you, we listed a house a couple days ago that has its own vehicle lift in the garage. It made me think of your husband and sons."

"But now they can just take their vehicles to a shop to be fixed," I point out. "Though I doubt if they will. They seem to enjoy tinkering. Though I wonder if that will change. I mean, I tinkered with the way my thrift shop clothes fit, too, but I'm hoping I'm through with all that. If I can buy stuff that fits right and that I can wash and dry at home, then I would rather buy it."

I maneuver the car into the right hand lane, to exit onto I-40. A few minutes later, I say, "So, we'll be there shortly. Have you ever met my sister-in-law Ruby? I can't remember."

"I think she was at your Christmas potluck last year. The short skinny woman with the blond highlights and too much jewelry?"

"Well, I thought it was too much jewelry. She thinks she's the height of fashion."

"And she's going to be your fashion consultant?"

I grin at her as we pull into the ABQ Uptown parking lot. "That's why I invited you along. To protect me."

As we're getting out of the car, Gloria says, "Okay, now remind me. Simple clothes that fit and don't require a trip to the cleaners. And I get to express my opinions freely."

"Yep. You get to be the bad cop."

"Or the good one, depending on the point of view."

Laughing, we enter the store. Ruby swoops down on us from the opposite corner. "Ruthie, it's so good to see you! And I'm so excited about helping you find your new image!"

Introductions over, we take a tour, with Ruby explaining the styles that are in fashion or about to become so, Gloria and I pausing occasionally to touch the fabric of a sweater or admire a particular color.

Then Ruby guides us into the largest of the dressing rooms in the back, where she's already hung skirts, blouses, and dresses and stacked slacks and sweaters. "Now I'm assuming you need a few of everything," she says. "So I brought in a small selection to get you started. I'm assuming you're wearing good foundation garments."

Gloria and I exchange glances. "My bra and panties are new, if that's what you mean," I say dryly.

"Let's see how they fit." I pull off my jeans and long sleeved t-shirt and Ruby looks me over critically.

"Well, we could have outfitted you with a prettier bra," she says. "But I think those will do for now. So let's start with the pants, shall we?"

While we've been going through the underwear inspection, Gloria has lifted the stack of slacks into her lap and is reading tags. She hands me two pairs of the five Ruby has set aside. "These are the only washable ones."

"Washable?" Ruby says. "What does washable have to do with how they fit? You want to think about style and fit before you worry about fabric care. Besides, you should have all your clothes dry cleaned if you possibly can. They look so much more polished if they've been professionally cleaned."

I pull on the first pair. "I don't want to be running to the cleaners every time I turn around." I look over my shoulder into the mirror. "Do these seem baggy in back?"

"They do seem loose," Gloria says.

Ruby pushes the door open. "Come and look at it in the three way," she says. "You can't tell the fit if you're twisting around."

We hold a consultation in front of the three way mirror, which confirms that the pants really are too baggy in back, then go back in to try the other pair—also baggy—and then on to the skirts and tops.

I choose a denim skirt, two cotton blouses, and three sweaters that don't have any lace or sequins on them and don't require a trip to the cleaners.

"And now let's take a look at the dresses," Ruby says briskly. "And you'll want some costume jewelry to round out your look."

"I'm not sure that I need any dresses, since I'm not working anymore," I say, picking up my jeans. I'm getting tired and I'm chilly. "The skirt should be all I need."

"One skirt? Oh, sweetie, you're going to need more than that!" Ruby says. "Besides, you still don't have any slacks! That reminds me, I think I may have something that might work for pants. Let me just go get it while you try on this dress." She hands me a bright red gauzy construction and goes back into the front of the shop.

I lift the dress to my shoulders and look in the mirror. "It's a little flimsy," I say doubtfully.

"It's a great color, though," Gloria says. "You should try it on."

I make a face as I pull it over my head. "I'm starting to burn out."

Gloria nods. "We could always get these and go get some lunch and come back later."

I grin at her in the mirror. "But I don't want to come back," I whisper, then more loudly, "Can you zip this for me?"

Ruby opens the door. She has some black stretchy fabric in her hand. "Found them," she says triumphantly. "These are going to be the next big thing— Oh Ruth, that is gorgeous!"

I look in the mirror and then at Gloria. She's smiling.

"It's perfect," Gloria says.

I look at myself again. It is pretty, but I'm not sure where or when I would wear it. "I don't usually wear this kind of fabric," I say. I look at Gloria. "Is it washable?"

"Yep. You don't even have to iron it."

"Oh, Joe is just gonna love you in that," Ruby says.

"He always has liked me in red," I say slowly. I smile at my image. I'll find somewhere to wear it. I nod at Ruby. "Okay, this is a definite yes."

"And now I want you to try these," Ruby says. "We just got them in yesterday. They're the latest thing. They look great with everything."

I take off the dress and pull on the pants. I don't recognize myself in the mirror. "Well, they do make me look thinner," I say, trying not to laugh. "But I can hardly breathe."

"Oh, you get used to that," Ruby says.

"They certainly aren't baggy in the back," Gloria says, grinning.

I look over my shoulder at my back side. Tight is hardly the word for these things. Compression might be more accurate. "I feel a little exposed."

"Are they washable?" Gloria asks.

"Probably hand washable," I say. "Like nylons or tights." I shake my head and begin pealing them off. It feels good to breathe again. "These just don't feel right, Ruby."

"But you still haven't chosen any slacks," Ruby says. "Do you want to look at more skirts, instead?"

We'll be here until midnight if I don't put a stop to it. Thank goodness it's almost noon. Lunch is a great excuse. "I think I need to stop for now," I tell her. "I need to get some food in my system."

"Well, before you do that, let's look at accessories," Ruby says. She gathers up the clothes in my "to buy" pile and carries them to the front while I dress. I look at myself in the mirror.

"Those tops will be an improvement," I tell Gloria. "But I personally like the way these jeans fit better than any of the pants I tried on."

"Are you telling me you're just a jeans and sweater woman?" Gloria grins at me.

"Maybe." I push back my hair and straighten my shoulders. I take a deep breath. "Okay, let's go look at accessories. I'm going to need your help, or we're going to wind up buying stuff I won't ever wear."

Ruby has laid out the sweaters and blouses on the counter and is collecting jewelry to match each one. Beside each top she's placed a bracelet, a long chunky necklace, and large earrings to match.

"Where would I wear all this?" I ask.

"Well, to charity events. Or to the grocery store. Or at home while you're waiting for the cable guy." Gloria laughs. "Or shopping for more."

"This elevates your style to a whole new level," Ruby says, coming up behind us with jewelry for the last sweater. "Doesn't this turquoise set off this dark red sweater beautifully? And it will look great with the new dress, too."

"Actually, that necklace isn't too bad," Gloria says. "It's shorter than the others."

We select three necklaces with earrings to match. I wonder how much of any of them I'll actually wear. Finally, we're done. When the total rings up, I gulp. That can't be right. Gloria nudges me. "Just get out your credit card. I told you, no price checking."

"I don't think I've spent this much on clothes in my entire life," I tell her.

Ruby hands me the receipt. "You're going to look so great!" she says. "Do you want to go change your outfit before you leave?"

"You know, that would be fun," Gloria says. "What do you want to wear first?"

Ruby is wrapping items and slipping them into the shop's exclusive red bag. As she reaches for the red sweater, I put my hand out.

"And the turquoise necklace and earrings, too?" Ruby asks. I grin at her and nod.

I change quickly. As Gloria and I head out the door with bags full of clothes, Ruby says, "Now I've put your information on our distribution list, so you'll get the latest catalogs and flyers. And we have some slacks coming in next week that I think might work for you, so I'll give you a call when they arrive."

"Okay, thanks," I answer automatically. But my stomach drops as I say it. I'm not sure how much more shopping I can take. When we're outside, I turn to Gloria. "I may need more protection again, since she's so determined to sell me slacks that don't fit."

Gloria laughs. "Any time! I'm having fun being your personal fashion expert. But I think I know where you might be able to find some washable pants that actually fit."

"Not before we get some food," I tell her. "I'm feeling pretty frazzled all of a sudden."

Even as I say it, I know that hunger isn't my real problem. It isn't even the amount on the sales slip. Well, maybe that's part of it. All of my energy has disappeared and the new necklace feels too heavy for my neck.

We head to a nearby deli to eat lunch. Even with food in my system, I feel no interest in more shopping.

I stir the ice in my soda and shake my head at Gloria. "You know, I like the clothes I got, but why does it make me feel so cranky to buy them? And kind of sad."

"Guilt, I suppose," she answers. "You always have acted like you felt life wasn't supposed to be easy."

"But life isn't supposed to be easy," I say in surprise.

"Who says so?"

"I don't know." I shrug. "Everyone I know, except you. It's just the way I was raised. Isn't everyone taught that?"

She puts down her sandwich. "Yeah, I think most people are taught that, or they just sort of absorb it from the atmosphere. But that doesn't make it true, does it?"

I nod to acknowledge her point, then shake my head. "But the amount I just spent on clothes would pay most people's mortgage for a couple of months," I point out. "Why should I have it easier than other people?"

"So you should feel guilty if life isn't hard for you?"

I can feel my shoulders hunching inward. The new necklace feels enormous. "Well, what's so special about me that I should have it easier?"

"Maybe it's not so much that you're more special than anyone else, but because you're supposed to be doing something more productive than babysitting a State Legislator," Gloria says.

My shoulders straighten, ready for battle, but she waves a hand at me. "Oh, don't look at me like that. Though I hate the word 'productive.' There we go with duty and guilt again." She laughs. "But I suppose if you want to use language that makes things not easy, 'productive' does work."

"That's the problem, though," I say, slumping over my food. "I don't know what it is I want to do. And I think 'productive' is a perfectly adequate word."

"I should have said 'fulfilling' or 'fun,'" Gloria says. "Or maybe 'soulful.' Something that makes you really happy and feel good all the way down to your toes."

"Does real estate do that for you?" There's a sense of relief in turning the conversation away from myself.

"Actually it does. I mean, there are days when I wonder if I'm crazy, given some of my fellow realtors and their attitudes. But for the most part it does make me feel good."

She bites into her sandwich and chews thoughtfully. "You know, I don't think I would have survived real estate if it hadn't been for you."

"Me? You weren't even doing real estate when we bought the house." I shake my head, remembering. "That was a long time ago, wasn't it?"

"Remember what it was like when you bought it? How grubby it was?"

"Oh, it just needed some paint and some grout, is all. And new linoleum in the kitchen."

"And yard work and curtains and God only knows what else. I thought you were crazy to buy that house. It was so awful. But watching you fix it up made me realize how to see what a house could be, not just what it currently was. I've used that lesson often, when I'm talking to clients about a potential purchase."

"I had a lot of fun fixing that house up," I tell her. "It was something I enjoyed doing. If you don't like that kind of thing, it probably wouldn't be a good idea to buy a place that needed work."

Gloria laughs. "That's for sure. But I can generally tell whether the person I'm talking to likes handyman work."

I smile, remembering. "Which I still do, actually. It made me feel good to fix that house up. It was like the house itself wanted me to. Like my work on it made the very walls happier."

"What I've discovered is that people can be happier, when they're in the right house. I love matching people with the right place to live, the place that helps them blossom and be happy."

"I wonder if it's possible for me to find something to do that makes me blossom and be happy," I say wistfully.

"I think that's why you have this money," Gloria says. "To give you that chance." She grins and puts her napkin beside her plate. "And clothes are a part of that process, too. At least for me. Let's see if we can find you some pants."

And we do find some, at what seem like exorbitant prices. But I have to admit that I like the way they fit. I also buy another dress and a couple pairs of shoes. We haul our stuff back to the car and get in.

"Wow," I say. "I can't believe I just spent almost two hundred dollars on a pair of pants. And bought three pairs of them." I shake my head. "And Joe must be wondering where on earth we've gotten to."

I ask Gloria to drive on the way back, so I can call Joe and tell him I haven't forgotten him. Or dinner.

"Oh, dinner's not a problem," he says. "I ordered some pizza. It should be here about the time you get home. And there's still salad stuff in the fridge. By the way, Ruby called and we set a date to have dinner with her on Sunday."

I grimace. So, in addition to spending an exorbitant amount at her shop I'm going to have to endure dinner with her, too.

When I get off the phone, I turn to Gloria. "Can you come and have pizza and salad with us? I need help deciding what to wear to dinner with Ruby on Sunday."

She grins at me. "You mean whether to wear the red dress you bought at the shop or the blue one you bought at Macy's?"

The clothes and the dinner with Ruby are the primary topics of conversation at dinner, with Gloria and I trying to convey to Joe the difference in fashion styles between me and Ruby.

He finally gives up trying to understand, but remains loyal to both of us by saying he likes my style best, and that the red dress is perfect on me, so Ruby obviously has an eye for what works.

Gloria praises his gift for diplomacy and leaves laughing at both of us. As her car lights turn out of the driveway, my cell phone rings.

It's Sam. "Hey, Mom. What are you up to?" he asks.

"Not much. Clothes shopping at Aunt Ruby's shop."

"Sounds like fun. Hey, I was wondering if you guys would be interested in a business investment that a friend of mine has going."

"Um, I don't know. What is it?" I look at Joe, who has stopped in the middle of putting the leftover pizza in the refrigerator and is watching me.

"It's a pizza parlor that would serve only healthy pizza. You know, gluten free, and lactose free and vegan and stuff."

"How old is your friend?"

"He's like in his mid-thirties."

"What does he want?" Joe asks.

"Just a second," I say into the phone. "It's Sam," I tell Joe. "He has a friend who wants to start a vegan pizza business."

Joe closes the refrigerator door. "That's what we have a financial team for."

I nod at him. "If he has a business plan or proposal or something, we can run it by our financial advisers," I say to Sam.

"He needs the money like yesterday," Sam says impatiently.

I frown. "Sam, that doesn't make any sense. You mean he already has the business in place but he's looking for more money?"

"Well, he's behind on his rent and his doors aren't open yet. It's costing him more than he thought to get it started."

My lips tighten. "You haven't given him anything, have you?"

"Well, a little bit."

"How much is a little bit?"

"About five."

"Hundred?"

There's a pause on the other end. "Thousand."

"That's a fifth of what you had. That was supposed to be for your new truck and to keep you going until you started getting the trust fund payments."

"I know, but I didn't have to put as much down on the truck as I thought, so I still had plenty. I may be a little short before the payments kick in, though."

Joe is leaning against the refrigerator door, drumming his fingernails on the countertop beside him, raising his eyebrows at me questioningly. I can't deal with both Sam and him at the same time. I turn and go into the living room. I hear the dishwasher open and dishes rattling into it.

"Look, Sam, you need to be careful," I say. "That money is for you to spend on yourself, not invest in your friends' business schemes."

"Jeanette's investing hers."

"Jeanette has a business degree. She knows what to look for. She also has a steady job. And she's better at saying no than you are."

"Yeah, she's always been good at saying no."

To bratty little brothers who wouldn't leave her alone. But all I say is, "I'm not going to get into your past arguments with your sister. Just give this guy my email address and don't give him any more money, okay?"

"I'll try."

"Oh, Sammie, come on. Do more than try, okay? Just tell him no."

"But he's a good guy, Mom."

"If he was a good guy, he wouldn't be taking your money and asking for more. Do you have anything from him that says when you're going to get that five thousand back, and how much interest he's going to pay you?"

"Well, not exactly."

I sit down on the edge of the couch and smile in spite of my irritation. He's such a soft touch, for all of his macho attitude. I might have known he'd be the child who'd have the toughest time with this.

I take a deep breath. "Okay. So, I tell you what. In the future, if someone asks you to invest in something, tell them you need to run it by your team of financial advisers, okay? Then send me or your Dad the information and we'll ask our team to take a look at it."

He chuckles. "My team of financial advisers. That's cool. Yeah, I can do that."

Okay, that's settled for the moment. Time to change the subject. "So what does the new truck look like?" I ask.

"It's hot! It has a hemi engine and chrome wheels and a wicked paint job. Wait 'til you see it!"

"We're going to Aunt Ruby's for dinner on Sunday. Do you want to join us? It sounds like a truck she would appreciate."

Joe's in the doorway, grinning and shaking his head at me.

"Maybe. Sara might be home for the weekend, and we were talking about going to a movie with a couple of people."

"Okay. Well, let me know so I can tell Ruby whether to set a place for you."

"Okay. Thanks Mom. Love you."

"You're welcome sweetie. Love you, too."

Joe sits across from me in the overstuffed chair. "Trying to create a bit of Ruby buffer?" he asks with a grin.

"Wherever and whenever possible. She's always had a soft spot for Sam. She won't mind. But I don't think it's going to work. Sara may be in town this weekend."

He makes a face.

"But that's the least of our Sam worries," I say. I tell him about the pizza business loan.

"The level of that kid's immaturity never ceases to amaze me," he says.

"He's only twenty, Joe."

"He acts like he's sixteen."

"Well, he's never had this kind of money before and he doesn't know how to handle it." I explain that I've offered our financial team as a vetting mechanism.

"I just hope he does what you said." Joe shakes his head. "I have a feeling this isn't going to be the first of this kind of news. And who knows what bright ideas Sara will come up with. In some ways she's my biggest worry about that youngest son of ours. If she decides he should marry her, life will really get interesting."

"Oh man, I hadn't thought of that."

I get up and cross the room to kiss the top of his head. "But, as long as you're willing to call him 'that son of ours' instead of 'that son of yours,' I think we can weather it. By the way, Gloria tells me that the real estate agency has just listed a house with a vehicle lift in the garage. Does that sound interesting to you?" I begin straightening the magazines on the coffee table.

"Well, if it also has enough space for offices that don't double as guest rooms, that could be a possibility," he says, retrieving a magazine from the stack. "Don't throw out this Writers Digest.

I'm not done with it yet. But even more than a house, I'm interested in getting someone to help market my books. Are you available to come to Santa Fe with me on Friday to meet with Carol Pastioni?"

Chapter 14

We're in Santa Fe bright and early Friday morning, me wearing my new denim skirt, a new blouse, and the chunky silver necklace and earring set. "I feel a little silly," I say to Joe as we drive toward Canyon Road, where Carol Pastioni has her office. "Like I'm overdressed."

"You look great," he says. "And you look a lot more confident than I feel."

I raise an eyebrow at him. "Why should you be anxious? You're thinking about giving her work, not the other way around."

"But what if she thinks it's not marketable? Or she wants to charge us some outrageous fee and I agree to it and then discover it's way more than it should be?"

"I don't see why she would think it's not marketable. You've been selling, just not as much as you'd like. And the only way to find out what she'd charge is to talk to her. Let's just not pull a Sam and agree to something before we've considered all our options."

He grins. "So you agree that your son is impulsive?"

I stick my tongue out at him. "Yes, your son is rather impulsive at times!"

"Here's the building."

We sit and look at the low adobe with its bright blue window shutters and door.

"Well, here we go," Joe says.

"There's only one way to find out," I say.

Neither of us has made a move to open our respective doors. We grin at each other. "We make a great team," Joe says. "So decisive."

I laugh. "Race you to the door."

The blue door opens before we get to it and a slender middle-aged woman with long wavy red hair and no makeup smiles at us. "You must be the Marshes," she says. "I was just about to make a pot of herb tea. Would you like some?"

We follow her into a tiny Saltillo-floored kitchen. "I hope you don't mind sitting in here," she says, filling the kettle. "My office is filled with marketing samples for a new beauty care product I'm working on."

"So what kind of products do you have experience with?" I ask.

Carol puts the kettle on the stove and sits down at the table with us. "This beauty product is a new venture for me. I've marketed everything from sports teams to pen and pencil sets to books. And quite a few things in between."

She nudges several brochures and a paperback mystery that are lying on the table. "These are some samples of my work. I developed the marketing campaign for the products advertised in the brochures as well as for the mystery series."

Joe picks up the book. "I've heard of this author, even though I don't usually read mysteries," he says. "Are you still working with him?"

She shakes her head. "That was when I was working on Madison Avenue. His publishing company was a major client for us."

"So you were an account manager there?" I ask.

Carol nods. The tea kettle starts to whistle and she gets up to tend to it. "Did you get a copy of my resume from the web site?" she asks over her shoulder.

"I did, but Ruth hasn't had a chance to look at it," Joe tells her. "It looked like you spent most of your marketing career in New York working on really big projects."

"Yes, I did. Some I led, and some I worked on as part of a team. It was pretty high powered. Eventually, I burned out. Now I'm in Santa Fe looking to use my skills and achieve a better work/life balance. That's produced some interesting opportunities, like the beauty product project. What kind of writing do you do?"

"I write literary fiction," Joe says, as I dig into my bag. "Primarily novels. We brought a couple with us, if you want to take a look at them." I put copies of the two most recent books on the table.

Carol comes back to the table with some mugs, then brings the tea pot and a plate of cookies. She nods at the books as she puts the pot down. "Who designed the covers?" she asks.

"The publisher, with some input from me," Joe says. "The publisher is a small press out of Las Cruces."

"So tell me about your books."

"They're generally set in the Southwest. I've published three novels and a collection of short stories a long time ago." He picks up the most recent book. "This is a love story about a U.S. park ranger and a woman who's gotten involved with a gang running drugs across the border. The other two are set in the Albuquerque area. One is about high school kids trying to get out of the barrio. The other is about a small town mayor who wins his election by one vote."

"So they're all local, basically."

"It's what I know."

"No, no, that wasn't a criticism," she says. "People elsewhere in the country don't really know much about New Mexico. That's actually a selling point. It's exotic to them. So how were you thinking I could help you?"

"Because the publisher is so small, they haven't been able to really market the books," Joe tells her. "So sales haven't been very good, even though they're available on the internet. And of course, I'm continuing to write, so I haven't been able to really get out and do book fairs or that kind of thing. It all takes money, which is something we just haven't had up to now."

Carol nods. "So what kind of budget do you have for a marketing campaign?"

"Well, that's part of what we need to figure out. What would a high quality campaign cost?"

She spreads her hands. "It depends on what you want to do. With books, you typically want to create some buzz around the product and accompany that with appearances on radio and television programs. You need to hire a publicist who has the contacts to set up appearances. But before you start a campaign, you need to make sure you have a strong print run already available to meet the demand when it occurs. So the publisher would need to invest in the print run."

I pull a small notebook from my bag and start taking notes. "So we'd need to talk to them about that. Then what would happen?"

"In the meantime, we'd develop a campaign tag and a press kit. I can work with you on that and contract with a publicist to go after media interviews once the books are available," Carol says. "My other focus would be on developing and placing print advertising." She turns to Joe. "And we'll need to refresh your website to reflect the campaign."

Joe glances at me. "I don't have a website," he tells Carol. "Until just recently, we haven't had the finances for something like that, either."

Carol reaches for the teapot and begins pouring tea into mugs. "The website alone is likely to cost anywhere from a thousand to fifteen hundred dollars."

"Okay," Joe says. "So what would a marketing campaign run us? With a tag and a press kit and publicist and everything?"

I look up from my notes to see Carol watching Joe's face.

"Anywhere from ten to twenty thousand for the publicity portion," she says. "Even a minimal advertising budget will double that."

"Okay," Joe says.

Carol blinks.

I lean forward. "We've recently come into a legacy," I tell her. "So we're able to afford to do this."

Carol nods. It looks like she's trying not to look relieved. "Forgive me," she says. "I was a little confused. You don't seem to have been doing much, so I just assumed you had a minimal budget."

Joe chuckles. "Sorry about that. I guess it's beginning to seem normal to us. We haven't had the funds up until now, so we haven't done anything, really. That's why there's no web site or anything."

"We've also just been kind of assuming that this is something you'd want to do," I say. "I guess you'll need to look at the books before you can make a decision or give us a good cost estimate."

Carol nods again and reaches for the books. "Well, a product is a product, so I don't have to be in love with your work to sell it, but it does help. Can you leave these with me for a few days? I can take a look at them and then sketch out a preliminary marketing plan and some costs."

We talk a while longer about the books and ways to research website design, then Joe and I leave Carol at the door, holding the two novels.

It's almost lunch time, so we find a parking spot near the Cathedral and walk to the Plaza.

We walk by an art gallery and pause for a minute to contemplate the folk art paintings in the window. "It's so strange looking at these expensive shops that I've never dared to even browse in and know that I could actually spend money there if I wanted to," I muse.

"You with your legacy," Joe says. "I'm impressed. What a great way to explain ourselves."

I chuckle. I'm still not sure where that had come from, but it worked well. "It just kind of popped out," I admit. "But it seems so much simpler than going into the whole lottery thing."

"Until someone asks where the legacy came from," Joe points out as we cross the plaza to the portal of the Governor's Mansion. "Do you want to look at jewelry or go get something to eat first?"

I grin. "I guess I was heading toward the jewelry, wasn't I? I suppose we could walk through and then go around to the restaurant."

Halfway down the covered walkway, I pause to look at some Zuni earrings. "These are all Native crafted," the elderly man on the stool beside the low table tells me.

I smile at him. "I know. I'm from New Mexico." I point to some narrow, delicately engraved silver earrings. "These are different. Are they Zuni, too?"

He smiles proudly. "My grandson. He's seventeen but he has a gift."

"I can see that," I agree. "How much?"

"Seventy-five dollars."

"Do you take credit cards?" Joe asks.

"Oh yes."

We complete the transaction and go on to the restaurant on the other side of the plaza, where we ask for a seat on the balcony. It's just warm enough to make it comfortable there. As soon as we're seated I replace the earrings I'm wearing with the new pair.

"You know you could have probably bought those for fifty," Joe says.

"I know. And once upon a time I wouldn't have even asked how much they were, because fifty would have been more than we could afford. But now I can. And I'm supporting some seventeen year old in his calling. Besides, I like them. Aren't they pretty?"

"They are pretty," he agrees, as the waitress approaches us. "But not as pretty as the lady wearing them."

"You're sweet," I say as I glance up at the waitress beside me. "Becky! Of all people!"

Becky stands there beaming at us, order pad and pen in hand. There's a glow about her that I hadn't seen in all the time we worked together.

"What are you doing here?" I demand. I reach up to touch her arm. "I'm sorry. That was rude. I've been trying to get in touch with you, but I never thought you'd be in Santa Fe!"

"Well, when you left the agency, there was really no reason for me to stay." Becky shakes her head. "I could see that things were going to change for the worse. I'd known for quite a while that I needed to make a change. So that was the proverbial straw, you might say."

I open my mouth but she holds up a hand. "Although in a good way! So I packed what I needed to make a fresh start, and I left Al without telling him where I was going, and I came to Santa Fe." She gestures toward the main dining area. "I'm waitressing here and going to school to become a massage therapist. It's something I've always wanted to do but didn't think I could."

"Wow, that was quick," Joe says.

Becky nods at him. "All the pieces just sort of fell into place. The next session at the school was beginning and it turned out I was eligible for federal educational assistance." She grins at me. "Sometimes it pays to not get paid very much."

She poises her pen above her order pad and smiles at us. "I do need this job though, to help pay the rent. What can I get you to eat?"

We order and she goes inside. "She looks so much happier," I observe.

"So your leaving the agency was a good thing for her," Joe says.

"Yes, it looks like it. You just never can tell, can you? I just wish I knew it was a good thing for Flora."

"Oh, Flora will land on her feet," he says. "And I hope you feel that you've helped her enough."

"I don't know. I haven't heard from her, so hopefully things have settled down. And the money should help to get her over this rough spot."

"And then some. And now you're going to want to do something for Becky."

"Well, I did something for Flora."

"Will Becky want it?"

"I would think so. I mean, she's not exactly rolling in money if she's waitressing."

"Just be careful what you get yourself into."

"Becky's not like that."

"I was thinking of Flora."

"That could get sticky," I admit. "But I haven't heard from her since I gave her the check, so it may be okay."

Becky comes back with our food a few minutes later. "The lunch crowd has descended," she says. "So I'm swamped. I'll see you in a bit."

I watch her as we eat. She moves smoothly among the tables, taking orders and bringing meals, making it look easy.

"I guess she's found her rhythm," Joe comments. "From what you told me, I thought she was kind of slow."

"She was, at office work," I tell him. "I guess she just needed something more physical. If that's the case, massage therapy may be a good fit for her."

"Do massage therapists make a decent living?"

"I have no idea. But if she's happy, that's the main thing. And she sure looks happier."

When we're finished, I write out a check to Becky while Joe fills out the credit card slip. We leave them in the small plastic folder on the table, but Becky picks up the folder before we're out the door, and follows us down the stairs. "Oh no you don't," she says from behind us as I reach the bottom step.

I turn and look up at her, past Joe. "I wanted to do something for you and Flora," I explain. "We gave the same amount to her."

"The best gift you gave me was working for you," Becky says. "You gave me unconditional acceptance, even when I messed up the paperwork and had trouble staying awake in front of the computer. And you leaving gave me the kick I needed to start a new life. A life I love."

From above, a voice calls, "Becky?"

Becky turns her head. "Coming," Becky answers. She turns back and smiles at me as she hands the check to Joe. "Since she won't take it, I'm giving it back to you." She edges past him and comes down the steps to give me a hug. "Thank you for the thought. Once I have my license, I'm hoping to move back to Los Lunas and set up a business. I want you to be my first client, okay?"

The tears in my eyes are making me speechless. I nod.

"Bye now," she says.

"I put the phone number on the credit card slip," Joe tells her.

"Oh good! Thanks!" She waves a hand at us and starts up the steps. "I'm coming, Marina," she calls. "See you two later," she says over her shoulder.

"We're in the way," Joe tells me. I turn and move out of the path of the customers coming in. Joe is folding the check and putting it into his wallet.

"I can't believe she did that," I say once we're on the sidewalk.

"She's quite a young woman," Joe says. "And she may need some help setting up that business. So I wouldn't feel too sorry about it just yet."

"That's true." I nod at the sunlight shining through the leaves of the trees in the Plaza. "Now there's an investment I wouldn't need to run past our team of financial advisers."

Chapter 15

On our way home from Santa Fe, we stop at a big box electronics store in Albuquerque and buy a new laptop for Joe. We spend Saturday afternoon at a training session learning how to "maximize the potential" of our new computers. I spend most of Sunday setting up our accounts on the new financial software. I'm describing its capabilities to Joe as we pull into the parking lot of Ruby's apartment complex.

"Damn," Joe says. "There's Sam. And he has Sara with him. Sorry, Ruth. And I wouldn't automatically reject the idea of setting up ongoing online bill payments. It might come in handy."

"We just need to make sure it's really secure," I tell him. "And Sara's not that bad, Joe. At least she's a known quantity."

"Tattoos and all."

Sam and Sara have seen us and are waiting on the sidewalk near the new truck, his arm around her shoulders, which are covered only with clear plastic rhinestone-sprinkled straps. "Hey Mom, Dad," Sam says. "Sara wasn't busy, so I brought her along."

"Hi Sara, how are you?" I say as I hug Sam.

"Did you let your Aunt know?" Joe asks.

"Uh no. I guess I should've called her." He and Sara glance at each other.

"I'm sure it'll be fine," I tell them. I smile reassuringly at Sara. It's a good thing Sam can pretty much do no wrong in Ruby's eyes.

Two apartments down, a door opens and Ruby peers out. "Are we moving the party out there?" she calls. She comes down the sidewalk, moving quickly despite her three inch heels. "Sam, I'm so glad you could join us."

"Aunt Ruby, this is Sara," Sam says. "Is it okay if she comes, too?"

"Of course, of course. There's always room for one more!" Ruby hugs him and beams at Sara.

She turns to Joe and me. "Come in, come in! Oh, Ruth, you look so great in that dress! I told you it was perfect, now didn't I? And the earrings are a perfect match with that necklace. You're developing a great eye."

I open my mouth and shut it again as Ruby turns away and moves toward her apartment door. I follow the rest of them into the small, immaculately decorated apartment. Everything is carefully arranged and looks like it's just come from the store. I look for some place to put my purse without disturbing the décor.

Ruby disappears into the kitchen while we settle into chairs. When she reappears with a tray full of drinks, Sam leaps to help her. Sara perches on the edge of the couch with her bare legs carefully together under her miniskirt. She has a rose tattoo on her right ankle and a flower tattooed on her left shoulder. They actually look nice on her slender young body.

"So how is school, Sara?" I ask. "You're a senior now, right?"

"A junior," Sara says. "It's going well. I'll be glad when I'm finished. Las Cruces is too hot, and the spring winds blow even harder there than they do here."

Sam sits down beside her and puts his arm along the back of the couch behind her. "Yeah, I keep telling her she should transfer," he says. "UNM has a merchandising program that's got to be at least as good as State's."

Sara gives him a little smile and turns back to me. "He thinks everything at UNM is better than NMSU."

"That's not what I said," Sam protests.

"So Joe, what do you think of Ruth's new look?" Ruby asks. "We dressed her up nicely, didn't we? Quite a change, huh?"

My lips tighten.

"Looks good," Joe says, putting down his glass. "And what have you been doing lately, Ruby, besides working?"

"Oh, nothing much. Work, work, work, that's what I do. Have you been having fun spending all your money?"

"Actually, he's been mostly working," I say evenly. I smile at Joe. "I think Joe would write even if the house caved in."

He chuckles. "Probably. Although it looks like we may have found someone to help market the novels more thoroughly, so that's good news."

"So that's where the winnings are going?" Sara asks. "Into marketing your books?"

"And into computers," I say. "We bought new laptops for each of us. Learning how to really use them is going to take a while, I think. They have so much software loaded on them, it's a little overwhelming."

"Poor you!" Ruby laughs. She stands up. "I'm going to check on that roast. I think it should be just about ready."

"Let me help," Sara says. She follows Ruby into the kitchen. I grin. The heels of her shoes are even taller than Ruby's.

Joe turns to Sam. "So are you guys back together, or is she just along for the ride?"

"I don't know," Sam says. "Maybe."

"That's decisive," Joe says dryly. "Just be careful, okay?"

"She's not what you think, Dad," Sam says. He glances toward the kitchen door. "She's actually really smart."

"Umph," Joe says as Ruby appears in the doorway.

"Dinner is served," she says.

The roast is perfect and the French bread crispy and hot. As we eat, Ruby says, "So tell me the news. I haven't seen you guys for so long. I know what Sam's up to. And he seems to have a nice and very chic girl friend." She shoots a smile at Sara, who smiles back at her. "So what are Jeanette and Paul doing these days?"

Joe gives her a synopsis of the activities of both. Ruby expresses envy of Jeanette's Japanese business contacts and declares that Paul's school plans don't surprise her at all. "I always knew he had more going for him than auto mechanic work," she declares. "Didn't I always say so, Ruth?"

My mouth twitches. I hadn't been aware that Ruby had any opinion at all about Paul's career choice or intellectual capacity.

"I think we all knew he wasn't really making the most of his potential," Joe says. "But he wanted to find a career that didn't put any financial pressure on us, and the mechanic work was a way to do that."

"Unlike another son, who shall remain nameless," Sam tells Sara dryly.

I shake my head at him and turn to Ruby. "We're just so glad that the lottery ticket will make it possible for him to go back to school," I tell her. "It seems to have come at just the right time for him."

"And Jeanette? Is she just going to invest hers or is she going to have some fun with it?"

"She's having fun working, just like Dad is," Sam says. "She's just going to use it to work more."

"Well, she loves what she does," Joe tells him. "Work isn't a burden if you like what you do. There's a kind of fulfillment in it."

"It's figuring out what you like doing that's the hard part," Sara observes.

I nod at her. "That's for sure."

"A person needs fun in their life, too," Sam says.

Ruby laughs. "So what's your idea of fun, Sam? Working on your truck?"

"Not hardly," he says. "I hated working on that truck. I bought a new one and it's got a sweet engine that someone else will get to tinker with when I want to soup it up some more."

Joe snorts. "You might try maintenance work first. Even new engines need regular oil changes."

"I'm gonna have enough money that I can get someone else to do it."

Ruby chuckles. "I guess you'll need to if your brother is getting out of the repair business. But you'll have your trust fund money, so you'll be okay."

"I'll still have to work," Sam says.

"The trust fund money is designed to give them a foundation, not make them dependent on it," I explain. "So they won't be rich, just stable."

"Ah, stability," Ruby says. "What a wonderful concept. I wonder what that feels like."

"It all depends on how much you need to be stable," Sam says. "Especially if you want to get married or something."

My head swivels. "Married?" I ask.

"And how would you know how much it would take for stability?" Joe asks.

Sam looks at Sara. "Yeah, married," he tells me. "Maybe. And I don't know how much, Dad, but I'm betting it's not forty thousand."

"Which seemed like a lot only a few weeks ago," Joe says, pushing back his chair.

"Oh, and we have baked alaska for dessert," Ruby says brightly. "Joe, can you bring it in for me? It's kind of heavy."

Joe and Ruby go into the kitchen. I look at Sam, who's holding Sara's left hand, which lies on top of the table. Sara isn't wearing any rings.

"This wasn't my idea," Sara says to me. Her face is tight under the carefully applied makeup.

"What is it you want, Sam?" I ask gently.

"For Dad to stop treating me like a two year old," he says sullenly. He leans back in his chair, still holding Sara's hand.

I shake my head. "No, I meant what do you want to do with your life? If you had more money, what would you do with it? How would you spend your days?"

He shrugs. "I don't know. How do you spend yours?"

I wince. "I'm trying to figure that out," I admit. "Right now I'm just trying to support your Dad with his work and get our lives organized. I might go back to school. I might start a business. I don't know."

"What would you study?" Sara asks.

I shrug. I don't really want to talk about it, but I don't want to push Sam, either. "I don't know. I really like helping people. I've had a lot of fun lately being a kind of Secret Santa, using some of our money to make people's lives easier. Paying for their dinners, or gas in their cars, that kind of thing."

"Oh how fun!" Sara says.

"Mom, you're amazing." Sam lets go of Sara's hand and leans toward me. "So you just go around looking for people you can help and finding a way to slip them some cash?"

I chuckle. "Well, it's not a deliberate campaign. But when I run across someone I can help, I try to figure out how to do it without making a big production of it."

"Isn't there some kind of formal way you can do that?" Sara asks. "Like a foundation or something?"

"Then it wouldn't be a secret," Sam points out.

"True. But it's a cool idea," Sara tells him. "You could set something up where you could buy prom dresses for poor high school girls and give them to them anonymously. But do it so the girls didn't feel like they were getting them because they were poor."

"So the girls wouldn't have to ask for help, you mean?" I ask. It's an interesting idea.

"Yeah." Sara fingers her left earring. "I mean, a lot of people won't ask for help even though they really could use it. They're either too proud, or they don't think they deserve it. And they're probably the ones who need it the most—the psychological boost of being considered worth being helped, I mean."

She has a point. "I wonder if anyone's figured out how to get past that problem," I say.

Joe comes back into the room carrying the dessert, with Ruby behind him with more plates.

"So Mom's going to set up a foundation that helps people who don't ask for help," Sam tells them.

"That looks beautiful, Ruby," I say, trying to distract him.

"It did turn out nicely, didn't it?" Ruby asks. "So, how big a piece do you want, Sam?"

"Oh, half of it." He grins at her. "No, just a small piece, Aunt Ruby. I ate a lot of that roast, remember?"

She cuts into the dessert. "I do like cooking for a man who will eat," she says, smiling at him.

"So what's this about a foundation?" Joe asks.

"We were just talking," I tell him.

"I think it's a great idea," Ruby says. "And I could help. I could be like a spy in the community, looking for people who needed help, and then the foundation could give them money or whatever it was they needed."

"That would be an interesting approach," I say evasively. Leave it to Ruby to take over and make it dramatic. A spy indeed.

"So this would be like a job?" Joe asks. He waves his fork at Ruby. "This is delicious."

"I don't know," I tell him. "Could you make a full time job out of spending money?"

Ruby laughs. "Well, I know I sure could! But I don't know how much I would spend on other people."

"I think it sounds cool," Sam says. "And I run across people on campus all the time who need money. I could help."

"Being in the American Studies department, I'll bet you do," Joe says dryly.

"I'm not sure I'm going to stay in American Studies," Sam tells him. "It's interesting and all, but it's not really all that exciting, once you get into it."

"What is it you want to do, Sam?"

"I don't know, Dad. If I did, I would tell you. Art, maybe."

Joe opens his mouth to reply. I try to head him off. "This was wonderful, Ruby," I say. "Joe, why don't we clear up, and let Ruby spend some time with Sam and Sara?"

As I unload the tray of glasses onto the counter beside the sink, I say, "Joe, it's not going to do any good to keep harping at Sam. And be careful with those saucers or you're going to chip them."

The saucers still rattle as he puts them on the counter. "I just get the feeling that he's going to spend the rest of his life living off the lottery money instead of doing something constructive."

"We were having this discussion about what he wanted to do with himself long before you bought that ticket."

"I know, but it seems worse now."

"And maybe this foundation idea would help him focus. It could be kind of fun."

"So you're really going to do it?"

"I don't know. It's just an idea. It might be worth exploring." Though not with Ruby's help, I think irritably. Aloud, I say, "Sara's right. There are a lot of people out there who need help but would never ask for it, for one reason or another." But even as I say it, I know the foundation idea doesn't feel right. It's too structured or something. It would take all the impromptu fun out of what I've been doing.

"And now you have Sara involved. And Ruby, too."

I turn on the water, pull on Ruby's bright red dishwashing gloves, and begin rinsing plates. "Sara's not involved, Joe. She just made some observations, is all. She actually seems like a very sensitive and sensible girl. I think it's the first time I've ever actually talked to her. She was always so quiet when they were dating in high school."

"Sullen, is more like it." He begins filling the dishwasher with the plates.

I start cleaning silverware. "Well, she doesn't seem sullen now. She seems very nice. And a girlfriend who knows what she wants in life may be just what Sam needs."

"As long as it's not our money she wants. You'll notice she came back into the picture after the ticket."

"I don't know about that. They were apparently talking before that, or he wouldn't have been able to tell her about it."

"Okay, okay. I realize you like her. But he's talking marriage, for God's sake. Where did that come from?"

"Well, at least he's thinking about the future. And someone besides himself."

"Is he?" Joe shakes his head at me. "I know he's your baby, but he needs to grow up. And everything he does can't always be justified or explained away, no matter how hard you try."

My lips tighten. I turn off the water and pull Ruby's gloves off. "Maybe, but everything he does or thinks isn't necessarily wrong, either. You actually treat him more like a child than I do. He does have a brain, Joe. Just because he doesn't think like you, doesn't mean he doesn't think."

"I know he's an adult," Joe says. "I just wish he'd act like one and take some responsibility for a change." He sighs. "I'm sorry. Do you know how many times we've had this conversation in the last few years?" He touches my shoulder.

"About a million." I move into his arms. "Sorry," I say into his shoulder. "I do love you. The problem is, I love you both."

"I love you too." He kisses my forehead. "I suppose we should go into the living room."

"Just try to be civil to him, okay?"

He kisses me again. "Okay. I'll do my best." He chuckles. "If you'll try to be civil to Ruby."

"She makes it difficult," I grumble. "You need to decide pretty soon what you want to do for her from the ticket money. She's becoming more irritating than usual. 'I don't know how much I'd spend on other people,' she says. Good grief." I move away from him. "I wonder how they're doing in there."

They're fine, although Sam is looking a little bored, because Ruby and Sara are discussing regional differences in fashion style and which magazines provide the best sense of the trends for coming seasons. But, being Ruby, by the end of their conversation, she's irritated Sara, as well.

"You should apply for a summer job at the shop," Ruby tells her. "That will give you a reference for when you graduate. We're trying to reach out to a younger market, so we could really use someone from your demographic."

Sara shakes her head. "I'm already set for the summer," she says. "I have an internship lined up at the Gap's headquarters in San Francisco. The internships there are very competitive. It's going to look great on my resume."

"Oh, the Gap." Ruby waves her hand dismissively. "They're so hyper trendy. No staying power. Now, if you want to know how to do it right for the long term, we're the place. My chain was around before anyone dreamed of the Gap."

Sara's lips tighten but she doesn't reply. Instead, she turns to Sam "What time does the movie start?" she asks him.

Ruby turns toward me, "Well, I don't approve of Sara's choice of summer jobs, but she's got a great personal look," she says. "You should get her to go shopping with you when she's home on a weekend. She could really help you lighten your look."

Before I can reply, Joe says, "Looks light enough to me!" and steers me out the door.

"You know, she has a real talent," I mutter as we head down the sidewalk. "No matter what she says, it always has an edge. Even when I'm wearing clothes from her shop, she still insists on telling me how frumpy I am"

He clicks open the car door. "I don't think she meant it like that, Ruth."

"Oh yes she did." I yank the car door open. "And she was rude to Sara in the process." I raise my hand to wave at Sam and Sara as they head toward the truck. "It was good seeing you, Sara. Bye Sam!"

Chapter 16

In spite of what I've told Joe, I'm still thinking about what I'm calling my "Secret Santa Foundation" on Monday, as I sit down to continue exploring my new laptop's capabilities. The foundation idea is better than nothing. At least it would give me something to do.

I've carried an end table from the living room into the sun porch and placed it beside the old wooden bench. I'm perched on the bench with a glass of ice tea beside me, the computer on my lap, wirelessly connected to the internet. The spring sun is shining through the porch windows.

I lift my face to it appreciatively. Ah, sunshine without New Mexico's spring winds and the grit the winds bring with it. This is the way to work.

I check the email account, then begin clicking links aimlessly, looking for foundation information but not actually reading any of it in depth. I have to admit that I don't really want to do anything formal.

But what *am* I going to do? Without the need to bring in money to pay the bills, I don't even know how to start thinking about where to focus my energies. This kind of decision making was a lot easier before we won the lottery. Life was pretty straight-forward: we needed a steady income and I'd found a way to make that happen. That little piece of paper has sure complicated my life.

My back is starting to hurt. This leaning over the end table isn't very comfortable. I glance around the sun porch. Speaking of money—

Maybe I should do a bit of furniture shopping for this space. It contains three potted plants and two benches. A table and chair would be nice. And a cushion for this bench. It's a little hard after you've sat on it for a while. Actually, I can probably find something online.

I do a quick search for outdoor furniture. Sure enough, there are kits available. There are also sales going on at the big box home improvement stores, including both the stores in Los Lunas. It looks like I need to go shopping.

Of course, anything I buy will probably need to be assembled. Maybe I can talk Paul into coming for a weekend. Or Sam. Actually, it isn't something either of them really likes doing, although Paul is the most likely of my three men to volunteer.

I type in another search for handymen in the Los Lunas area, and come up with a few ideas. I jot them down. The trouble with working on the porch is that I don't have access to the printer, which is in Joe's office. Maybe I should buy a portable one for myself. I can stop by Staples on my way to Home Depot and Lowe's.

"Boy, you're hard at work," Joe says, coming out the front door.

I grin at him. "I'm concentrating on spending money. I started out checking email."

"Actually, I came out to talk to you about spending money," he says. "Carol Pastioni called. She has a couple of proposals for us to consider and wants to know if we can meet with her sometime next week."

"She didn't give you a price range on the proposals?"

"I think she's still afraid of scaring us off." He grins. "After all, you didn't say how big that legacy was."

I chuckle. "I didn't, did I? Any time next week is fine with me. Are we meeting in Santa Fe?"

"I'm going to try to talk her into meeting in Albuquerque. It'll reduce the amount of time I have to take from this draft."

"That reminds me, did you tell her about the book you're working on?"

"No, I keep forgetting. I don't know why. Help me to remember when we meet with her, okay?"

"Shouldn't you tell her about it before we meet, so she can fold it into her proposal?"

"I guess so." He frowns and looks out across the yard. "I don't know why I have this block about it. I guess I don't see how I can start marketing it when it's not even done yet."

"Afraid the marketing ideas will get in the way of what you're trying to do?"

"Yeah, I think so. Too much market focus and not enough on the work itself. I think I'll just keep quiet about it, for now, unless she asks."

"Whatever you want to do." My fingers move across the computer mouse pad. "I got thoroughly sidetracked with new furniture for the sun porch. I'm thinking about going down to Lowe's and Home Depot. They both have sales on and some of the items are on the Net. Wanta see?"

I show him what I'm thinking about buying, and we discuss options for assembly, then Joe goes back to work.

I stretch my arms out in front of me, relaxing my shoulders. Maybe I should look into the cost of window shades, too. That would make the porch more usable in the summertime.

I grin. I have to admit the shopping part of winning the lottery is kind of fun. But it isn't going to keep me busy forever. There has to be more to life.

While I'm out, I come across a lamp that reminds me of Aunt Marsha. I feel a stab of guilt. In all the excitement about the ticket, I've been neglecting my semi-weekly visits to my mother's older sister in the nursing home in Belen.

Impulsively, I buy the lamp and head south on the freeway. To my left, the cottonwoods in the river bosque are beginning to put on their spring green. This is a sight I anticipate every year, but today it just makes me feel sad. Everything and everybody is leafing out in new directions, except me. And Aunt Marsha.

When I get to the nursing home, I find her asleep. This has been happening more often lately, as she becomes more and more fragile. I think it's part of the reason I'm beginning to forget to come.

I feel a sort of guilty relief. It's becoming harder to know what to say to the once-vibrant woman on the bed. And when she is awake, she seldom seems to remember who I am.

I find a nurse's aid and ask her to install the lamp on the bedside table. I go back into the room and stand at the foot of the bed, watching Aunt Marsha sleep, her mouth slightly open, her hands so transparent they're more bone than skin. At ninety two, she is sleeping through her days, waiting to die. She has nothing left to do.

My own breathing is constricting, my lungs tightening. The old body smell is overwhelming. I move hurriedly out the door. Halfway down the hall, I stop and lean against the wall, trying to catch my breath, closing my eyes against the sudden tears.

"Are you all right, lovie?" A frail female voice asks.

I open my eyes and stand away from the wall. "I'm not sure why I'm crying," I tell the old woman hunched in the wheelchair on the other side of the hallway. I cross the hall and sit down in the brown plastic chair beside her. "I have nothing to complain about."

The old woman chuckles. "I didn't ask what you had to complain about," she says. "But it seems to me that you're feeling disappointed and frightened."

I bite my lip. It's silly, but "disappointed" probably *is* the best word for the way I feel. "My husband and I came into some money," I tell her. Her eyes darken in sympathy. "Nobody died," I add quickly. I look away. "I don't have to work now."

"Did you like your job?"

"I liked some of the people I worked with."

She chuckles again. "An important distinction." She looks into my face with shrewd eyes. "And now you feel you have no purpose and that frightens you."

It isn't a question. I nod, grateful to this woman I've never seen before for speaking my thoughts. That someone has finally figured it out.

She's silent for a long minute, then she says, "You're on a journey, my dear. It may take a while, but you will find your heart's delight."

I look at her in surprise. Her voice has changed. It's stronger, somehow.

"You have a gift you haven't unearthed just yet," she tells me. "But you will. Don't fret about it."

I swallow the pain in my throat. "How?" I croak.

But she has fallen silent, her chin against her chest. Is she asleep? Disappointed, I start to get up.

The white head lifts and I sit back down. "Trust yourself," the frail old voice says. I lean closer and it strengthens. "Trust yourself. Look inside. You'll find it."

Just then a male nurse's aide materializes from a nearby doorway.

"Ready to go back, Margaret?" he asks cheerfully, reaching for the wheelchair handles.

She raises her head and lifts a finger at him. He pauses. She looks at me. "I'll be praying for you." She smiles mischievously. "We also serve who only sit and wait."

Then she nods to the aide, and he maneuvers the wheelchair away from the wall and down the hallway. I say goodbye to the back of her head. I sit for a long time on the hard plastic chair before I get up to leave. When I do, I drive home slowly.

Chapter 17

I'm still pondering the old woman's words several days later. She had said that I'm on a journey, that I have a gift I haven't discovered yet. And not to fret about it. That's certainly easier said than done. And being on a journey implies that there will be an end to this, that I'll find an answer to this question of what I'm here for, the purpose of my life.

But how to find that out? There are people who work as career coaches. I could go talk to someone like that. Is there anyone doing that in Los Lunas, though? I've never heard of any, and pretty much every kind of business came through the insurance agency door at one time or another. Maybe I should look in Albuquerque.

Or just see if there are some books I can read that would give me some kind of direction. I feel a little embarrassed asking for help with these questions at my age. I turn on my computer. Maybe an internet search will turn something up.

My phone rings. I frown at the number, which isn't familiar, then tap the Answer button. Maybe it'll be Becky.

"Mrs. Marsh? This is Sara. I hate to bother you, but I had a weird voice mail from Sam, and now I can't get a hold of him."

My stomach clenches. "What do you mean 'weird'?"

"I'm sure it's fine, but I wanted to make sure he was okay, and I thought maybe you would have talked to him in the last couple days and that way I would know that he was just mad at me, and he was actually all right."

"Sara, could you start at the beginning again? What do you mean 'weird'?"

"Have you talked to him since Monday?"

"No, actually, I haven't. But that's not unusual. It's only Thursday."

"Well, then maybe his phone isn't working or something."

"Sara, you said you had a weird message from him. What did he say?"

"He said he was going to make sure that I knew he wasn't a kid, and he did too know what he wanted and that I would be sorry that I didn't care about him. And then he hung up, and when I tried to call him to tell him I really did care, he didn't answer." Her voice rises. "And I've left messages and texted him and Facebooked him, and he's not responding to anything!"

"What on earth was he talking about? Did you have a fight?"

"Well, sort of. I told him I wasn't ready to marry him and that I didn't think he was serious. He's just trying to get his Dad's attention, is all."

"When did this happen?"

"Sunday night. And then I came back to school Monday morning, and that afternoon while I was in class I got this phone message from him. He knows I have class that afternoon. I'm sure that's why he called then, so he wouldn't have to actually talk to me." She's crying now, her voice breaking on the other end of the connection.

I'm pacing up and down the length of the porch, forcing my thoughts into sequence, my stomach to stop churning. "Tell me again what he said in the message."

"He said he wasn't a kid, even though I seemed to think so, and he was going to prove it. And that he knew what he wanted and that I would be sorry I didn't care about him."

Her voice rises in exasperation. "Of course I care about him! I've had feelings for him since I was fourteen! Hasn't he noticed that I've never had another boyfriend? But I haven't finished school or had a career or anything. How am I supposed to know if I want to marry him, for God's sake? And he doesn't have a clue what he wants to do with himself. What kind of life is that?"

I smile in spite of my anxiety. She sounds so much like Joe right now. "Okay, so I haven't heard from him, but that doesn't mean there's a problem," I say, as much to myself as to Sara. "He may just be mad, so he's ignoring you."

"I know. And I don't want to worry you. But the 'you're gonna be sorry' part kind of freaked me out."

I nod. The knot in my stomach tightens every time she repeats that part of Sam's message. "I'm going to try calling him," I tell her. "I'll let you know when I hear from him, okay?"

"Okay, but can you not tell him that I called you?"

I smile in spite of myself. She sounds so young. "I'll try. But I can't promise you anything."

We say goodbye, and I stand there for a minute, looking down at my phone. I need a reason for calling Sam. Joe and I talked yesterday about going to Elephant Butte Lake on Saturday. I could invite Sam along. Normally, I'd ask Joe if he wanted company. But this is something of an emergency.

I tap in Sam's speed dial number. The call goes to his voice mail. I leave a message asking him to call and then sit staring out at the yard, biting my lip. It's probably nothing. Just Sam being temperamental. I call his roommate's number. No answer there, either. Great.

It's three o'clock. I can be in the city and at Sam's apartment in the University District in less than forty minutes. Am I overreacting? Probably. But still— Sara isn't the only person spooked by Sam's message. It's probably just Sam being dramatic to get her attention. But she's right: The "you'll be sorry" stuff is scary.

But if I go into the city, what am I going to tell Joe? He'll just get irritated and try to talk me out of it by ranting about Sam's immaturity again. Which maybe he is, but Joe's ranting isn't going to reassure me that Sam is okay.

Though I'm going to have to tell Joe that I'm going. It's too far to just leave without letting him know where I'll be. I suppose I can look for "finding your life purpose" books at the bookstore in the Mall.

When I look in the door of Joe's office a few minutes later, he's surrounded by paper and frowning at his laptop screen. He gives me a preoccupied look.

"Okay," he says when I tell him where I'm headed. "And if you happen to run across something that contains a calendar for the early 1980's along with the lunar calendar and tides, I could sure use it about now."

"You can't find it on the internet?"

"Not so far." He waves his hand at the pages in front of him. "I have a sequencing complication and need to know when the moon was full on a Sunday during the summer of 1983."

"Okay, I'll see what I can find. I'm going to take some of that jam I bought the other day to Sam while I'm in town."

"Okay. Tell him I said hi, and Sara does seem like a nice girl." He moves the computer mouse.

I shake my head as I close the door. I'm not sure that message will be appropriate, even if I do see Sam. But then, maybe it will be. Who knows?

But Sam isn't there when I knock on his apartment door, and his roommate Andrew says he hasn't seen him since Monday afternoon.

"How was he?" I ask. "I mean, did he seem upset or anything?"

Andrew shrugs his shoulders. "Seemed okay. Not very talkative. Said he was going for a drive and didn't come back. I figured he was with Junie."

"Junie? I didn't think they were together anymore."

"He was talking to her on the phone that afternoon before he left."

"Do you have a phone number for her?"

He shakes his head. "No. Sorry."

I go from there to the bookstore, but my mind keeps drifting from the books I'm looking for. "I'm sure it's fine," I tell myself.

But I'm not sure, and the knot in my stomach keeps getting tighter. It's been three days since anyone's seen or talked to him. Should I call the police? Sam won't thank me for that, when he does show up.

And I'll have to tell Joe, who's going to vacillate between anxiety and anger. Which is only fair, because that's about how I feel at the moment. Idiot kid. Where is he, anyway? And why can't he just answer his damn phone?

But maybe he's hurt. I'm still standing in the bookstore's Careers section. I look at the titles in front of me and grab three at random. They all seem irrelevant at the moment, but I'd said I was coming for books, so I should buy something. Not that I'm likely to read any of them until I've heard from Sam.

I find a clerk and explain what Joe needs. He leads me to a shelf and hands me a book. I glance at it without really seeing it and take my armload to the register.

As soon as I'm out of the store, I try Sam's number again. No answer. Where can he be? I take a deep breath, forcing myself calm against the rising tide of panic.

Surely he's okay. I wonder whether the University has a record of whether he's been in class the last few days. I can't call the restaurant. He quit a couple weeks ago.

And I don't want to call Sara to ask if he's been in touch with her. Though the poor girl probably isn't paying much attention to her own classes, between being worried about Sam and being mad at him. I smile ruefully. Just like his parents.

Or at least like his mother. I still haven't told Joe. There's no point in calling him, though. For all I know, Sam will answer my voice mail before I pull into the driveway.

But he doesn't. I sit in the car looking at my phone, wondering if I should try calling again. It's only been about forty-five minutes since I called the last time.

Instead, I send him a text message: "What's up? Love you, Mom." I don't want him to think I'm monitoring his every move, but I really do need to hear from him.

Joe is in the kitchen, refilling his coffee cup.

"Sam wasn't home," I tell him.

"Probably in class," he says. "We can only hope."

"I wish there was a way of making sure of that," I say, trying to keep my voice even. "I had a weird call from Sara this morning. That's really why I went by his apartment."

He looks at me over the top of his coffee cup. "What do you mean, weird?"

"She said Sam asked her to marry him Sunday night."

"Oh God. What an idiot."

"She told him no," I say impatiently. "That's not the weird part. He called her on Monday—"

"It shows that she has more sense than I gave her credit for."

"It was when he called her Monday afternoon while she was in class that things got weird. He left a message saying he wasn't a child, and he was going to prove that he wasn't, and she would be sorry she'd turned him down."

"So he was acting as immature as usual."

"And she hasn't heard from him since then, even though she's called him half a dozen times with messages to call her."

"So he's sulking."

"He's not returning my calls either, and his roommate says he hasn't seen him since Monday evening."

I must be doing a good job of seeming calm because Joe only takes another sip of coffee and says, "Maybe they're just missing each other."

"His roommate said he assumed Sam was staying somewhere else."

Joe raises an eyebrow. "He assumed? He hasn't actually talked to him?"

I shake my head.

"So he's taken off somewhere to sulk and hasn't bothered to let anyone know where he's gone," Joe says, putting his cup on the counter with a clink. "Damn it, when is he going to learn a little responsibility?"

"I wish I knew who to call at the University to find out if he's been going to class." I pace restlessly across the kitchen and begin unloading the dishwasher. I need something to do or I'm going to go crazy.

"Even if he wasn't, that doesn't mean there's anything wrong," Joe points out.

"If he was, then I wouldn't be feeling like we need to call the police." I open a cupboard and begin filling it with cups and glasses.

"And tell them what? That we have a stupid son who can't bother to let his roommate or his parents know where he is?"

I turn toward him. "I guess I could call the Parents' Resource Office. They should know if it's possible tofind out if he's been going to class." There's a sense of relief in having a definite task to do.

"You do that," he says, moving toward the hall door. "I have a time schedule issue to resolve."

"Oh, I found a book for you," I say. "I don't know if it will be work. I didn't really look at it too closely. I went to the bookstore after I went to the apartment." I dig it out of my shopping bag and hand it to him.

"Thanks," he says. He turns it over to glance at the back cover, then looks up at me. "I'm not trying to be a jerk, Ruth. I just know that monitoring Sam can take all of our time and energy, if we let it. It's not productive for us or for him."

"I know, but he's still our child," I say. "And that part about making her sorry is just scary."

"I'm sure he had nothing more in mind than not answering her phone and text messages for a week or so."

"That's pretty childish."

"We're talking about Sam, remember?"

"I don't think he's as immature as you think, Joe."

"I hope not, because doing something really dangerous to himself would be pretty immature. And I do love him, even if he does act like a five year old at times." He gives me a quick hug. "Let me know what you find out from the school, okay?"

He heads back to his office. I stand in the middle of the kitchen. Maybe he's right: Sam is probably fine, and I'm probably overreacting. I hope so. But it can't hurt to see what I can find out from the University.

I set up my laptop on the kitchen table. As I'm waiting for the modem and laptop to connect to each other, my phone rings. I rummage frantically through my purse for it, but the call has ended by the time I find it.

I sigh and lay the phone on the table. Well, it wasn't Sam's number or Sara's, so it must not be too important. I type in the address for the UNM parent resource site. As it comes up, the phone's message signal beeps. I'd better answer it, though it's distracting me from my primary purpose at the moment.

I glance at my watch. It's only four fifteen. Someone is bound to be in the Resource Office until five.

I pull up the message. It's from the Bernalillo County Sheriff's Department. They have an abandoned truck registered to a Samuel Marsh. My contact information was found in the glove compartment. Could I please call and let them know how they can get in touch with Mr. Marsh and discuss the truck with him?

I frown. Didn't the dealer change the registration on the old truck when Sam traded it in? I dial the number and explain who I am and why I'm calling.

"Sam traded that truck in on a new one a few weeks ago," I tell the deputy. "The dealer must have resold it and not transferred the registration."

"Ma'am, this one is pretty new," the deputy says. "It's a 2011 yellow Dodge Ram with a custom paint job. Some kind of red firebird design."

My throat tightens. I can't swallow. My heart is pounding, and there's a buzzing sound in my ears. I swallow hard and force myself to speak. "Where was it?"

"It was on Old Route 66," he tells me. "Out in Tijeras Canyon. It had gone off the road and collided with a drainage culvert."

The buzzing is louder. I feel myself swaying forward and make an effort to grip the edge of the table with my free hand. "When?" I gasp.

"We found it early Tuesday morning. We've been trying to track down the driver, but haven't been able to locate him. We're assuming it was Samuel Marsh, since we don't have a record of the vehicle being reported stolen."

I'm swinging forward again. My eyes close. I push myself back, gasping for air. "I don't know where he is." My voice sounds far away and raspy. I force myself to breathe. "I haven't heard from him since Sunday night."

"And how are you related, ma'am?"

"I'm his mother."

"I'm sorry to have to ask these questions, ma'am, but we do need to talk with him. Given the circumstances, we can't just file an accident report. We'll need to investigate."

"Investigate?" My spine straightens in alarm. "What circumstances? Was someone hurt?"

"No, ma'am, there doesn't appear to have been anyone else involved. But there were empty beer cans in the cab of the truck."

"Oh, no. Oh, Sam. For heaven's sake."

"I'm sorry, ma'am. We're going to have to make a report. The longer he waits, the worse it's going to look on the record."

"I don't know where he is," I say again. "If I did, I would tell you."

"I'm sure you would, ma'am. Let me give you my name and number so if he calls or shows up, you can have him contact me directly."

"Okay." I take the information woodenly, hardly aware of what I'm doing. A pain is starting in the back of my head, and I'm having trouble focusing. Or breathing, for that matter. Finally, the call is over. I stare at the piece of paper on which I've written the Deputy's name and phone number.

Oh, God. Oh, Sam. Well, I was right. I haven't been overreacting. I wish I had. What do I do now? I need to tell Joe. A sense of panic overtakes me. It's one thing to argue that there's a problem. To actually have proof is another thing entirely.

Get a grip. Deep breath. Okay, deep breath again. I get up slowly. I stand for a minute in the doorway, bracing myself against the wall. Okay, now I can make it down the hall.

I knock on Joe's office door and walk in at the same time. "I just had a call from the police," I announce. He stops typing and turns. "They've found Sam's truck in a drainage culvert in Tijeras Canyon. They want to know where he is."

"Oh, God," he says, starting up. He grabs me as I begin to weave again, and guides me to the edge of the guest bed.

"Oh, Joe, I'm so scared," I whisper. I feel like someone is strangling me.

He holds me tightly, patting me on the back like a child. "I'm sure it's fine," he says. "I'm sure he's okay. I'm sorry I was such a jerk. It's going to be fine, Ruthie. He's probably off somewhere having a beer with his buddies."

"They found empty beer cans in the truck."

"Shit. What an idiot," he growls. He squeezes my shoulders. "I'm sure there's a perfectly reasonable explanation. But the longer he goes without explaining, the harder it's going to be."

I nod against his shoulder. "That's what the Sheriff's deputy said."

Joe gets up to hit a button on the computer. "Just let me save this, and we'll start figuring out how to find him."

"Okay. Do you think we should file a missing persons report?"

"What with the beer cans and all, that may just complicate things," he says over his shoulder. "I wonder if he's talked to either Paul or Jeanette in the last few days."

"We can start there." It feels good to have a plan. Any plan. "And I can call the restaurant. Maybe someone there has seen him." Oh God, Sam. Where *are* you?

"Yeah, it hasn't been that long since he quit, he may still be hanging around there." Joe groans. "You don't realize how much you don't know about your kid's routine until something like this happens."

"He could be out in the woods with a concussion, Joe. Or worse." I feel like I'm going to throw up.

"Let's make some phone calls before we start imagining worst case scenarios." He switches the computer off and turns back to me. "Besides, I would think the police would have noticed if there were tracks leading away from the truck."

"I hope so. Can you call the kids while I get in touch with the restaurant?"

But no one has seen or heard from Sam since the previous weekend. After an hour of phone calls, we know nothing more than that. And that it's too late to get in touch with UNM to find out if Sam was in class on Tuesday or Wednesday.

"Now what?" I ask, after I've talked to his roommate again and tried to leave another message for Sam, only to find that his voice mail box is full.

"Do you want to call Sara?"

"I don't know. It just seems like it would be worse to tell her what we know."

"I'm surprised she hasn't called you again."

"She's probably trying to keep herself busy. Or calling him every hour on the hour. His phone message box is full. I'd be willing to bet it's mostly messages from her with a few from me mixed in. And I'm sure she would call if she'd heard from him."

"And knowing his truck was left on the side of the road in the canyon with a crushed fender isn't going to make her feel any less anxious."

I smile at him wearily. "I think that's the most sympathetically I've ever heard you talk about her."

"If it wasn't for her, we wouldn't have even known there was a problem before the Sheriff's office called. Or have any idea why there might be a problem. So, yeah, I guess my attitude has changed a little."

"I feel so helpless."

"I know. So do I. I don't know what else we can do, though. I suppose we could check to see if Ruby has heard from him."

My stomach clenches. "The last thing we need is Ruby's opinion," I say sharply.

"And if she knew he was in trouble, she would have called me," Joe says. "They don't normally talk that often."

"Yeah, for all of her 'Sam is my favorite' routine on Sunday, it's not like she sees him more than once in a blue moon," I agree. This is hard enough. Ruby will just make it worse. Oh Sam, where *are* you? "I feel so helpless," I say again.

"About the only thing we can do at this point is get something to eat and go to bed."

Which we do, though we don't get much sleep. Somewhere in the middle of the night, we decide to go in to Albuquerque on Friday and try to talk to the Sheriff's deputy. If he'll tell us where the truck was found, we can take a look at the site ourselves.

"I know it's not logical, but I just feel like maybe we'd see something they missed," I say, my head on Joe's shoulder. "It'll at least make me feel like we've tried."

Joe nods. "At least we'll have something to do while we wait."

Chapter 18

When I wake the next morning, I have a moment of sleepy peacefulness. Then I remember, and the fog of fear rolls in again. I feel like I'm drowning—panic and heaviness combined. I push it back firmly and sit up.

I can't cave in now. There's a perfectly reasonable explanation for all this and when I do see Sam again, I don't know whether I'm going to hug him or yell at him. Or both at the same time.

I shake my head against the darker fear. I'd know if something truly terrible had happened. I would have felt it. I swing my feet out of the bed and head to the bathroom.

We have a quick breakfast and drive to the Sheriff's office. The deputy we talk to isn't the same person I spoke with on the phone, but she's still helpful, telling us where the truck was found, and explaining that we can't see it, since it's been taken to the impound yard until the investigation is complete.

My stomach tightens at the word "investigation." It makes Sam seem like a criminal, even though no one has any idea what actually happened.

The word also makes me angry. The Sherriff's deputies don't seem overly concerned that something really bad might have happened to Sam. They seem to think that he's simply hiding from a DUI conviction. No one seems to even be considering the possibility that there could be another explanation. For all they know, he was the passenger in the truck, and someone else had been driving and drinking that beer.

I tell Joe this theory as we're driving east across the city toward Tijeras Canyon. He shakes his head.

"Not likely," he says. "But it's sweet of you to think so. You know he drinks, Ruth. Not anything heavy, I don't think, but it's probably not possible these days to go to college and not drink."

He reaches for my hand. "But I'm sure there's an explanation. And even if he gets charged with DUI, I really don't care, as long as we know where he is and that he's all right."

I stare out the window at the vehicles beside us, tears welling into my eyes. "Yes, as long as we know he's okay, nothing else really matters. Oh God, Joe. I just can't believe this is happening."

We visit the crash site and learn nothing except that the truck skidded before it went off the road and smashed into the end of the concrete culvert. There's no sign of anyone walking away and into the woods. This is a relief in one sense but, as Joe puts it, "If he didn't do that, then where the hell is he?"

By the time we get home, I've called the University on my cell phone to start the process for finding out if Sam has been in class this week, and Joe has agreed that we should file a missing person report. I had discovered yesterday evening that it's possible to file one on-line, so we do that after dinner, too exhausted and anxious to do much else.

But on Saturday morning, we have nothing left to do. "This is awful," I tell Joe as we eat breakfast. "I don't even feel like doing laundry, much less read those new books. At the moment all I can think about is whether Sam is okay."

He nods. "I know. I feel like I'm going to have to move mountains just to get up from the table."

"I think I'll call his roommate again."

"It won't do any good," Joe says, his elbows on the table. "If Sam had come back, he would have let us know."

"Not if Sam had asked him not to."

"Why would he do that? He's not mad at us, he's mad at Sara."

"That's true. I guess I'm just losing all perspective on this." I get up and move restlessly around the kitchen. "I really need something active to do. Maybe some yard work would be a good idea."

"The flower beds need to be cleaned up. We could do them together."

"Yeah, we need to start thinking about what we want to plant. I noticed yesterday that the daffodils are coming up."

He puts his head in his hands. "I'm so sorry for all the mean things I ever said to and about that kid. Maybe he *is* mad at us."

I stand behind him and put my arms around his shoulders. "It's not your fault, Joe," I say into his hair. "He's just Sam, that's all."

"When we do find him, I'm going to give him a piece of my mind," Joe says, touching my hands. "After I hug him for an hour, that is."

I chuckle. "Only after I'm through doing the same thing."

An hour later, we're raking dead leaves off the flower beds when Joe's cell phone rings. My stomach clenches as he pulls it out of his pocket, then relaxes as he says "Hi, Ruby. How are you?"

He listens for a second, then says, "Hold on for a second, okay? I need to tell Ruth." He pulls the phone away from his face. "He's at Ruby's." Somehow he manages to grin and look disgusted at the same time. "Been there since late Monday night."

He shakes his head and returns to the phone. "Sorry. She's been pretty worried."

My knees buckle. I sink to the ground and cover my face. My stomach heaves and I take deep ragged breaths of spring air, forcing myself not to throw up. Sam is okay. A deep sense of relief washes over me. He's okay.

I look up at Joe, who's still listening to Ruby, and grin at him through my tears. Like I've been the only one who was worried. And saying I was "pretty worried" is the understatement of the century. The relief floods over me again. Sam is okay. He's okay.

And then a wave of shame washes over me. We hadn't called Ruby because I was so irritated about her snide comments about my clothes. My anger seems so petty now. And just stupid. Sam is safe. Nothing else really matters. He's okay.

"We'll be in shortly," Joe says into the phone. He hangs up and shoves it back into his pocket. "He's been at Ruby's all this time. He showed up early Tuesday morning looking crazy and said he needed a place to crash. Apparently he hitchhiked into town from the Canyon. So she put him in her guest room and he's been there ever since. Not saying much. Just sleeping and eating and staying in his room." He shook his head. "She's had late shifts every day this week, so she's been gone a lot. She didn't realize until this morning that he hadn't let us know where he was."

"So we're going in? Does he want to talk?" I chew on my lower lip. "Should we let the Sheriff's department know where he is?"

Joe shakes his head. "Let's find out what happened before we call them. But we should let Sara know he's all right."

"And I put us through hell because I was too proud to let you call Ruby."

"Well, I went along with you," Joe says. "I'm sorry. I should have insisted."

I gulp back my tears and lean into him. "Oh God, Joe. He's really okay. I was so scared."

He puts his arms around me. "I know. So was I. But Ruby says he's fine. Physically anyway. She's not sure what's going on inside his head."

I giggle against his shoulder. "Well, if she was, she'd be the first person in a while to know that. Including Sam, I think."

Joe chuckles. "That's for sure." He looks at the dead leaves on the grass beside us. "I guess we should just stop where we are and get cleaned up so we can go talk to him."

I nod and pull away from him. "Though I need to call Sara."

He starts gathering up the gardening equipment. "You go ahead. I'll put these away while you call her." He grins. "And probably be out of the shower by the time you're done talking."

I stick my tongue out at him and smile at the same time. "It shouldn't take that long."

But it takes longer than I expect. Sara answers the phone immediately, but she has a lot of questions about Sam, the truck, and what happened. I can't answer most of them, but it takes a while for Sara to realize that and to stop repeating, "Oh, thank God!"

When she finally does, she asks, "Do you think he'll call me?"

"I don't know, Sara," I say. "I haven't actually talked to him. Ruby called his Dad to tell us he was with her."

"So you haven't seen him?"

"No. We're going into town now to try to find out what happened."

Sara's voice changes. "Will you ask him to call me?" she asks meekly.

I smile. "I will. But I can't promise you anything."

"I know. But just— If you could tell him I really want to talk to him, I'd appreciate it."

"I will."

"And could you let me know how he is?"

I hesitate. Should I be getting into the middle of this? But it was Sara who told us Sam was missing in the first place. "Sure, I'll let you know. But it may be late tonight before I can call you."

"That's fine," she says. "I'm not going anywhere, anyway. I have a paper due on Monday. Maybe I'll be able to concentrate on it now."

We finish our conversation, and I go to shower and change. Joe and I are on the freeway forty minutes later, heading into Albuquerque. The sky is so blue and the cumulus clouds are enormous. Everything looks so beautiful now that I know Sam is in one piece.

But the beautiful day isn't evident in Ruby's apartment. The living room drapes are drawn against the light, and Sam is slouched at the end of the couch with the television remote in his hand. He's watching an auto racing event, and he doesn't turn it off when we come in, although he does mute the sound.

"Hi," he says gruffly, not getting up and clearly not wanting to be hugged.

I feel Joe tense. "That's all you can say for yourself?" he demands. "You had your mother worried sick."

Sam's eyes flick up toward his father and back to the television. "You weren't worried though, huh?" he asks the screen.

My lips tighten. "Yes, as a matter of fact, he was. We both were."

Ruby walks across the room and takes the remote from Sam's hand. She turns off the TV. "Come on, Sam," she says. "That scowl really doesn't look good on you."

"I just don't want to be lectured," he says to the floor.

Joe opens his mouth, but I put my hand on his arm. "No one wants to lecture you, Sam," I say. "We love you, and we just want to know how to help, if that's what you want."

"Why should I need help?"

"Well, I assume you want your truck back."

He shrugs. "I guess. I suppose someone's towed it by now."

Joe opens his mouth again, but again I forestall him. "Someone has towed it, Sam," I say. "The police have it."

His head jerks, and he finally looks up at me. I sink into one of Ruby's upholstered side chairs.

"The police?" he asks.

"The sheriff's department, actually," Joe says. He sits down in the other chair. Ruby perches on the end of the couch opposite Sam.

"They found it abandoned, and they towed it in," Joe explains. "That's what they do with vehicles left beside the road. They called us Thursday afternoon asking where you were. We were pretty worried, I can tell you."

"Oh shit." Sam sits up. "I'm sorry, Mom."

"We already knew you were missing," I tell him. "Sara called earlier saying she hadn't been able to get in touch with you. She was pretty freaked out."

He closes his eyes and slouches back against the couch again. "Great," he mutters. He opens his eyes. "Did she tell you what she did?"

"You mean that she told you she wouldn't marry you?"

Ruby raises an eyebrow at me. I nod at her and look at Sam.

"That's not all she said," he says sullenly. "She said I was immature and that she wasn't interested in getting involved with a kid. She needs a *man* in her life."

My lips twist into a grin at the way he says "man," but I suppress it quickly. Joe opens his mouth, and I shoot him a warning glance.

"Don't even say it, Dad," Sam says. "I know you've always thought I was immature." He sits up suddenly. "Why doesn't anyone ever look at the good side of who I am?"

"But we do, Sam," Ruby says. "We know that you're smart and talented and good looking and loving. And you have a real gift for words, when you choose to use it."

"Gift for words?" He frowns at her. "What makes you think that?"

"I saw the poem you wrote to Sara," she says, looking guilty. "When I was picking up in the guest room this morning. You left it on the bedside table."

He slouches deeper into the couch.

"I'm sorry Sam," she says. "You left it out. I didn't know it was private."

"I'm not a writer," he says.

"Why not?" Joe asks. "What's wrong with being a writer?"

Sam glances at him, then looks up at the ceiling. "I'm not going to compete with you, Dad."

Joe is staring at Sam as if he's never seen him before. "But every writer is different," he says slowly. "Different styles, different genres, different subject matter. There doesn't need to be competition."

"I don't need your permission." Sam glares at him.

"I'm glad to hear that," Joe says. "I just want you to have a sense of direction. I really don't care what you do."

I bite my lip. Sam looks at the blank television screen.

"I don't mean I don't care," Joe clarifies. "I mean that whatever you do is fine with me. I would just like you to have a goal, and so far it hasn't seemed like you had one."

Sam is still talking to the blank television screen. "So if I change majors again, are you going to be all over me about it?"

"What were you thinking of changing to?" Ruby asks.

He glances at her, then speaks to the blank television again. "There's a creative writing program at UNM that I might be interested in. Or maybe somewhere else. Maybe the one at

Southern Methodist. They're in Dallas. They have that summer program in Taos every year."

Joe opens his mouth and then shuts it.

"That's great, Sam," Ruby says. "And with the money from the ticket you won't need to make your choice based on cost." She looks at Joe and me, then back at Sam. "Or not completely, anyway. I don't have any idea how much those programs are."

He sits up. "I've been doing some research online while you were at work," he tells her. "I think the money will be enough. And I emailed a couple writing samples to the UNM program. It's a concentration at the BA level, and I've taken some Lit courses as part of my American Studies work, so I think it would be pretty painless to switch, if they think I'm good enough. The Dallas program looks pretty cool, too."

"Though you'll need to get the investigation over with before you can go out of state," Joe says.

Sam's head swivels toward his father. "What investigation?"

The knot in my stomach is back. In my relief at finding him alive and well, I've forgotten about the legal side of Sam's truck crash. "The Sheriff's department found beer cans in the truck, Sam."

"Oh, shit. Sorry, Mom. Damn, I forgot about those."

"Oh, Sam," Ruby says.

"It's not what it looks like," he tells her. "It was too late for the movie, so Sara and I went to a party on Sunday night after we left here. Some of the guys were sitting in the bed of the truck drinking. They left the cans there. There weren't any trash cans, and I didn't want them flying out on the road, so I tossed them into the cab behind the seat. I forgot all about them."

"So you hadn't been drinking when you went off the road?" I ask.

"No, I swerved to keep from hitting a deer. But I can see how the Sheriff would think that I was." He looks at his Dad. "Now what do I do?"

"We're going to have to hope they believe your story," Joe says.

"Well, it's the truth," Sam snaps.

"I didn't say it wasn't," Joe answers. "But I'm not the one you're going to have to convince."

Ruby stands up. "I just realized that I didn't offer you anything to drink when you came in. Joe, can I get you anything? Ruth? Ice tea? Water? Soda?"

"I could use some ice tea," I tell her.

"A Coke would be great," Joe says.

"Sam, can you come and help me?" Ruby asks. "I want some water for myself, and I don't have enough hands for it all."

I start to get up, but sink back into my chair at a warning head-shake from Ruby. When she and Sam are safely in the kitchen, I turn to Joe. "Do you think they'll believe him?"

He shrugs. "I don't know. I doubt it, but I'm hoping I'm wrong. We'll find out."

Chapter 19

Joe is right. The Sheriff's deputy we talk to that afternoon is skeptical of Sam's story.

"It sounds to me like you must have been feeling guilty about something, to just leave a brand new vehicle like that beside the road," she says. She's a small woman with severe short black hair and bulky inside her deputy uniform. Her name tag says she's Helena Meek. Her intense black eyes never leave Sam's face.

We're sitting in a small cluttered conference room in the Bernalillo County Sheriff's offices in downtown Albuquerque. Sam spreads his hands, palms up. "That's what happened," he says. "The deer jumped out from the other side of the road, and I swerved to miss it. I know I should have held steady—" He glances at his father. "But it was just instinct, like when you duck when something's coming toward you. Next thing I knew the truck was rammed into the culvert. I must've hit the brakes when I swerved, but I don't remember."

"You did." I tell him. "We saw the skid marks. That's how we knew for sure where you'd gone off the road."

Deputy Meek looks at me. "You went out there?"

"We were trying to find him," Joe says. "We didn't know where he was."

The deputy makes a note on the pad in front of her, then looks at Sam. "So where were you?"

"Some guy stopped to see if I was okay, and I asked him to take me to my aunt's." He shrugs. "She lives in Uptown and it was closer than my apartment in the U District or my brother's place in Rio Rancho. And then once I got there I just didn't feel like leaving. Everything just went on hold."

She makes another note. "Do you know the name of the guy who picked you up?"

"He didn't say. He was driving a white GMC truck, probably ten years old or so. Older guy with dark gray hair, kinda longish. Has a mustache."

"Why didn't you call your parents?"

He sinks lower into his chair. "I was embarrassed. My Dad's always telling me how immature I am, and here I went and smashed the fender on my new truck. And Aunt Ruby was closer."

"And more sympathetic?" She looks from Sam to Joe, then back at Sam. "Accidents happen. It sounds to me like you didn't want your Dad to know you'd been drinking."

"I wasn't drinking." Sam's voice rises. "I told you. The cans were in the truck because I didn't want them flying out the back."

"I'll need to talk to your aunt."

"That's fine," Joe says grimly. "You do that."

She looks at Joe. "I'm just doing my job. You have to admit it's a convenient story."

"Sometimes convenience also happens to be the truth."

"Sometimes. But I have to try to figure out if it really is. And you're his Dad, so you're going to try to protect him, aren't you?"

"Not always," Sam says.

She taps her pencil on her notepad. "You'd be surprised at what fathers will do for sons, even when they don't get along with them. We see all sorts of things."

"So what happens next?" I ask.

"So, I can't arrest him right now on a DUI. We don't have a breathalyzer test, since he didn't call the police." She turns to Sam. "Why didn't you call 911?"

He shrugs. "It was really late, nobody else was involved, I felt like an idiot. It was my own fault, and I was okay, so why would I call 911? It wasn't an emergency. And this guy came along right away, so I had a ride into town."

"Accidents are supposed to be reported, you know." She makes another note on her pad and then looks at me. "He committed a crime when he didn't call 911. Accidents are supposed to be reported, whether or not the person involved believes it to be an emergency. We'll have to issue him a ticket for that. And we still need to talk to your sister."

"My sister," Joe says. He hands her a piece of paper. "Here's her contact information. I'm not sure what her work hours are right now, so you may have to call her at the shop."

"We'll be keeping the truck until then," Deputy Meek says. "And possibly longer." She rifles through the papers on the table. "A complete search of the truck apparently hasn't been completed yet. I don't have the report."

"You found the cans behind the seat," I say. "And my contact information in the glove box. How much more searching do you have to do?"

"You'd be surprised what we find in impounded vehicles," she tells me.

Sam chuckles. "Don't worry Mom. They won't find anything else, unless they put it there." Deputy Meek looks up from her paperwork and frowns. "Sorry, Deputy. That wasn't funny, I know. Sorry. Too many TV shows, I guess."

"You're right. It wasn't funny." She stands up. "Now, I'm going to fill out this paperwork with what you've told me, and then I'm going to need you to read through and sign it. That's going to take me some time, so if you all will wait outside, I'll get that done and you can leave." She holds open the door.

As we're filing out, she says, "One of the things I need to include on the form is where Sam can be reached. So I need an address and phone number."

"Can I just go back to my apartment?"

"Where is it?"

"The University District."

"Are you in school?"

"Yes."

"Working?"

"No."

"And your parents live in Los Lunas?"

"Yes."

"My advice would be to stay with your parents until all this has been sorted out," she says. "Judges favor parental supervision."

"Judges?" My stomach tightens again.

"He's going to have to go to court, at least for the ticket." She leads the way to the waiting area. "It typically takes four to six weeks to come up on the docket."

She turns to Sam. "When you've decided on an address, my office is right down this hall. Otherwise, I'll just use what's on the registration."

"Actually, the house is on the registration. I didn't use the apartment address." He turns to me. "Since it was on the old truck's, I just left it like that."

"That's fine." I turn to the deputy. "So he'll be moving back home for the next couple months."

Deputy Meek nods and disappears. We sit down to wait. "I'll bet she makes us wait a while longer than she needs to, just to give you time to think about that crack about finding stuff," Joe says to Sam.

Sam grimaces. "I know. I should've kept my mouth shut. But she was really starting to get to me."

I chuckle. "She'd already gotten to your Dad."

"She probably just assumes that Ruby will lie to protect him," Joe grumbles. "I don't know why they would even bother contacting her, if they're so sure she's not going to tell them the truth."

"Gotta cover all the bases, I suppose," Sam says. "I wonder how long they'll keep the truck."

"That reminds me," I say. "Have you called the insurance company?"

He shakes his head and grimaces. "I never even thought of it. I was too busy feeling sorry for myself. This is going to raise my rates, isn't it?"

"Unless the damage is minimal enough that you can just get it repaired and not report it," Joe says.

I shake my head. "If there's a police report, the insurance company will eventually find out. You're going to have to let them know." I groan. "Darn. Andy's still your agent, isn't he? We'll need to go through the main switchboard and try to keep him out of it."

"How come?"

The story of Andy's rumor-spreading keeps us occupied until Deputy Meek comes back with the forms. Sam follows her into her office to sign them and comes back with a traffic citation in his hand.

"Okay, I'm free to go," he says cheerfully. "A ticket instead of a truck, but at least I'm not behind bars."

I glare at him. "Your sense of humor really is not funny at the moment. And don't you dare tell me it's just gallows humor."

"Sorry," he says sheepishly. "I'm just trying to keep some balance. So I guess we need to go by my apartment so I can pick up my laptop and clothes and let Andrew know where I've been and where I'm going."

Once this is accomplished we head onto the freeway back toward Los Lunas. "I hate doing this to you, Mom," Sam says. "You're not going to have an office space while I'm under house arrest."

I chuckle. "Well, house arrest may be a bit strong, Sam, but it's okay. I've been doing most of my reading on the sun porch lately, anyway."

"And you'll have decent internet access, for a change," Joe says. "Your mother got us hooked up on cable, and we have a modem so you can access it anywhere in the house."

"Sweet," Sam says. "So I can keep on researching the writing programs."

"What about classes?" I ask.

After a long pause, Sam says, "I guess I'd better go back. I didn't go at all last week. I brought my books with me. It's only another six weeks. And I'll need decent transcripts to send to the programs that I apply to."

I let out a breath I hadn't realized I was holding. Out of the corner of my eye, I see Joe's hands relax on the steering wheel.

"Though you're going to have a transportation problem," Joe observes.

"I think I can take the Railrunner," Sam tells him. "Though I'll need to get to the train station. It's what, about five miles from the house? I suppose I could use my old bike. It's still in the garage, isn't it?"

"There aren't any bike lanes for most of the way between the house and the station," I point out. "It's not very safe. I can drop you off and pick you up, if you want to."

"Isn't that going to be a hassle?"

"Depends on how early the train is." I turn and grin at him. "Something tells me you don't have any seven a.m. classes."

He chuckles. "No, I don't actually. The earliest one is at nine fifteen. Do you mind if we go by the station and pick up a schedule on the way home?"

"And when we get home, you might want to call Sara." I turn to look at him again. "She asked me to ask you."

He nods and looks out the window.

Chapter 20

We settle into our new routine quickly. I find that I enjoy having Sam in and out of the house. The place feels more alive with him here, somehow. He decides that he can get to the train station safely on his bike and doesn't need me to ferry him back and forth.

I don't agree, but I have to admit that it's something of a relief to not have to plan my schedule around his. He's gone enough that Joe and I can pretty much follow our old routine, and we're able to keep our appointment with Carol Pastioni.

Joe arranges for her to meet us for lunch at a pizza place in ABQ Uptown. "We should stop by Ruby's shop after lunch," he says as we cross the parking lot to the restaurant. "Find out if she's talked to the Sheriff's department yet and see what they have on sale."

I shrug. "I'm not really in the mood for shopping. I think I'm still adjusting to how much I spent the last time I was there."

"It wasn't all that much," he says. "Besides, you could buy half the shops in this place."

"No thank you!"

"You really don't like to shop, do you?"

I shake my head. "Not for clothes. Speaking of Ruby, have you decided yet what we're going to give her from the ticket money?"

"No, and now with Sam's situation, it's gotten complicated. There's Carol, looking at the menu board."

We consult, decide to risk the spring winds by sitting outside, and are escorted to a table. We each order a large salad, then Carol pulls a folder from her bag and hands it to Joe.

"I found quite a bit about your books on line," she says. "You get positive reviews, although there aren't a lot of them. So I assume that's an area we can work on—getting reviews, I mean. I've put together a couple different ideas for advertising approaches. One is more print oriented and the other emphasizes social media. We didn't talk about appearances, but I went ahead and consulted with a publicist and put together a few suggestions for personal interviews, as well. Basically, you can tour the country chatting to radio stations and appearing on television—"

He looks at her in alarm. "Appearing? You mean like on talk shows?"

Carol smiles. "It's not quite as intimidating as it sounds. The worst part of it is that after about the third one, you begin to feel like you're repeating yourself, and it can be hard to keep your enthusiasm up."

His mouth twists. "I think the worst part of it for me would be talking on camera. I've never been good at public speaking kinds of things."

I look over Joe's shoulder at the proposal. "Did you add a cost for the web site?"

Carol nods. "I've included some cost estimates for that, using my contact here in Albuquerque. That's actually one of the first things I would suggest doing, since we'll want to include the site on the promotional material."

Joe turns a page. "Yeah, I see it's at the top of the time line. So what's the total cost likely to be?"

"Well, it depends on what you want to do," Carol answers. She fiddles with a lock of her hair. "I've structured the proposal as a kind of menu, so you have a list of the various components and then different options for how much emphasis you want to place on that piece and what media you want to use. So you can pretty much pick and choose and then we can put a package together, depending on what current themes we can tie into—seasonal or political topics, that kind of thing. By the way, I really enjoyed both the books. I especially liked the one about the small town mayor who wins his election by one vote."

Joe smiles at her. "Thanks, I think it's my favorite. It's based on an actual election." He frowns. "I'm not sure what you're going to find that's really topical though. I don't tend to think about that kind of thing while I'm writing."

Carol shakes her head. "And I don't think you should. But once they're written that can be my job. By the way, do you have other, shorter material you can place in literary magazines? If you do, that's another way of elevating your profile."

Joe nods. "Actually, I do. I tend to focus on shorter works between novels. It helps clear my head. But the submission process for them takes time that I could be devoting to writing."

She nods. "Another option would be to hire someone part time to help you with queries and submissions, and that sort of thing."

"You mean like a personal assistant?"

"If we're going to start hiring staff, we really are going to need a bigger house," I murmur.

Carol grins at me. "There never seems to be quite enough space, does there?"

"So what are we talking about, in terms of price?" I ask.

She hesitates. "Well, as I said, it depends on what you want to do. You could spend a couple hundred thousand on print marketing alone, although I wouldn't recommend it. For the type of work Joe is doing, a modest print campaign in the literary magazines, and a solid set of reviews and interviews—"

Joe opens his mouth and she grins at him. "Radio interviews, at least at first," she says reassuringly. "And then a web presence, which I believe is vital. Those, together with some social media activity, should result in an uptick in sales. Of course, whether the sales you generate will cover the amount you spend, at least in the short term, is another question entirely. You are working on another book, aren't you?"

He nods.

"Similar in tone and concept?"

He nods again.

"Then you're more likely to see a cost benefit from the initial round of marketing when you publish that book, because the market awareness of your work will already have created an interest in the new novel."

Joe is flipping through pages. "So, what would all that cost?"

"Depending on what you do, anywhere from thirty to seventy five thousand."

"Wow," Joe says. He looks at me. "That's a lot of money."

"That's what it's for, Joe," I tell him. "To get your work out there."

Carol pushes her long red hair behind her shoulders. "There's no need to make a decision today. And you'll need to get that web site up, no matter what you decide." She glances at her watch. "I actually have another appointment that I need to get to, so I'll toddle on off and you two can discuss this at your leisure. Will that work?"

"I appreciate all the effort you've put into this," Joe says. "It just added up to more than I thought it would."

"Marketing isn't cheap, if you want to do it right," she tells him. "If you don't do it right, then it's even more expensive, because you've just thrown your money into the wind."

"I knew that," Joe says ruefully. "I just didn't realize how cheap it wasn't."

Carol starts to lay money for her meal on the table.

"No, no, we'll take care of lunch," I tell her. "And we appreciate your coming into Albuquerque to talk with us. This would have been even more daunting if we'd just received an email."

"No problem." She retrieves her money and stands up. "And I appreciate the lunch. Just let me know in the next couple weeks what you want to do, okay?"

We say our goodbyes and Joe closes the folder. He moves the food around on his plate. "Seventy five thousand dollars. I don't know what to think."

"That was the high end of the price range," I point out. "And we have it to spend. This has always been at the top of your wish list. Before cruises or houses or trucks or anything else."

"It has. But still—"

"Let's just give it some time," I suggest. "In any case, you really ought to do the web site."

"That's true. I could do that. Maybe I should start checking out other author sites and getting ideas."

"I don't think it should be a maybe, Joe." I peer at him over the top of my glass of ice tea. "Are you getting cold feet about marketing?"

"I'm not sure what it is." He moves his food around with his fork. "What if it fails? What if no one responds and I discover that there really isn't a market for my stuff? That I've been deluding myself all these years, and the reason the books haven't sold well is that they're really not any good? That the lack of sales has nothing to do with whether or not they've been marketed effectively?"

I stare at him. I've never heard this from him before. "Well, I think they're good," I say, finally.

"You're my wife," he points out. "You're bound to be biased."

"Carol likes them."

"Carol has to like them if she's going to get a contract to market them."

I frown. "This is so unlike you. You've always been so positive about the value of what you're doing."

"I've never had to test it. I don't know how much of that attitude was a defense mechanism and how much it was belief in the books' value."

"There's only one way to find out."

"And what happens if I find out that they aren't any good?"

I raise an eyebrow. "Aren't you confusing literary quality with marketability? You've always insisted that there's a difference. That the quality of your work is part of the reason they haven't become best sellers. Aside from the fact that we didn't have the money to market them, that is."

"And now that it's come right down to it, I guess I'm not so sure I want to test that theory," he says ruefully.

"You might want to start testing it by going online and seeing what those reviews say. Have you ever done that?"

"I've been afraid to. Afraid that I wouldn't agree with the reviewers about what was good or bad about the books. Afraid I'd start listening to opinions instead of my own instincts." He pushes his plate away. "I'm not really hungry, I guess. Are you ready?"

There's no more talk about going shopping. Instead, we drive to the Rio Grande Nature Center and spend an hour walking in the river bosque. We chat aimlessly, carefully avoiding the question before us. Back in the parking lot, Joe says, "I'm glad we did that. I feel better now."

"Any decision?" I ask lightly.

"I'm not sure." He clicks the unlock button on the key and we get in the car. "Wow, it got warm in here. I think I'm going to go ahead with the website research. And look at what Carol's proposing to see if we could put together a small campaign that would give the books some exposure without overwhelming me."

I nod. "I wondered about the time aspect of the whole thing. What about getting an assistant?"

He shakes his head. "That seems a bit much. Not unless we run across someone who needs a job, anyway. I'm not sure I could keep them busy."

"And we'd have to find someplace to put them, unless they could work from home or something."

"Which reminds me." He turns the key in the ignition. "Did I hear a slight give on the whole subject of a new house when you said we'd need a bigger one?"

I chuckle. "So you heard that, did you?" I click my seatbelt into place. "It was just a comment about hiring staff."

"Hmm. It sounded to me like you were actually beginning to think more space would be nice." He maneuvers the car into the traffic on Rio Grande Boulevard and into the lane to access the freeway.

"More space would be nice," I admit. "But I'm not sure I'm ready to go house hunting. It just seems like a huge hassle. And do you realize how much work moving would be? Remember what that was like?"

"That was almost twenty years ago and we had three small kids in tow and did it all ourselves," he points out. "Sam could actually help this time, instead of losing his bottle constantly. Besides, we could hire someone to move it all for us."

I laugh. "I still don't know what happened to that yellow plastic bottle." I tilt my head back, against the headrest. "I suppose we could have someone do it for us, couldn't we? But the search just seems complicated."

"Why don't you sit down with Gloria and tell her what you want and then wait and see what she comes up with? I don't think she'd take you to places she knew weren't going to work for us."

"So this has just turned into my project." I grin and shake my head at him.

"There's no point in making it a project for myself unless you want it," he says. "So yeah, I guess so." He raises an eyebrow at me. "Is that okay?"

"I think so." I stare out the window. We're on I-25 now, heading south. Beyond the high rise buildings downtown, the extinct volcanoes on the west side of the river gaze back at me, as remote as ever.

Suddenly, I feel a surge of energy. The idea of a new house does feel good, as long as we don't have to move everything ourselves. "A pantry, and guest rooms and offices, and a garage with enough space for you to work on the truck inside, instead of in the driveway," I say aloud. "And maybe an extra room for an assistant, if and when you need one."

Joe laughs. "Sounds good to me!"

Chapter 21

That night we expand my initial house wish list. More space for storage. Offices for both of us, Joe's preferably in a separate building. Maybe a den. Guest rooms. A larger dining space. Everything on one floor. A yard that doesn't require a lot of maintenance.

"So when we do take that big trip, I don't have to worry about whether the grass needs to be mowed while we're gone," Joe says.

"You know, we could hire a maintenance service," I point out.

"I suppose so," he says. "Though I'm not sure you could handle someone else messing with the flower beds."

I laugh. "That's probably true. So let's see how long it takes Gloria to meet all these requirements. It's quite a list."

Which is exactly what Gloria says after I read her the list on the phone. "Are you looking for a particular architectural style, as well?" she asks.

"No, I don't think so. Though we both like the adobe look. Oh, and we'll want a porch large enough to hold the new porch furniture."

She laughs again. "I'm so glad you're finally doing this, Ruth," she says. "You two deserve to enjoy. As a matter of fact we have a house on our list that may meet pretty much all your requirements. But I'm going to have to check the number of bedrooms and the size of the porch. Are you going to be around this afternoon?"

I chuckle. "Joe thought you'd have something. Yeah, I'm going to be around this afternoon. I have some laundry to catch up on, but that's about it. And the usual e-mail clean-out."

"How's Sam doing, by the way? I saw him the other day on the train. He seemed much more relaxed than the last time I saw him."

"He does seem more relaxed. I hadn't thought of it that way. He's more fun to be around, that's for sure. Joe says he's lost his chip, so he's more balanced now."

"You mean like chip on his shoulder? That's funny. I'll call you later when I know more about the house. It's in Bosque Farms. Would that be an okay location for you?"

"We've always liked Bosque Farms," I tell her. We hang up and I go into the garage, where the washer and dryer are housed, to sort laundry.

Bosque Farms. Which would mean a couple acres of land. Green land with cottonwoods, if it's typical of Bosque Farms lots. That would be nice. I shake my head and drop one of my new blouses into the machine. Having money is nice, I have to admit.

I finish sorting, get the first load started, and decide to reorganize the storage cupboard. There's no point in moving stuff we don't need.

"Hey Mom." Sam puts his head in the door. "What are you up to?"

We chat for a few minutes, then he disappears to get a snack. I smile again. I know it's not permanent, but I do like having him home. Having a son who has worked past some of his adolescent issues is also nice. Even nicer than money. What a relief his attitude change has been.

Though he's looking tense when I go into the kitchen a few minutes later. He's pacing back and forth between the stove and kitchen table.

"Aunt Ruby called," he says. "I'm not sure having her talk to Deputy Meek was such a good idea. She sounded really pissed off."

"Ruby or Deputy Meek?" I open the cupboard where the canned food is stored. It looks like I'm going to need to get more groceries pretty soon. Supplies are going down more quickly with Sam in the house.

"Aunt Ruby. Though probably Deputy Meek by the time Aunt Ruby was done with her."

I turn. "What happened, exactly?"

"As far as I can tell, Deputy Meek accused Aunt Ruby of covering for me, and she blew her top. She was still mad when she called me, and the deputy had left a couple hours before that."

"Wow. Ruby's pretty good at keeping her cool and finessing any situation, so Deputy Meek must have been really irritating."

"Sounds like it." Sam grins. "It's nice to know that I'm not the only one who wanted to slug her."

"Did Ruby say that?"

He chuckles. "Well, she said she wanted to slap her."

"I hope she didn't get too aggressive."

"It sounded like she did give her a tongue lashing."

Joe comes into the kitchen just then.

"Are you done already?" I ask.

"I got interrupted by a sister who was madder than I've seen her since I borrowed her car in high school," Joe says. He grimaces. "My ears are still burning. I'd hate to be that deputy."

"So is her little explosion going to make Deputy Meek believe that I'm innocent of DUI or think that Aunt Ruby is just covering for me?" Sam asks.

"We're just going to have to wait and see," Joe says.

Sam slumps into a chair at the table. "This waiting stuff is getting old."

I put my hands on my hips. "You have no idea what really anxious waiting is like, young man." I'm not as irritated as I sound, but he needs to get some perspective.

He winces. "Sorry. I did say I was sorry for that, didn't I?"

Joe chuckles. "I think it's going to take a few more 'sorries'." He pours himself the last of the coffee. "Anyone want any more?"

Sam and I shake our heads, and Joe turns to head back to his office. "I talked to Gloria," I tell him. "She may have something that will fit our needs. She's going to try to call me this afternoon."

He chuckles. "Told you," he says as he goes through the door.

"Needs?" Sam asks.

"It's not so much that I want to hear you say 'I'm sorry' a dozen more times," I tell him. "I just want you to never do anything like that ever again."

I open the refrigerator. We definitely need groceries. There are two apples and one avocado left in their respective bins. "The needs, so-called, is our wish list for a new house."

"So Dad finally talked you into it, huh? We've been placing bets on how long it would take."

"Who's 'we'?"

"Paul and Jeanette and Aunt Ruby and me. We've got a Facebook discussion going."

I frown at him. "You're not talking about the ticket on Facebook are you?"

"No, just the idea of a new house."

"I'm surprised Jeanette is on there. I'd think she'd be too busy."

"She's not on it much."

"So what do your siblings think about your latest adventure?"

"You mean the truck? They haven't said much. Jeanette's fussed about what she calls 'the potential impact of a DUI,' but she's been pretty cool about it. And you know Paul. He just asks me if I saw the game last night or tells me about the latest custom job at the shop. He's got some sweet pictures up on Facebook. Do you think I could get him to repair the fender for me?"

"You'll have to find out if he has time. And get the truck towed to Rio Rancho."

He slumps down in his chair again. "Maybe I'll wait to see how it all shakes out. What do you think Deputy Meek will do now?"

"I have no idea. You're just going to have to wait and see." I touch his shoulder. "I know the waiting is tough, Sam. I was just bugging you."

He pats my hand. "I know." He sits up and stretches his arms out. "I need to get back to work on my paper." He shakes his head. "I had no idea that Aunt Ruby could get that wound up about anything." He grins at me. "I guess she likes me. Or really doesn't like Deputy Meek."

"Some of both, I suspect. And doesn't like being accused of lying." I laugh. "I'm glad you guys talked to her instead of me. It sounds like she was practically bouncing off the walls. Uh oh, there goes my phone. Surely she doesn't need to tell me about this, as well!"

But when I pick up the phone, it isn't Ruby, it's Flora.

"Ruth, I want to thank you for what you've done for me," Flora says after we say hello. "You dashed off so fast I wasn't able to tell you how much that meant to me and the girls."

"I wanted to help," I tell her. "And I felt really bad about the way you had to leave the agency. I just wasn't expecting Andy to do that."

"I know. It was pretty unbelievable." She sighs heavily. "It's still hard to believe that he could do that after all the time and effort I put into that place."

My lips twitch. Well, when Flora was there, she actually was a hard worker. Though not necessarily thorough.

"So the reason I was calling," Flora says, "is that I have this amazing opportunity and I wondered if you would be interested in supporting it."

There's a murmur in the background, then she says, "Well, not exactly supporting. I mean investing. I met this guy who has a laundromat that he's been managing, and he's getting ready to buy it. He's willing to take me on as a partner, but I'd need to buy into it, first."

"A laundromat?" Joe had been right. I'd been crazy to think Flora wouldn't come asking for more.

"Yeah, it's the one on Main Street across from the flower shop. He says they gross about five thousand a month."

I should just refer this to the financial team, but I can't help myself. This is Flora, after all. "Are you expecting to live on the proceeds?" I ask.

"Well, the idea is that we'd split the net."

"So what is the net?"

"Well, the gross is about five thousand, like I said." There's another murmur in the background. "I guess the net's about twenty five hundred, on a slow month."

Which, after taxes, is going to be less than what Flora was making at the agency. "Is this guy there?" I ask her.

"Umm, yeah, actually. Do you want to talk to him?"

"No. No I don't." That comes out more sharply than I mean it to. I soften my voice. "Flora, you're not dating this guy, are you?"

"Well, yeah. Kinda."

My eyes close. Damn. "Joe and I don't make investment decisions ourselves." I move from the kitchen into the living room as I say it. "We have a financial team that looks at proposals and makes recommendations to us. We don't do anything without a positive analysis from them. So if you want to send me something, I can forward it to them."

And their review is going to take a while, I think grimly. "It typically takes a couple months."

"But I need this now," Flora says. There's another murmur. "Or at least within the next couple weeks."

Her voice rises. "This isn't just an investment proposal, Ruth. This is me, Flora. The Flora you worked with, remember? The one who got fired because of you?"

I flinch and feel my jaw clench at the same time. "And I'm ready to provide you with a good job recommendation, any time you need it," I say evenly. "But I can't just hand you another check, Flora. Our finances don't work like that. That was a one-time thing. And investment proposals have to be vetted through our financial advisors. That's how it's been set up, and I can't go out of that structure."

"Can't or won't."

"Are you sleeping with him?"

"That's none of your business."

"It is if you're asking me for money."

"Meaning you'll give it to me if I tell you I'm not?"

"Meaning you need to be careful, or you're going to get yourself really hurt," I say calmly. "And that's going to really hurt the twins. How are they, by the way?"

"Oh, they're fine," Flora says impatiently. "So if I can put a what you call it proposal together, will you give it to your committee?"

"Yes, I'll do that. Just mail it to the house."

"Okay, I'll see what we can put together," she says reluctantly.

We say goodbye. I click off my phone and stare out the living room window into the yard. Well, that was pretty awful. And how did this guy know that Flora knew someone who might be interested in his so-called investment?

I bite my lower lip. I've already started letting phone numbers I don't recognize go to voice mail. I'm going to have to start doing that with Flora, too, as much as I hate the idea. I do feel responsible for her. But this laundromat investment sounds like a disaster waiting to happen.

The spring wind is picking up outside. I stare out at the moving bushes without really seeing them. I hired and trained Flora. And she's a good worker, when she puts her mind to it. But Andy knew that Flora was often late and took long lunch hours or left early on a fairly regular basis. It had been only a matter of time—or his wife's involvement—before he told me that Flora needed to clean up her act or find another job.

I feel a little guilty offering to act as a job reference, knowing what I do of Flora's habits. But what can I do? She's lost her job because of me. Well, she'd lost it sooner than she would have otherwise. That's the reason I made the effort to visit and give her that check. The money had really been more to absolve my own conscience than out of generosity.

But it seems to have backfired. Not only has Flora apparently already spent the money I gave her, she wants more. And as a partner with a man she's sleeping with. I don't even want to think about how long this so-called opportunity will last. Probably until whatever I invest is gone.

Then she'll be back on the phone or showing up at the door, implying that her situation is all my fault. I shake my head at the tossing bushes. I just hope Flora has enough sense to keep those twins away from this guy.

I know that's not fair. The man is probably a perfectly decent person. But it just doesn't sound like a good situation. And he apparently hasn't been clear with Flora about the amount of return she can expect on her investment. Or she's so infatuated she hasn't thought it through clearly.

Well, if Joe and I don't give her the money, Flora isn't going to have anything to invest, and she'll find out pretty quickly whether or not this guy is truly interested in her. I don't really expect to get a proposal in the mail and if it does come, the financial team is likely to pick it to pieces.

I grin at myself. "Okay, conscience satisfied," I say aloud.

"You arguing with your conscience again?" Joe asks from the doorway.

I make a face and drop into the easy chair. "Flora called. She wanted to know if we would be interested in investing in a laundromat. Actually, she wanted to know if we would give her the money to invest."

"I hope you told her no." He drops onto the couch. "I had a feeling she was going to be trouble."

"Yes, I told her no. There's a guy involved. Now she's going to be mad at me for driving him away, I suppose."

"Good, then maybe she won't come up with any more investment schemes."

I shake my head. "I doubt it. I think I'm going to start sending her phone calls to voice mail, though. Then she can leave a message and I'll be able to think about how to respond before I call her back."

"Because of course you'll call her back." He shakes his head. "You're just too nice, Ruth, that's your problem."

"That seems like it ought to be a good thing, not a problem. Besides, she might really need my help."

"See, this is what concerns me about the foundation idea," he says. "Every request would be a valid one, and once you open the flood gates, you'd want to help everybody you run across."

"I'm not a complete pushover. I could handle a foundation if I wanted to," I say defensively. "But I already told you I don't want to do that. And I did tell Flora no."

"Only because you've already given her money."

"And because the guy who wants her to invest in the laundromat is also her boyfriend. Well, for the moment, anyway. They're sleeping together."

"Where'd she meet this guy?"

"Who knows?"

"Well, I hope she hasn't quit her real job, or she'll be coming to you for help again, after he dumps her."

"You don't know that."

"I'm about ninety-nine percent sure. But we'll see. So what did Gloria have to say?"

"I haven't heard from her. She did say that we had quite a list, but she thought they had something that would fit our needs. But she had to check on the number of bedrooms and whether or not it had a porch."

"Was a porch on our list?"

I grin at him. "It is now. I thought of it while I was talking to her."

He chuckles. "If we're going to do it, we might as well go whole hog, huh?"

Sam saunters in, an apple in his hand. "So I was thinking about this house thing," he says to his father. "Didn't you say you still hadn't decided what to do for Aunt Ruby?"

"Yeah. And now, if I just give her a check and the Sheriff's Department finds out, it's going to look like we're paying her off."

Sam frowns. "Shit, I hadn't thought about that. Sorry, Mom." He leans against the door frame. "I was going to say that maybe you could help her with a down payment on a house. She's been in that apartment complex a long time, and I think she's pretty sick of it."

Joe and I exchange glances. The kid is brilliant. "That makes a lot of sense," Joe says.

"And she could start looking now," I say. "By the time she finds what she wants and actually needs the money, we should know what's going to happen with the DUI thing, and we can figure it out from there."

"She's my sister, after all," Joe says. "Who cares what the Sheriff's Department thinks?"

I raise an eyebrow at him.

"I guess I'll give it a couple days before I call her, though," he says.

Chapter 22

So now everybody has something to do but me, I think resentfully the next morning as I roam the almost-empty house. Joe is hard at work on his current revision, Sam is at the University studying, Ruby will be house-hunting soon. Gloria is doing what she loves best—finding the perfect home for yet another family.

And I'm wandering down a dark hall, bored out of my mind. At this moment, I'd be happy to be back at the insurance agency prodding Becky and covering for Flora.

I rub the back of my neck. I need to get out of this house. I tell Joe I'm going grocery shopping and grab my keys.

But I don't head directly to the store. Instead, I find myself at River Park with the car window down, listening to the breeze in the newly formed cottonwood leaves overhead.

I get out and locate a trail heading west into the bosque but paralleling the river. I follow it about a half a mile and then sit down on a log beside the path. The leaves overhead cast patches of shadow on the path and the new grass forming nearby.

I watch the moving shadows. I sat in this bosque often when I was a teenager, escaping from the dark house where my mother was either wandering aimlessly or painting walls like a crazy person. It had all felt like my fault somehow. After all, from what Aunt Marsha told me, the postpartum depression that set in shortly after I was born seems to have triggered the agoraphobia.

"We didn't know what that was, back then," my Aunt had said. "The doctors gave her Valium, but it did as much harm as good. She stopped crying so much, but it turned her into a zombie. And it all just got worse after she had Carl. It was really hard to watch. She had the babies that she wanted, but she could barely enjoy either you or Carl. I hate to say it, but it almost made me glad I couldn't have children." I remember her chuckling at that. "Of course, with the bakery, that would have been difficult, anyway."

Marsha had owned a small but successful donut shop in Belen. When I was a teenager, I loved helping out there on the weekends. The tips were great, and the place buzzed with energy. But I'd also seen the physical toll it took on Aunt Marsha and decided that I preferred an office job as a full-time occupation.

Now I have to make a new choice, carve out a new path for myself. Or do I? Can I just relax, as Margaret, the old lady at the nursing home, had said? Can I just let go and stop trying to force a decision on myself? Let it come naturally?

I look up at the cottonwood leaves. They just come out every year; it's just part of the process of life.

Can I do that? Just allow myself to leaf out, to unfold, so to speak, without worrying about every step of the process?

I sit there for a long time, watching the leaves move in the breeze. Not thinking; just feeling the sun's warmth on my face.

After a long while, I hear voices. Two small children are trotting down the path toward me. A young woman carrying a cooler lags behind them. "Juanita! Ernesto! Come back here!" she calls.

The children stop in front of me. We look at at each other.

"Hello," I say. They giggle shyly.

When the young woman reaches them, she puts the cooler down and places a hand on each child's shoulder. "You stay by me, you hear?" she scolds. She looks at me apologetically. "I'm sorry. I hope we didn't disturb you. I worry about the river."

"You didn't." I smile at her. "I understand. I also had restless little ones."

"Mama, I'm hungry," the little girl says, pushing at her mother's hand.

The young woman and I exchange bemused glances, then she and the children move away. I stretch my arms. I feel so much calmer now, so much more able to just see what will happen. Able to wait for the gift that is my life to unfold.

But I do need to fill the cupboards. And Sam has mentioned a particular type of cookie that he's hungry for. I stand up and head to the car.

Gloria calls the next morning.

"I think this is it!" she says. "It's in Bosque Farms on three acres and it has great big cottonwoods and access to the ditch bank and six bedrooms and a den. Actually, I think I mentioned it to you before, because it also has something I think Joe and the boys will like. It has a garage workshop with a vehicle lift."

"It sounds great. Is it all on one floor?"

"Yes, and it's adobe. And it has a porch along the back that overlooks the ditch bank and the bosque. I think you'll really like it."

"So, how much are we talking, money wise?"

"They're listing at four hundred thousand."

"Wow." Could we really buy something that expensive? I shake my head.

"But I don't think you'll need to pay that much," Gloria tells me. "It's been on the market for a while, and there's not a huge demand for houses that big or at that price point. I think they'll settle for three fifty."

I chuckle. "It's just hard to believe we're talking seriously about those kinds of numbers."

Gloria laughs. "I know. It's great isn't it? So do you want to take a look? This afternoon is a good time, since the owners won't be home."

"Umm, let me check with Joe."

"Are you chickening out?"

"No, no, I'm not chickening out. I just thought Joe would want to come."

"Okay. Well, let me know as soon as you can, okay? So they can straighten up before we get there. She's picky about the place being spotless when we bring anyone in."

We hang up and I look around the kitchen. The lace curtains I sewed from $2 a yard Wal-Mart fabric. The carefully sanded and repainted cupboards. The chip in the door jamb where Sam and Paul bumped it bringing in my second-hand desk. It was their birthday gift to me two years ago, after Sam left home for school. Do I really want to leave this? So many memories. But it is small and cramped.

We could renovate. A new stove and refrigerator alone would do wonders, along with a new sink and countertop. But what a hassle a renovation would be. And we really could use more space.

I grin. We've been fine with the space we have, until now. But I have to admit that the idea of having more room is enticing, if a little scary. Having Joe with me to look at the house would be good. I really might chicken out if he doesn't come along.

But when I knock on his office door, he's deep in the middle of his manuscript. He puts a tick mark on the papers in front of him and looks up with glazed eyes. "House? Today? I have to trace this theme through to make sure I didn't drop it."

He runs his hand through his hair. "Or twist it. I feel like there's something wrong but I can't put my finger on it."

"Never mind. I'll tell you about it when you come back up for air." I move across the room and kiss the top of his head. "It'll be okay. You'll figure it out."

He erases the tick mark. "I hope so. I hate this part. First drafts are so much more fun."

I kiss him again and go to call Gloria.

A couple hours later I'm driving through an area of large homes under large trees on large lots, many of which house llamas, sheep, or horses as well as homes. Bosque Farms is a suburb that really doesn't feel like one. And I'll need to pay attention to how the house is situated on the lot, or we'll end up paying flood insurance. With the price of these homes, that could get pretty outrageous.

I chuckle at myself. You can take an insurance person out of the business, but they're still going to think like an insurance person, no matter how much money they have.

Ah, this is it. I pull into the driveway of a long cream-colored adobe house with a colonnade along the front. There appears to be a garage on one end and a separate building on the other, all connected by a columned walkway.

It's beautiful. And when Gloria and I walk through the house, I see that it meets all the items on our list, and then some. I hadn't thought to ask for an island in the kitchen, or saltillo tiles on the floor. Or two fireplaces, one of which serves both the living and dining areas.

The cottonwood trees on the property are huge and full of the gnarly character I love about Rio Grande cottonwoods. Living here would be like having my own River Park. Gloria and I sit in the dual rocking chairs beside the rustic bench on the back porch and admire the trees and the river bosque beyond them, bordering the property.

"The bosque being so close means there is some fire danger," I say. "That's likely to increase the insurance premiums." I glance at the house. "Though the foundation looks like it's raised enough to make flood insurance requirements unlikely."

"So you're thinking you'd take out a mortgage?"

"I have no idea. I guess we'll need to talk to the financial people." I grin. "Listen to me. Joe hasn't even seen it yet."

"So you like it?"

"It's wonderful, Gloria. How long has it been on the market?"

"About a year. The owners want to sell and downsize. They're getting older and just can't maintain it the way they'd like to. She's pushing 80 and he's almost 90. She says the cleaning has just gotten too much for her. He says he's tired of the yard work."

"It looks to me like they've done a great job."

"They're both pretty picky, I think. But you can get someone in to clean, if you're worried about keeping it dusted and vacuumed."

"Yeah, we've been talking about getting someone to do yard work, but Joe seems convinced that they won't do it right. I may have the same problem. I suppose it will depend on how busy I am." I grimace. "Not that I know what else I'd be busy at."

We sit, watching the trees in the afternoon light. "It just seems like a dream," I muse. "I mean, could this really be mine? Could I sit here every morning? Or in the evening, and watch the sun go down across the river?"

Gloria smiles. "It still really hasn't sunk in, has it?"

"Not really. I mean, not working has sunk in, I think." I grin. "I have to admit that I like not getting up early to go to the office every day. And buying whatever strikes my fancy at the grocery store has sunk in, although I'm still startled at the totals sometimes. And new shoes are always fun. But the idea of this being ours—" I gesture at the lawn and the cottonwoods, the bosque beyond. "This seems like a dream that's just too big for me."

"Trying to wear shoes that are too big for you, huh?"

"I guess. It's just something we were brought up with, you know?"

"Yeah, I know. I've been working hard for the last twenty years to get it out of my system."

I turn my gaze away from the trees. "What do you mean?"

"We get taught that we aren't good enough, that we need to be obedient little girls and boys and always do what the grownups tell us. That we're not as smart as we think we are and don't deserve what we want unless we've been granted permission by those in authority—the principal, the priest, God, society at large. Whoever."

I look at her in surprise. "Wow, you sound really bitter."

"It took me a long time to even realize what was going on, much less try to figure out how to deal with it. I feel like I've wasted a lot of time."

"I guess we all do get those messages," I say slowly. "I hadn't really thought about it that way—that I'm waiting for permission from someone to enjoy my good fortune. To live my life, even. I suppose it's why I keep trying to find something to do, something I can tell people 'this is what I do.' Like I have to have an excuse for being alive."

I shake my head. "But I feel guilty, Gloria. I mean, other people don't have this kind of money. Shouldn't I be doing something productive with it? And who am I to flaunt myself?"

"You don't have a flaunting bone in your body," she says. "I think what you really mean is, who are you to think you deserve your good luck, when others don't have it? Is that why you keep trying to give it away?"

I shake my head. "No, I have fun doing unexpected things for people to make their lives easier. I really enjoy it. It gets tricky, though. I'm discovering some people don't want temporary help. They want to just live off you."

"They just don't know how to help themselves. But yeah, you have to be careful, because helping someone with that kind of dependency isn't going to help them at all, in the long run."

"Hmmm." We rock companionably for a while. Finally, I rouse myself. "So, what's the next step, after Joe sees the house?"

"You think he'll like it?"

"With that garage and the separate office?" I grin. "He'll be wanting to know when we can move in."

"Well, we'll need to fill out some paperwork so you can make a formal offer. Then we'll see if they accept it. And you'll have to decide how you're going to pay for it. A bank mortgage will take a while, no matter how much income you have. Even with cash, there'll still be the survey and title work and stuff. Then, knowing you, you'll probably want to paint and have it cleaned before you move in. So the answer to Joe's question is, when can he get here to see it?"

I chuckle. "When I can tear him away from this revision. Maybe tomorrow or the next day?"

I pose the question to him when I get home. Tomorrow is fine, he says, pouring himself another cup of coffee. He needs a break, anyway. He's made some changes, but he isn't sure if he's caught everything. He's getting so he can't see the damn thing.

"And in the middle of a difficult section, Ruby called me back," he adds. "I told her we want to give her money for a down payment on a house, and I thought she was going to hyperventilate right there on the phone. When she stopped saying, 'I can't believe it,' she immediately started making plans."

"That's great, Joe. I'm glad she liked the idea."

"Hmmm." He looks at me out of the corner of his eye. "One of her plans is to look for something in Los Lunas. Maybe that new subdivision in Huning Ranch."

My mouth opens, then closes again.

He laughs. "Life is never simple, is it?"

"When she hears about the new house, she's going to want to help me decorate," I say ruefully. "And she'll be close enough to do it."

Sam comes in just then. "So I got a call from the Sheriff's office," he says. "They're ready to release the truck, but they want to know where to have it towed. They don't think it's drivable."

"What do you mean, release it?" Joe asks. "What about the DUI?"

"They've completed their investigation and concluded they can't press charges," Sam says laconically. He opens the refrigerator.

My knees buckle. I grab the edge of the counter. "Thank God!"

Joe raises his coffee cup. "I could throw this at you," he tells Sam.

Sam grins at him and shuts the refrigerator door. "Sorry, Dad. Couldn't resist."

I pick up the dishtowel on the counter and throw it at him. He catches it in midair and comes to hug me. "Oh, Sam," I say into his chest. "Oh, thank God. Oh, Sam."

"And if I just pay the ticket, I don't have to go to court," he tells me. "Deputy Meek was just messing with us about that."

I sit down at the kitchen table, my knees still weak. "What a relief."

Joe pats Sam's shoulder. "I hope this is the last time you have to talk to a Sheriff's deputy," he says.

"I sure don't plan on having any more conversations with Deputy Meek." Sam grins at his father. "I suppose it's all experience that can go into my writing though, huh?"

"You need to milk this one experience for everything it has in it," Joe tells him. "For your mother's sake, if nothing else. Though getting that truck drivable may produce your next set of writing ideas."

"You'll need to get in touch with the insurance company and find out where to have it towed," I say.

"I called, but no one called me back."

"You called the 800 number?"

"Yeah, they told me to call my agent. He hasn't gotten back to me."

"I could tell you where to go, but they might have changed the list, so that would be risky. You couldn't find anything online?"

"Everything says 'contact your agent'."

"Did you go by the office?"

"Yeah, but I was on my bike, so by the time I got there they were closed. And I have class tomorrow, so I'm not sure when I'm going to be able to get down there during office hours."

"I guess I can do it," I say slowly.

"Why don't you wait and see if they call tomorrow," Joe suggests. "Then if you have to, you can go by. I hate the thought of you going in there if you don't have to. Or we can stop tomorrow after we see the house."

I nod. And it would be good to have Joe with me. "I'm not sure the house will be available to be seen tomorrow, but I'll check with Gloria. Will it be okay to wait that long, Sam?"

"Well, I'm kinda in a hurry to get the truck back, but another day of bike riding isn't gonna kill me," he says. "So what house are you going to see?"

I describe the house, and he seems enthusiastic. "And a separate space for writing even when people are visiting," he says. "That's cool, Dad."

"It sounds like it," Joe says. "I haven't seen it yet, though. It's still in the possibility stage."

"It's too bad I have class tomorrow," Sam says. "I'd like to see it."

But when Joe and I stop at the insurance agency on the way home the following day, I'm glad Sam's not with us.

Christine is at the reception area desk. She looks up expectantly, then her face becomes carefully blank.

"Hello Christine," I say. "Is Andy here?"

"He's out of the office at a meeting," she says. "How can I help you?"

"Our son's truck was in an accident, and we need to find out where he should have it towed to get it fixed," Joe tells him. "He called to ask, but no one has called him back."

"He should call the 800 number." She picks up the paperwork in front of her.

"He did," I say. "He was told to call his agent."

The door opens behind us. "Hi honey, I'm—" The jovial tone in Andy's voice ends abruptly when we turn to face him. "Ruth. Joe," he says formally. "How can I help you?"

We explain the situation again.

"Ahh, yes." He strokes his chin. "Come into my office."

The office is dustier and smaller than I remember it. And the blinds are grubby from being handled when Andy looks out the window. Was it always like this, but I just hadn't noticed?

Andy sits down behind his desk. "Have a seat, have a seat," he says jovially. "I did receive a phone message from your son, and he said something about the Bernalillo County Sheriff's Department, so I wanted to get in touch with them before I called him back."

I frown. "And why would you do that?"

"To find out who was at fault, whether there'd been a police report filed, of course." He looks at me reproachfully. "You know the procedures."

"Why didn't you just call Sam and ask him?" I ask. "Then he would have known that you'd received his message."

"I would have had to verify his version of events, anyway," Andy points out. "You know we do that."

"His version?" Joe asks. "Whose side are you on, anyway?"

"Well, the side of truth, of course." Andy winks at him. Then his face grows solemn. "I understand there was alcohol found in the truck. He'll be lucky if we don't just cancel his insurance."

"There were alcohol containers," I tell him. "Not alcohol. And he wasn't DUI."

"We should have just paid for the repairs ourselves," Joe mutters to me.

I nod at him and turn to Andy. "Aren't you getting ahead of yourself? The repairs will need to be made, one way or another. And the company can't raise his rates when he hasn't even been accused of anything. And if you try, we will be changing our insurance coverage. And not just for the vehicles."

Chapter 23

He leans towards us. "Well, aren't we the high and mighty ones," he says. I've never seen him this angry. "You think you've got money now and you can just do what you want, don't you? Cover for your son's alcohol use and reckless driving. Bully me into trying to help you make it look like he was trying to protect some poor little animal. Strong arm the company into not raising his rates, even though that's what he deserves."

He half rises from his chair. "Well, I know what the sheriff's report says. Do you really think that won't follow you if you try to transfer to another insurer?"

"I thought you said you hadn't talked to the Sheriff's office yet," Joe says.

"You apparently haven't seen the final report," I tell Andy. "Because he wasn't charged with DUI. And won't be. And even if he was being charged, we would still change companies. You can expect to get a cancellation notice from us."

"If you cancel now, the company is unlikely to really take pains with the claim on the truck," Andy points out.

I nod. "I understand that. I know how this works, remember? But the company is obligated by law to pay claims that occur as the result of activity while the vehicle is covered by them. So we will be expecting that they do so. And if we have a problem with that, then I guess we'll just have to get our legal team involved."

He flinches. He hates legal wrangling, partly because of the potential bad publicity, partly because of the cost. I'm suddenly overwhelmed with weariness. "I hope it won't come to that," I say gently.

"But if we need to, it will." Joe's voice is grim.

Andy's eyes flicker from Joe back to me and then back to Joe again. He picks up the papers on his desk and taps their bottom edge against the desktop, lining them up. "So, I don't actually have a statement from your son about what happened," he says. "Or an estimate for the repairs."

"He wants to make sure he takes it to an authorized repair shop," Joe says evenly. "Who would you suggest?"

Andy gives us a couple options and we leave. Outside, Joe squeezes my arm. "Wow, you've become quite the negotiator," he said. "I'm impressed."

"It helps to have worked with your opponent for almost twenty years," I say dryly. "You have some idea how he thinks."

He clicks the car doors open and we get in. "Really hates legal wrangles, huh?"

I nod. "Though if I was really good at it, I'd be psyched up because we won that round. Instead I just feel really really tired."

"But just a little pleased with yourself?"

I chuckle and buckle my seat belt. "Well, pleased to be able to call on our legal team if we need to. And to be able to say so knowing that we really can. I have to admit that was a nice feeling. I don't know how many times I've heard him cow people with the 'we don't really want to get the lawyers involved, do we?' routine."

I shake my head. "The funny thing is, he really doesn't want to get the lawyers involved. Which is one of the reasons his saying that is usually so effective. He actually means it. Though, generally, the people he's talking to take it as a threat and promptly cave in to whatever he's proposing."

"Well, I don't think we'll have any more trouble with him." Joe starts the car. "Do you want to go out to eat, or go home?"

"Let's go out. I could use some enchiladas. Is Teofilo's open tonight, do you know? We can take some back for Sam."

"We'll find out." He swings the car out of the parking lot. "So were you serious about switching insurance companies?"

"Yeah, I should have done it already. I guess I should start doing some research, so we have something in place for the new house."

He laughs. "That has a good sound, doesn't it?"

I grin at him. "What, me doing research?"

He lifts an eyebrow at me. "What do you think?"

"Oh, you mean 'new house'?" I tease. "Yeah, it does have a good sound. It's beautiful, isn't it, Joe? Like something out of a movie set. I can hardly believe it might really be ours."

He chuckles. "I don't think you need to worry about the 'might' part. Gloria seemed to think they'd be willing to sell for the price she suggested. And we can always go higher if we need to."

"So it looks like that part is settled. Have you thought any more about web site designs? Or decided on a set of marketing strategies?"

"Yeah, I've marked up the list Carol gave us. I think it will run about thirty five thousand, to start. I'd like to go over it with you. Maybe tomorrow?"

We discuss our plans through dinner and then put in phone calls to Jeanette and Paul after we get home, to tell them about the house.

"And I have news of my own," Jeanette says to me. "We may be able to start up the nonprofit sooner than we thought. Ken's grandfather died a couple months ago and left him funds sufficient to cover Ken's expenses, going in. We're costing it out, but I may be leaving the firm at the end of the year."

"Wow, that's great, sweetie. So will you stay in Oklahoma City?"

"Ken's parents are here, so yeah, I think so. They're starting to have some health problems, and he's an only child, so he wants to stay nearby."

"So—" I didn't want to ask, but I really wanted to know.

Jeanette chuckles. "He's just a friend, Mom. Business partners. That's all."

"No potential for anything more?"

Jeanette hesitates. "I don't think so, no. I mean, actually, no. Definitely not. He has a partner."

"I thought you said you were going to be partners."

"No, I mean he has a life partner. He's gay."

"Oh. Well. That puts that to rest, doesn't it?"

"There is someone I've been seeing," Jeanette says slowly. "I'm not sure where it's going to go, though. He has a five year old daughter, and he has sole custody."

"Wow, that would be a change for you." Jeanette has never been the maternal type. There was no gushing over babies when she was in high school.

Jeanette chuckles. "It hasn't gotten to that point yet. Of discussing possible changes, I mean. And I don't know that it will. It's not like you and Dad, knowing so instantly."

"You never know."

Jeanette laughs. "My mother, the hopeless romantic."

As we finish talking and are saying goodbye, Joe comes into the living room. He's been in the kitchen, talking with Paul.

"Paul says 'hi' and he's glad about the house and the shop sounds great," Joe tells me. "He has some news of his own. You know how he applied for that program late? Well, he's been accepted. He's already put in his notice at the shop."

Joe sits down in the easy chair. "So we're going to have two kids in school at the same time."

"But without the financial burden," Sam says, appearing in the doorway. He leans against the door frame. "How was the house?"

"Really great," I say. Joe tells him about the hydraulic lift.

"Cool," he says. "So you can really take your truck apart and put it back together, huh Dad?"

"Or your fender, if you want to wait that long," I point out.

"Well, I need to get that taken care of pretty soon," Sam says. "It's getting a little warm for bicycling back and forth to the train station."

"We stopped by the agency and saw Andy," I tell him. "You have a couple different options for repairs."

"Thanks. I really don't want to work on it myself, anyway. I don't find auto repair work quite as much fun as Paul and Dad do."

"I could maybe get a classic to tinker with," Joe says thoughtfully. "That would be fun. If I have time. I still need to get this manuscript to the publisher and then get a website put together."

"You think the house will happen before you get that done?" Sam asks.

"It sounds like the sellers are pretty motivated."

When Gloria calls the next afternoon, she echoes Joe's observation. "They sound pretty motivated," she tells me. "So as soon as you guys want to come by and sign the offer, we can start the process. Or we can do it online. Would that be easier than pulling Joe away from his latest draft?"

"It might be. What does that mean? You can just send us the form in an email?"

"Yeah, and then you just sign and scan it and send it back to me. We don't need a notary for this part. Oh, Ruthie, I'm so excited for you. And have you thought about when you want to put the current house on the market?"

"I think we're going to wait until we're completely moved out," I tell her. "Since we have the luxury of doing that. And we'll need to get it cleaned up and ready to be sold, anyway. That should be easier to do if it's empty."

On the other end, Gloria groans dramatically. "You're not thinking about doing the cleaning and touching up yourselves, are you?"

"Well, we'll know what needs to be done—"

"You could have someone come in and do it for you," she points out. "There are people who do that for a living. And that kind of work has been kind of slow lately, so you'd be helping them out."

I chuckle. "And you happen to know someone who could do it for us?"

Gloria laughs. "How'd you guess? By the way, are you available for another spa treatment in the near future? I'm about to make a really big sale, and I want to celebrate. This time, I'm not waiting until the final paperwork is signed."

I laugh and we make a date for the following week. I head to the living room with my laptop and portable printer and set up on the coffee table. I need to look at insurance options and email the accountant member of our financial team. We're going to need advice about how to pay for the house.

I lean forward and turn on the computer. It's weird to think that in another couple months I could be sitting in my own office, even if Sam is still living with us. I make a mental note that I'll need a bigger desk. The second-hand one in Sam's room isn't big enough for both the laptop and printer.

He comes into the living room as I'm printing off the forms Gloria has sent.

"So they towed the truck this morning and I've already had a call from the shop," he says, flopping onto the couch.

I pull the forms from the printer. "And?"

"It looks like it's going to cost a quarter of what the truck is worth to repair it."

"Vehicle repairs are expensive, Sam. That's what insurance is for."

"You're sure they'll cover it?"

"After the deductable, of course. But yes, they'll cover it," I tell him. But his face is still glum. "What's the matter?" I ask.

"I'm just not sure it's worth it."

"The truck? Why not?"

"Well, not the truck exactly. The hassle." He moves restlessly. "I don't mean the truck isn't worth the hassle. I mean I'm not sure I want to keep the truck after it's repaired."

I lift the laptop onto the coffee table beside the printer. "I thought you really liked that truck."

"I did. I mean, I do. It's got a hemi engine and a cool paint job and a great sound system. But I'm not sure it really represents me anymore. I'm wondering if I should sell it and look for something a little calmer."

"Is it paid off?"

He shakes his head. "That's the problem. I didn't pay cash. And now that it's damaged I'm not sure I can sell it for what it's going to be worth after it's repaired."

"You had the cash to pay for it outright. What happened?"

"Yeah, well, my reserves are a little low," he says reluctantly. "I spent quite a bit of it taking people from work out to eat and sending Sara flowers and stuff. And buying her a ring she won't accept." He stares out the window. "And then I loaned the gluten free pizza guy that money. He still hasn't paid me back."

I manage not to pursue that comment. Instead I ask, "Are you completely out of money?"

"No, but I need to make sure I have enough for tuition. Because of course I'm not eligible for a PELL grant anymore." He grins at me, then sobers. "And I want to visit a couple of those MFA writing programs before I make a final decision about applying. I've got a little time, because I'm still technically a sophomore. But I'm thinking if I take more credits next year, I can get caught up and maybe graduate in December. That's if I don't transfer into the undergraduate writing program. If I do, I might have to take some inter-semester classes to make the December graduation." He shrugs. "Either way, I need to rethink the whole vehicle thing. Do you think I can get enough for it to cover the loan?"

"It'll depend on how much you owe and how good a job the shop does," I tell him. "So what are you thinking about replacing it with?"

"Something used that gets good mileage, if that's possible. I thought maybe Paul and Dad could go with me."

"That sounds like a plan. And you'll have a shop with a lift in it, for working on it."

He grimaces. "I guess. If Paul has time. Or if I do. In order to graduate next winter, I'm going to have to take 18 credits all three semesters."

I grin at him. "Oh, you mean you're going to have to study?"

He tosses a couch pillow in my direction and stands up. "Funny, Mom, very funny." He stretches. "Actually, that's what I need to do right now, after I get a snack. Do you want anything from the kitchen?"

"No thanks."

He disappears. I shake my head and reach for the laptop. What a kid. He messed up and he's working to fix it, without whining or asking for help. If Sara can hang in there, he's going to be a great partner, one of these days. I know they're talking again. He was on the phone with her last night.

And Paul starting his own program in the Fall. And Jeanette starting her own business. And it turns out that there's a young man in the picture, after all.

I shake my head. My children are moving forward with their lives. The ticket seems to have actually helped that happen, instead of slowing them down. I'm the only one it's left feeling stranded.

Though I'm moving forward too; I just don't know exactly where. But right now, I'm just going to focus on the house-buying stuff and let the rest of my future take care of itself. As I think it, I realize that I actually feel pretty calm about that, which is pretty amazing.

Chapter 24

When she picks me up for our spa appointment the following week, Gloria says, "Before we head to the spa, I want to show you something."

I raise an eyebrow at her. "That sounds mysterious."

"Well, I have an idea that I want to run past you, but I think it would be easier if I show you what I have in mind. It's just down here." Gloria turns the car off Highway 47 onto a small dirt road leading east toward the mesa.

We drive about a half a mile down a narrow dirt road. There are old cottonwoods on one side and an alfalfa field on the other. Gloria pulls into the yard of an old adobe house that is obviously empty.

"What wonderful vigas!" I say. "But the house looks so sad. And kind of lonely."

"I have the keys," Gloria says. "Let's go look at it."

The door sticks and we have to push hard to get it open, but once we're inside, I can see that it was once cared for. The adobe walls are still in pretty good shape. There's a tin ceiling in the living room, saltillo tiles on the kitchen floor, and a wood-fired kitchen stove.

"What a great stove." I crouch down to look into the oven compartment. "I wonder if you could convert it to electricity or gas? It just fits this room, somehow."

Gloria grins and pushes her hair away from her face. "I was hoping you'd say that. The place is selling really cheap. The old man who lived in it died, and his kids want to realize their inheritance as soon as possible. It wouldn't take much to fix it up and make a profit on it."

I straighten and turn to look at Gloria as she stands in the dim light of the cobwebbed kitchen window. "And you're telling me this because—?"

"I'm wondering if maybe this would be something you'd want to do. Find homes that need some work, fix them up, and re-sell them. There are houses like this all over the county."

I frown. "You mean like flipping them? That's just for profit, and it's usually newer homes, isn't it?"

"No, I don't mean flipping exactly. I mean buying older homes that you put some love and care into and then reselling them. Not trying to make a profit so much as what you would probably call keeping the house alive and ready for a family that would appreciate it. Families who can't afford big new houses."

I move to the sink and look out the small window above it. The glass is wavy with age. I'd have to decide whether to replace it or not. It has character but it's probably not very well insulated.

There's a garden space fenced off in the backyard. I picture raised beds and a swing in the old cottonwood between the garden and ditch bank. Yes. This feels right. I feel my head nodding and turn to Gloria. "I like it."

"The house?" Gloria grins at me, knowing the answer.

"The whole idea." I frown. "Do you think I could, though? Don't you need a contractor's license to do something like that?"

"It would depend on how much you wanted to do. If you're going to gut the place and replace wiring and stuff like that, you might. Especially if you're going to do it all yourself. But if it's minor stuff like painting and flooring and having appliances replaced, you wouldn't need to."

"I could always take contractor's license classes," I hear myself saying. "If I needed to."

If I can learn the insurance industry, I can learn contractor stuff. I'll find a way. My back straightens and I look around. "A couple coats of paint and a new sink would do wonders for this room," I say. "And probably replacing the countertops. But not the floor tiles."

Gloria laughs. "You do like the idea, don't you?"

There's a gladness welling up inside me that I haven't felt since Sam was born. "This is awfully sudden," I say. "And I'll need to talk to Joe about it. But, yes. Yes, I do." I hug Gloria impulsively. "Oh Gloria, thank you!"

She laughs and hugs me back. "This is going to be fun," she says happily. "I can find them, and you can fix them up. And we're going to make a lot of families very happy."

"And houses," I tell her. "Starting with this one. How much are they asking for it?"

I tell Joe about the plan over dinner. Sam has borrowed his Dad's truck to go to the University to work on a group project for one of his classes.

"So the idea is that Gloria finds houses cheap, you buy them and fix them up and then resell them, using Gloria as your agent?" Joe asks.

"Um, yeah, that's the basic concept."

"Sounds like a good deal for Gloria. She gets a commission both ways."

"And gets to work with a seller who isn't trying to make a huge profit," I point out. "These are going to be smaller older homes going to families who don't have a lot of money, so the commissions aren't going to be very big."

Joe nods. "It's houses like our new one that really generate realtor income, isn't it?"

"Yeah, it is. But she seems really excited about this. Not only because I've finally found a purpose, but because she loves selling decent homes to families who might otherwise not be able to afford a place of their own. This would help her do that. And it would improve the local housing stock and preserve homes that would otherwise probably be torn down and replaced by big ugly new houses that most people can't afford."

"So why don't you two just go into business together?"

"I'm not sure that would be a good idea. It's better if we keep it separate, I think. Besides, I might want to do this as a nonprofit, and I don't think Gloria could afford to work that way."

"A nonprofit sounds like a great approach. Jeanette should be able to help you get that organized."

"I was thinking that. Maybe we'll be her first client."

"We?"

"M&R Enterprises. After my mother and me." I grin at him. "How she would have loved this. It's as much in honor of her memory as anything else. Mary and Ruth Enterprises."

And Marsha and Margaret, I think with a little smile. For all the old women in my life to whom I am so grateful. I stand up and come around the table to collect his now-empty plate. "What do you think?"

"I think the idea is perfect, and that any name you want to give it will be perfect," Joe reaches out to pull me to him. "Come and kiss me, oh real estate tycoon."

We've decided to use some of our mad money to pay cash for the Bosque Farms house, which has sped up the purchase process considerably. Two weeks later we have a closing date set. Gloria helps me find a woman to go through and clean it, and a young man to touch up the paint on the walls.

"I don't think you're going to need to do much," she tells me. "That house is one of the cleanest I've ever sold."

We also locate a moving company, and Joe and I begin sorting out all the items we've accumulated over the years that will go to the thrift shop. We're taking most of our old furniture with us. Shopping for new stuff can come later, after we've lived in the house a while and have a better sense of what we need.

Besides, I'm going to have to have a definite sense of what I want to do before I let Ruby help me shop. And I want to make sure Gloria has time to go with us. I'm thinking about how to arrange that the evening that Joe and I go through the hall coat closet.

"And then we need to start thinking about when and how we're going to put this house on the market," Joe says suddenly, interrupting my thoughts.

I frown at him. "What do you mean, when and how? There's no rush, is there?"

"Well of course we can afford the mortgage payment," he says. "But I don't want to leave it empty for long. It's not good for the house or the neighborhood. And I don't really want to be maintaining two yards. Or to become a landlord. I was thinking that maybe we should do something with it that's more of a donation than a sale. Kind of in keeping with your M&R Enterprises plan."

I pull out two pairs of children's snow boots and add them to the thrift shop pile. "Not to Ruby."

"No, she needs to find something she chooses. Besides, I think she's found a place. She called earlier to say there's a house in Peralta that she's looking at."

Right next door to Bosque Farms. I laugh and shake my head. I'm definitely going to need help from Gloria when it comes to decorating the new house.

Joe grins. "Sorry," he says.

"I'll cope," I tell him. "With Gloria's help. So were you thinking about actually giving the house away? If we do, the people we give it to might not take care of it."

"No, I was thinking more about selling it for what's left on the mortgage, rather than trying to recoup what we paid for it or make a profit."

I sit back on my heels. "You mean like finding a family that needs a home but can't afford one this size? We'd have to make sure they didn't know we were taking a loss on it, or they'd wonder if there was something wrong with it."

"We could just say that we're selling low because we want to move quickly, or something like that."

That makes sense. "I wonder if Gloria knows of a family that fits your description." I pull myself to my feet. "Ouch. I was kneeling too long. I'll go call her and ask."

"We still have a lot of cleaning out to do," he warns.

"There's nothing like a little incentive." I grin at him and go in search of my phone.

And Gloria does know of a family that fits Joe's description. As a matter of fact, she knows a couple of them.

"There's one in particular that I think could really use the help, though," she tells me. "He's an auto mechanic working for a shop in Albuquerque, and she cleans houses to supplement his income. They have four kids and they're renting a two bedroom house right now while they try to put together enough for closing costs for the First Homeowner program. But if you're willing to let the house go for fifty thousand, I think they probably already have enough to manage the costs on that amount. Do you want to meet them?"

"Let's have them come and look at the house as potential purchasers. That'll give us a chance to meet them," I tell her. "And you can just tell them the amount and that we want to sell quickly. That'll help explain why it's so low. We don't want this to seem like charity."

"Can I bring them by tomorrow evening? I already have an appointment with them to look at an older rental in Belen that they might be able to renovate. I can bring them by your place after we're through there. Say about seven thirty?"

I move the phone away from my mouth and say "Seven thirty tomorrow?" to Joe.

He laughs and nods. He's shaking his head at the old boxes of puzzles and games on the top shelf of the closet when I get off the phone. "She moves quickly, doesn't she?" he asks.

"Or maybe it was just serendipitous. She already had an appointment with these people." I tell him what Gloria told me about them.

"Sounds too good to be true," he responds. But at nine o'clock the next night he's telling me that they seem like the perfect family for the house. "Two boys and two girls, so they can split up the bedrooms. And those rooms are pretty decently sized, so they should be able to manage. And that littlest girl was sure excited about the tree swing."

"They do seem very nice," I say. "I hope they'll make an offer. They seemed a little concerned about the cost of the appraisal and stuff."

"I suppose we could help with the closing costs if they need it," he says. "I think the house is a good fit for them. The husband was telling me that the way we've maintained it is a big selling point for them. The other places they've looked at have required a lot of work they just don't have time to do, what with both of them working and the kids and everything."

"I can get in touch with Gloria tomorrow and tell her to offer help with the appraisal and other costs, if they need it." I look around the living room. "The wife told me something similar. Apparently her mother is really sick, so on top of everything else, she's been juggling her work schedule to make time for medical appointments. She's been worried about trying to repaint and clean and move and still work and ferry her mother to the doctor."

I stand up. "You know, in some ways, the house has seemed a little sad, since the kids all left home. I hadn't realized how much it needed young people around until Sam moved back in. I think it'll be in good hands with this family. This gives it an opportunity for a new life, with children occupying its bedrooms and playing in the yard again."

He grins at me. "You really do feel like buildings have souls, don't you?"

I laugh. "I do."

Sam comes in from the kitchen. "So the truck is officially repaired," he announces. "I'm gonna go pick it up tomorrow after I get home from class. The repair place is practically next door to the train station, so that makes it easy."

"Ah, the conveniences of suburban life," Joe says. "Are you still thinking about selling it?"

Sam nods. "I've been talking to the Auge Boys in Belen. They have a second hand V-4 truck with a standard transmission, so it's gonna get better mileage than this one. They'll consider a straight across trade. I was wondering if you and Paul could go down there with me on Saturday."

"Sure, I can do that, if Paul's going to be around. Though I'm having trouble believing you're really parting with your souped up vehicle, Sam."

Sam shrugs. "Well, I've got to cut costs if I'm gonna go to school full time and not work, and still get the finances together for an MFA program." He hesitates, then says, "Which brings me to something I've been wanting to ask you guys about."

"Hmmm?" I've been sorting through the magazines on the shelf of the lamp table while they talk. I look up at him. Even though he's leaning against the doorjamb, he looks taller to me somehow. More confident, even in his hesitation.

"Would it be okay with you if I moved into the new house with you?" he asks. "I mean, instead of going back into an apartment? I've been paying my part of the rent on the apartment, so Andrew wouldn't be stuck with the whole thing halfway through the year. But he's found a new roommate now, so he doesn't need me to do that anymore. I can pay you room and board. It would still be cheaper than living on my own, and it would help me save toward my MFA expenses, wherever I end up going."

He looks from Joe to me and back to Joe again. "If you don't mind."

Joe is looking at me with a bemused expression. "That'll make it even harder for you if he moves to another state for his Master's program," he says.

But so much nicer in the meantime. "That won't be for a while. He has to finish his B.A. first," I tell him.

I turn to Sam. "We love having you with us, Sam." I grin. "I've even been willing to give up my office space for you. I think it would be great if you moved into the new house with us." I chuckle. "Besides, you're going to need the garage capacity, if you're buying a second hand truck."

"Hey, we'll make sure it needs only minimal repairs," Joe says. "Between the three of us. Besides, I don't think Sam wants to spend all his time under his truck, even if it is on a lift."

Sam chuckles. "Not hardly."

I shake my head at Joe. "If I know you and Paul, you'll talk Sam into putting in a new engine so it gets the best mileage possible." I stand up. "I've finished sorting out the magazines in here. Have you started thinking about the bookcases in your office, Joe? This would be a great opportunity to do some cleaning out."

"I've thought about it," he tells me. "But I'm still working on the final review of my manuscript. I should be done some time next week. Then I'll start organizing stuff into boxes. But we're hiring someone to pack all this, remember?"

"Yes, and I also remember discussing the fact that there's no point in paying someone to move stuff that we don't actually need to move. Doesn't it feel better to have the coat closet cleaned out?"

"I'm sure the coat closet feels so much better," Sam snickers.

"You're a big help!" I tell him. "For that, you can go get me a box from the garage for these magazines."

He goes out, chuckling. I turn to Joe. "You okay with him moving with us?"

He nods. "I think it's a good idea. But I think we need to keep his room and board payments to a minimum, or bank them for him. Whatever program he decides on, he may find that it's more expensive than he expected. And I don't want us to get in the habit of giving him money."

I nod. It's an interesting tight rope we're walking with the kids. Wanting them to have enough, worried about making them dependent. I guess you worry about your kids no matter what your resources are like.

"It'll be nice to have an extra pair of hands for the move," I say. "Or the clean out, anyway."

And Sam is a help, when the time comes. It's late May before we actually make the move. Even before that he's been helping me with my business plan for M&R Construction. He's worked with me to make sure it's clear, and he's proofread it for me.

When we actually move, it turns out that the small local moving company that Gloria has suggested we use was started a couple years ago by two of Sam's high school friends. He works alongside them moving boxes and furniture and calls it supervising while they catch up on post-high school gossip.

It takes about three days before everything is transferred to the new place. Then there's another day of hauling the stuff we've decided we don't need to the thrift shop. Joe and Sam take the final load in the bed of Sam's new truck. The other vehicles are already at the new house.

I wave goodbye to them from the window of the empty living room and turn back into the room. I look around the room, indentations from the furniture still marking their places in the carpet. So many years in this house. So many memories. "I'm going to miss you, house," I whisper. "Thanks for all you've been to us."

The vacuum starts up in the master bedroom. The young woman Gloria suggested to help with the cleaning must be almost finished with the back of the house. I straighten my shoulders and go into the kitchen to wipe out cupboards. I'm scrubbing the sink when Gloria knocks on the kitchen door.

"I thought I'd find you here," she says. "I've come to play fairy godmother. Let someone else do the cleaning, Cinderella. She needs the money, and you need to go home. Put on your glass slippers."

I laugh and drop the scrubber. "Yes, ma'am. I guess I don't really need to be doing this, do I?" I pull off my cleaning gloves. "Do you have all the keys?"

"Yep, we're all set. Let me just tell Julie we're going, and we'll get out of here."

Gloria disappears into the back while I gather my purse and phone. I'm staring at the wall next to the kitchen door when Gloria comes back.

"See those marks, where we tracked the kids' heights?" I ask her. "I wish I could take that piece of wallboard right off of there and take it with me."

"That might kind of mess up the wall," Gloria observes.

"It'll probably get painted right over."

"And then marked up with another set of children's heights," Gloria says. "You're giving this family a wonderful opportunity, Ruth. I hope you know that."

I nod, unable to speak. I pat the wall. "Goodbye old house," I murmur. "You've been a good house to us." I take a deep breath and turn to Gloria. "I need to get out of here or I'm going to start crying."

"Your carriage awaits!" she says.

We stop at the grocery store to pick up a few items and then head to Bosque Farms. At the house, the movers are still unpacking boxes. While I offer them sodas, Gloria returns to her car and comes back with a shopping bag. "Come out to the porch," she orders me with a grin.

Joe and Sam are already there, sitting in the big wooden rocking chairs the previous owners have left behind and admiring the view.

"Sam and I have decided that we should go on a family vacation before the summer is over," Joe announces as Gloria and I cross the threshold. He stands and comes to put an arm around my shoulders.

"We'll get Jeanette to take some time off, and we'll schedule it before school starts so it'll fit into Sam's and Paul's schedules. And we'll go to Costa Rica or the Bahamas or something. Or Machu Pichu. Or all three. We can ask Ruby to watch the house for us, so it won't matter how long we're gone, as long as we're back before classes start. Then when we get back I'll start up the marketing campaign, and you can get moving on M&R Enterprises. What do you think?"

My back stiffens. It's all happening too quickly. We're not even settled into the new house yet. And these vacation plans are likely to be more complicated than he thinks.

"What a great idea!" Gloria says.

And then I laugh. On the other hand, we can probably find a travel agency to set it all up for us. It'll all work out. I've finally figured out that much, at least.

I grin at Joe and shake my head. "I think the ticket has gone to your head," I tell him. "And that I feel like I'm still trying on shoes that are too big for me. But I guess I'll get used to it."

"And like it," Gloria says. "Glass slippers look good on you."

She puts her shopping bag on the wooden bench beside the rocking chairs and begins removing its contents. "And now, to celebrate new houses, new shoes, new enterprises, and fantastic vacations, we have champagne in plastic glasses!"

As we raise our glasses to toast each other, the sunset flares in a burst of light across the trees in the bosque. Its golden glow bathes the lawn and deepens the shadows under the cottonwoods.

"They're very beautiful shoes," I murmur to Joe as his arm tightens around me.

www.ingramcontent.com/pod-product-compliance
Lightning Source LLC
Chambersburg PA
CBHW070010120726
47909CB00003B/872